IN THE RANCHER'S PROTECTION

Beth Cornelison

HARLEQUIN

ROMANTIC SUSPENSE

HARLEQUIN®
ROMANTIC SUSPENSE™

Recycling programs
for this product may
not exist in your area.

ISBN-13: 978-1-335-62662-2

In the Rancher's Protection

Copyright © 2020 by Beth Cornelison

This edition published by arrangement with Harlequin Books S.A.

For questions and comments about the quality of this book, please contact us at CustomerService@Harlequin.com.

Harlequin Enterprises ULC
22 Adelaide St. West, 40th Floor
Toronto, Ontario M5H 4E3, Canada
www.Harlequin.com

Printed in U.S.A.

A car behind them honked its horn, and Luke raised his gaze to his rearview mirror to frown at the impatient driver.

After checking for traffic, he pulled onto the crossroad, and his brow beetled. "And the adventure trip? How does that figure into your situation?"

Carrie wet her lips. "Well, Nina suggested that. I guess she thought that making me face some physical challenges would help build my confidence in the other battles I was facing. For me, it's just an opportunity to...escape my situation for a few days. Hit Pause. Take a breath."

The muscles in his jaw flexed as he, apparently, meditated on her answer. Then with a quick nod, he met her gaze again. "Then that's what it will be. I'll make sure these next few days are a relaxing, confidence-building escape for you. Okay?"

She exhaled heavily. *Escape.* The word taunted her. If only it could be a permanent escape, instead of just a few days. But for now, a few days of safety would be a gift. "I like that deal."

* * *

**Be sure to check out the other stories in
The McCall Adventure Ranch series!**

* * *

**If you're on Twitter, tell us what you
think of Harlequin Romantic Suspense!
#harlequinromsuspense**

Dear Reader,

Welcome back to Boyd Valley, Colorado, and the Double M Ranch! I couldn't resist the opportunity to peek in on the McCall family and the new ranch hands one more time. I checked in with Nina Abshire, who was introduced to readers in *Christmas Rodeo Rescue*, an online read at Harlequin.com, in November 2018, and renewed acquaintances with the characters from the previous four books in The McCall Adventure Ranch series. In this story, you meet a new hire, ranch hand Luke Wright, who has a tragic history and a penchant for wanting to be a knight in shining armor wherever he sees a need.

Carrie French might be in danger, but she doesn't want Luke getting involved in her plight. While Carrie hides out at the Double M, she's startled by the sizzling chemistry she shares with Luke. But someone dangerous is following Carrie, and she doesn't want anyone else put in harm's way—especially not the handsome and kind ranch hand with soul-piercing gray eyes!

Another special character in this story is Lylah Grace Douglas, named by Mickie Douglas, who won the chance to use her own name for a character of her choice through a fund-raising auction benefiting community projects in my hometown. Thanks, Mickie!

As always, I hope you enjoy this story and Carrie's journey to self-discovery, freedom and hope—and, of course, true love!

Happy reading,

Beth

Beth Cornelison began working in public relations before pursuing her love of writing romance. She has won numerous honors for her work, including a nomination for the RWA RITA® Award for *The Christmas Stranger*. She enjoys featuring her cats (or friends' pets) in her stories and always has another book in the pipeline! She currently lives in Louisiana with her husband, one son and three spoiled cats. Contact her via her website, bethcornelison.com.

Books by Beth Cornelison

Harlequin Romantic Suspense

The McCall Adventure Ranch

Rancher's Deadly Reunion
Rancher's High-Stakes Rescue
Rancher's Covert Christmas
Rancher's Hostage Rescue
In the Rancher's Protection

Colton 911

Colton 911: Deadly Texas Reunion

Cowboy Christmas Rescue
"Rescuing the Witness"

Rock-a-Bye Rescue
"Guarding Eve"

The Mansfield Brothers

The Return of Connor Mansfield
Protecting Her Royal Baby
The Mansfield Rescue

Black Ops Rescues

Soldier's Pregnancy Protocol
The Reunion Mission
Cowboy's Texas Rescue

Visit the Author Profile page at Harlequin.com for more titles.

Author's Note

Domestic abuse is a far-too-common reality in the United States. Statistics from the CDC's National Intimate Partner and Sexual Violence Survey (NISVS) indicate that one in four women and one in ten men experience some form of physical, emotional or sexual abuse or stalking by an intimate partner in their lifetime. If you or someone you love is experiencing abuse of any form from an intimate partner, help is available by contacting the National Domestic Violence Hotline at 1-800-799-SAFE (7233) or visiting www.thehotline.org.

Chapter 1

He'd found her. Again.

Carrie French stared out the dirty window of the hole-in-the-wall motel where she'd been hiding for the past week. Frustration and fear bit her stomach. Acid climbed her throat until she thought she might vomit.

Instead, she pulled a deep breath in through her nose and blew it out slowly through pursed lips, seizing her composure with both hands. If she panicked, she'd hurt her ability to think clearly. She had a few precious moments before Joseph would discover her here in room four. She could picture him flashing a wad of hundred-dollar bills to the front-desk clerk as he presented her picture and demanded to know where Carrie was.

Because she was used to having to run on a moment's notice, Carrie had kept her bag packed, her shoes lined up and ready to stuff on her feet, her burner phone fully

charged. With a few quick motions, her cell was un-
plugged, her feet covered, her bag in hand and she was
scrambling to the door. She cracked it open, peeked out.

Joseph was still in the small office, his back to the
window. She had no time to waste.

Covering her head with the hood of her jacket, she
jammed her sunglasses in place, shouldered the strap of
her canvas bag and fled the room. She didn't bother closing the door, didn't look back. She ran for the car she'd
parked around the corner, out of view of the office, and
whispered a prayer for divine intervention. *Help me get
out of here. Don't let him see me. Please!*

"Hey! Carrie? Stop!"

Her heart sank as she pushed her legs to go faster,
fumbled the ignition key one-handed while she tossed
her bag on the back seat. *So much for not being seen.*

She locked the doors, and tears blurred her vision as
she cranked the engine. He was at her window in seconds, pounding his fist on the glass. "Damn it, Carrie!
Get out of the car!"

She tried to ignore his presence, his feral growl as
he shouted at her. With trembling hands, she shifted the
transmission to Reverse. Twisted to look behind her as
she backed out of the lot.

A loud thump and sound of glass cracking drew a
startled gasp from her. She spun to see what he'd done.
Her windshield had a spiderweb break and a long fis-
sure snaking across the driver's side. He held a rock, his
arm raised, ready to smash it against her window again.

Carrie stomped the gas pedal. The car rocketed backward. The rock he held slammed down on her hood, leaving a dent, then tumbled to the ground. Joseph made a

grab for the door handle as she wheeled a hasty Y-turn and raced out of the side parking lot.

A car horn blasted as she cut into traffic and sped away, and from the motel parking lot, she could hear him scream, "Give up, Carrie! I will always find you!"

Carrie shuddered. Five years ago, that promise might have sounded like a romantic movie line. Now, after sixty months of watching everything she'd believed about the man she'd married melt away, she knew the shouted vow for what it was. A threat.

And all the reason she needed to keep running. Keep hiding. Because if Joseph ever caught her, she knew he would kill her.

Hours later, when she felt certain she'd escaped Joseph, Carrie stopped at a fast food restaurant in a tiny Oklahoma town and released a shuddering breath. Once she'd thought she could flee her abusive and manipulative husband simply by leaving him, filing for divorce and getting on with her life. Now she knew Joseph was a bad dream that would keep returning, no matter the lengths she went to. Desolation sat on her chest, suffocating her. What hope she'd had for a fresh start had eroded, little by little, each time he'd caught up with her.

She smacked her hand on the steering wheel, bitter tears stinging her eyes. How in the *hell* did he keep finding her? She didn't use credit cards. She changed burner phones every time he found her. She didn't use her real name when she paid cash and checked into motels at night. She'd driven hundreds of miles, randomly picking small towns or thriving cities to stop. She'd dyed her hair so many times, all the conditioner in the world would never rescue it from the brittleness and split ends.

She glanced in the rearview mirror, reminding herself what color she'd last used. That's right…a boring shade of light brown.

But no matter how smart she thought she was being, no matter how far she drove or how random her path, Joseph always showed up within days. Then he'd gloat. And he'd try to drag her back to Aurora, Colorado, with him. Often, he'd smack her around, taking out his frustrations over her determination to be free of him. One time, he forced her back to their sprawling estate outside Aurora, and she'd had to devise a new plan to slip away undetected.

The process was physically exhausting, emotionally draining and increasingly challenging. She had to find new ways to dodge him. New places to hide. And she felt herself becoming more and more isolated as she cut off contact with more and more of her friends.

The few friends that had a hint of her predicament had offered to take her in, but she refused to put them in danger, drawing them or their families into the line of fire. Joseph was too well connected, too cold and calculating.

Earlier in their marriage, when Carrie had confided in her best friend, Hanna, and taken refuge at Hanna's house after an argument with Joseph turned violent, Joseph had taken his revenge by getting Hanna fired from her management job and kidnapping Hanna's Yorkie from the doggie day care. Peanut had never been found.

Besides, Joseph knew most of the same people she did, so she didn't see those friends and business associates as safe places. She was one of the few who knew Joseph's dark side. He was good at presenting a charming, confident and gracious facade. After all, he'd fooled her before they were married, hadn't he?

Now, she sat at the edge of the gas station/minute market parking lot and stared through her cracked windshield at the rural Oklahoma terrain. She felt conspicuous in her black BMW M4 coupe with the broken windshield, as if she had a neon arrow pointing to her. *Flash. Out of place. Flash. On the run. Flash. Sore thumbsville.* She shrank down in the driver's seat, wishing she could simply disappear.

She watched a teenage couple climb out of a pickup truck, laughing and playfully poking at each other before exchanging a sloppy kiss and entering the store. Next came the man in the Sooners T-shirt, then a petite woman with two small children who were begging her in loud voices to buy them each a sugary frozen drink. Ordinary people with ordinary lives. She envied them. They had a place to go home at night. No one chasing them, wanting to hurt them. Or did they?

She knew that, to outsiders, she probably looked like the normal one. Appearances meant nothing. Just like wild animals, people learned to hide their vulnerabilities, their wounded hearts.

As she cranked her engine, preparing to get back on the road, a billboard across the road advertising the local rodeo snagged her attention. The ad featured pictures of both a cowboy and a cowgirl competing, and her thoughts flashed to a friend from high school who'd been a rodeo champion—until a car accident had left her severely injured and relearning how to walk. For years, she and Nina had stayed in touch. Carrie had visited Nina several times through her rehabilitation and cheered the progress of Nina's recovery. How long had it been since she'd heard from her old friend? Two years? Three? Since she'd broken ties with so many of her old friends, deleted her

Facebook and Twitter accounts, and essentially erased her past connections—to protect them from Joseph.

A sharp pang for her former life, for her dear high school and college friends, for days when her biggest worry was whether the Taylor Swift concert would sell out before she and her gal pals could land tickets. Carrie huffed a sigh of resentment toward Joseph and all the ways he'd wrecked her life. Taylor Swift concerts being the least of those ways. He'd stolen her freedom, her happiness, her peace of mind.

Blinking back tears, she continued to stare at the rodeo billboard, remembering how inspirational Nina's attitude and determination to heal from her setback had been. Nina had stayed so positive. She buoyed those around her as much as her friends had encouraged and comforted her. Carrie missed that mettle. Missed Nina.

Her heart beat faster as an idea tickled. Last she'd heard, Nina was in Colorado. Colorado was within a day's drive of here. Joseph didn't know Nina. Not well, anyway. She'd talked to him about her friend's remarkable accident recovery, but she'd given him few details.

She'd give almost anything to spend a few days with Nina and pretend for a short while that she was eighteen and carefree again. *Too risky.* The warning whispered in her head, while a desperate longing and nostalgia wrenched in her chest.

She dug her burner cell out of her bag and stared at it while she debated. Could she maybe just call Nina, hear her voice, receive the sort of pep talk Nina did so well? Before she could talk herself out of it, she was looking up the number for Zoe's Diner in Boyd Valley, the eatery that Nina's mother owned. Zoe would know how to reach Nina.

"Zoe's Diner, how can I help you?"

A smile spread across Carrie's face as the familiar maternal voice filled her ear—and her heart. She passed the next few minutes with generalized small talk with Zoe before getting Nina's phone number.

She stared at the number she'd inked on the palm of her hand but only debated for a moment before calling her friend. One phone call on a burner cell couldn't hurt. Could it? She prayed it wouldn't. Nina answered on the third ring, her voice sounding dubious—and who doesn't sound wary when they take a call from an unfamiliar phone number?

"Nina, it's Carrie French. Your mom gave me your number. How are you?"

"Carrie! Oh my gosh! It's so great to hear from you! How the heck are you? Where are you? Please tell me you are in town and can come by for a visit. We have so much to catch up on!"

"Well, I'm not in town. I just saw a rodeo billboard that made me think of you, and…" She paused for a deep breath before her voice could crack. "I wanted to hear your voice. See how you were."

"I'm good. Well, *great*, actually. I have a new job working at a ranch in Boyd Valley, and…wait for it…I'm getting married in six weeks!" Nina's happiness filled her voice and lifted Carrie's spirits.

"Married?" A double-edged pang slashed through her. Joy for her friend along with grief for her own lost dream of marital bliss. "Wow, that's fantastic! Who? How? I want details."

Nina explained how she'd been buried in her car by an avalanche just before Christmas a year and a half ago. Something special had sparked between her and the emergency operator who'd stayed on the line with her until she was rescued, and they'd been dating ever since.

"Buried by an avalanche?" Carrie shook her head. "You have the worst luck in cars!"

"Oh, I don't consider the accidents bad luck. Between the two, they brought me to Steve. I wouldn't change that for all the world." Nina paused, then said, "Gosh, I wish you were in town. I'd love for you to meet him."

"I'd like that, too. I hope someday I will."

"What about you? I'm not sure we've talked since your wedding. How's married life treating you?"

"Oh, uh…" Carrie opened her mouth to give the routine lie, the false cheer to hide her misery. But something made her stop. Nina had been too good of a friend in the past to feed her the fake sunshine and roses.

"Uh-oh," Nina said.

"What?"

"You hesitated. If things were hunky-dory, you wouldn't have needed time to consider how to answer."

"I, um…"

"It's okay. You don't have to tell me. I didn't mean to pry if—"

"I left him. We'll be divorced soon, but I…"

When Carrie let her sentence trail off, Nina murmured, "I'm so sorry, Carrie."

As much as it hurt to admit the truth of her failed marriage, admitting the truth for a change instead of perpetuating the myth of an ideal marriage to Joseph felt good—lifting a little of the weight of secrets and lies she'd been carrying for too long.

Nina changed the subject to her new job as a hand for the Double M Ranch. "The owners, the McCalls, hired me, even knowing there were a few jobs I couldn't do as well as the other hands because of my injuries from the old car wreck. But I'm in the saddle again, and I'm working with great people and…well, I just love it here!"

"That's so great, Nina. To think how far you've come in recent years—" Carrie sighed "—it gives me hope."

"Never give up hope." Nina's tone was kind but firm. "I learned that through all my trials, if nothing else. Good things can come from the most unexpected places and change your life. Like Steve did for me. And the McCalls. Good things are coming for you, too. I know they are."

Carrie wanted to believe that, but seeing a brighter future as long as her vengeful and violent husband was pursuing her was nearly impossible.

"Oh, Carrie!" Nina said, breaking into Carrie's gloomy thoughts. "Can't you come for a few days? I really miss hanging out with you, and it sounds like you need some girl time to cheer you up."

A wistful pang twisted in her chest. "If only. I could use some girl time right now. But I can't."

"May I ask why?" Nina pressed.

Carrie fumbled for one of the convenient lies she told when people asked why she passed up lunch dates or girls' night. Or why she wore long sleeves in warm weather. Or any of the many excuses to cover the dark truth of her unhappy marriage. The parade of lies was soul crushing. Each one felt like another piece of her that Joseph was stealing from her. Each one another concession to his cruelty. A knot formed in Carrie's throat, and she had to swallow hard in order to speak again. "I just…can't. I'm—" *Too busy? Not feeling well? Taking an early morning flight?*

She shuffled mentally through the deck of excuses,

and an elixir of shame, frustration and rage simmered in her belly.

"Carrie? What's going on? I can hear it in your voice. There's something more than your divorce troubling you."

Carrie squeezed her eyes shut, and twin tears leaked from her eyes. "Um, yeah. Sorta. But—"

"I'm your friend," Nina said, her tone gently encouraging. "I want to help. Please tell me."

She shook her head and wiped her cheeks with a finger. "There's nothing you can do."

"Not even listen? Pray for you? Offer a shoulder to cry on?"

Carrie drew a shuddering breath, and before she knew what she was doing, she blurted, "I'm in hiding. From Joseph. He…was abusive. *Is* abusive. And he's determined to find me and make me pay for leaving him."

She heard a soft, sharp inhale of breath before Nina whispered, "Oh, Carrie, that's awful! I'm so sorry. I—"

"So I can't come see you, because I can't risk bringing the danger he poses to you."

A heavy silence screamed through the phone, and the wings of panic flapped in Carrie's chest. What had she done? She'd shared her darkest secret with someone she hadn't seen in several years. She'd been close to Nina in high school and her early years of college, but how did she know she could still trust Nina?

Finally, Nina stammered, "I— H-have you reported him to the police?"

Carrie scoffed. "Yeah. For all the good it did."

Nina gave a frustrated-sounding huff. "Look, you'll be safe here. Steve and I will protect you."

Carrie shook her head even though she knew Nina

couldn't see it. "I can't put you in that position. He has an uncanny way of tracking me down that I can't explain. I don't use credit cards and I change phones frequently and… No, I can't risk him coming to your place and causing trouble for you."

"Carrie…" Nina paused, then said, "Then come to the ranch. At any time, there are at least three big, capable ranchers on hand that would gladly stand between you and an abusive husband. During the day, that number is more like six. He won't get to you even in the unlikely chance that he does find you there. I mean, it's a private ranch. Why would he look for you there?"

"Why would he have looked for me in any of the other random small towns where he's caught up to me? Thank you for the offer, but I really can't risk—"

"Please, Carrie. Let me help you! I know the McCalls. I know they'd want to do this for you. You could stay in the guesthouse they use for the adventure-trip guests." Again she heard Nina inhale. "In fact, they have another trip leaving in a couple days! You could join the trip. It's perfect! You'll spend a couple days here at the ranch before heading out into the nearby mountains to hike and camp and do adventure activities like rafting and rock climbing and zip-lining."

Carrie chuckled stiffly. "Because I don't have enough danger in my life already?"

"Trust me, the McCalls are sticklers for safety. After a mishap a couple years ago, they go above and beyond typical safety protocols and triple-check everything. You'll be with a group that includes one of the owners, Josh McCall, and one of the hands, Luke Wright. They'll protect you."

"You wouldn't be going?"

"Someday I might. I'm not physically up to some of the challenges yet since my accident. Another hand, Dave, and I stay back at the ranch to take care of the McCalls' herd while the group is away."

"I don't know, Nina," Carrie said. But the idea *did* intrigue her. Hiking through the mountains, away from civilization, for a few days? She'd have other people around her. For protection. For distraction. How great would it be to have a few days to simply catch her breath? To quit looking over her shoulder? And the chance to see Nina, a friendly, familiar face, after weeks on the road? *Sounds heavenly.*

"Does that mean yes? That you'll come?" Nina asked, her tone bright.

"Um, what?"

"You said it sounded heavenly."

Carrie's pulse tripped. "I said that aloud?"

Nina chuckled. "You did. So now you can't deny how much you want to do it."

"Wanting to come see you has never been the issue." Carrie dragged her fingers through her messy hair. "I told you why I can't. Joseph—"

"And I shot your excuses down. I'll tell the McCalls you're coming. My guest. You can do the paperwork when you get here."

Carrie scanned the small town where her car was still parked. Left, right, front, back. Carefully checking for evidence Joseph had caught up to her. The woman she'd watched earlier going into the convenience store now exited with her two small children, both kids carrying slushy red drinks. A sports coupe pulled into the parking lot with a loud roar of its powerful engine, and Carrie jolted.

Damn, but she needed downtime to chill. A place where she didn't spook at every sound and where she didn't feel the need to constantly search faces and keep her own hidden. Maybe the McCalls' Double M Ranch— or better yet, the wilds of the Colorado mountains—was the perfect place to just…get lost. Go off the grid, in a sense. Shake whatever means of tracking her Joseph had.

"Okay," she murmured softly, surprising herself. "I'll come."

"Great!" Nina's enthusiasm bubbled through the line. "How close are you? When can you get here?"

Carrie squeezed the steering wheel, already doubting the wisdom of her decision. "Is tonight too soon?"

"I'll make the arrangements and text directions to the ranch to this number. Okay?"

"Thank you, Nina." As she drove slowly back onto the highway, headed toward Colorado, Carrie sent up a silent prayer that going to the Double M Ranch, traveling with the adventure tour, didn't prove the most recent in a series of mistakes. Bad enough her life was at risk. How would she live with herself if anything happened to Nina or any of the other people at the Double M?

Chapter 2

Luke Wright stared at the abscess on the Double M's best breeding bull's flank and frowned at his boss, Josh McCall. "I'll get the medical kit. Think we should call the vet in?"

"Well, Dr. Germain's supposed to be out here on a routine visit later in the week. Let's treat it ourselves for now." Josh glanced up at Luke from his squat beside the bull. "But keep a real close eye on it. Check it three or four times a day. Dave will show you the treatment regimen."

"Do you think—" Luke broke off as the crunch of tires on gravel signaled the arrival of a car to the front drive of the Double M Ranch. The black coupe's windshield reflected the blue August sky and puffy white clouds, preventing him from seeing who was behind the wheel, but the BMW insignia on the hood said this was no ordinary visitor to the ranch. He didn't know anyone in Boyd Valley that drove a luxury vehicle like that.

The windshield also bore a large crack with spiderweb-like fissures that ran the width of the car. The crack was big enough to be a safety issue, and he wondered in passing why the windshield hadn't been replaced. It struck him as odd that the owner of such a nice car wouldn't have repaired the damage to the windshield.

The driver cut the engine, and a petite woman with light brown hair in a thick ponytail and wearing large-lens sunglasses emerged from the car. Slowly, the woman took off the sunglasses and cast a dubious gaze around the ranch yard.

The August sunlight hit the woman's hair, making it shine, and Luke caught his breath. Her delicate bone structure and full, bowed lips were at odds with each other. Fragile innocent versus seductress. Angel and temptation. Her figure continued the duality. Her petite frame suggested a childlike vulnerability, while her curves were all woman. "Wow. Who's that?"

Josh lifted a shoulder. "Guess I should go find out." He glanced at Luke, then added with a smirking grin, "Unless you want the excuse to talk to her, get her number, maybe?"

Luke snorted and raised an eyebrow, trying to minimize whatever Josh may have seen in his gaze. "Naw, you go ahead." He twisted his mouth in wry amusement. "Just remember you're married now. You're off the market."

Josh laughed. "Kate has nothing to worry about. I only have eyes for her."

Luke returned his gaze to the woman beside the beat-up coupe, and pure male lust kicked him hard in the groin. At the same time, a warning bell clanged in the recesses of his brain. No doubt about it. The visitor was attractive, but he'd learned that appearances could hide a multitude of inner scars.

About the time Josh left the corral where he'd been helping Luke with the wounded bull, a feminine squeal filled the air, and Nina Abshire, another of the Double M Ranch hands, raced past Josh from the stable to greet the newly arrived woman with an enthusiastic hug.

So…clearly Nina knew the lovely brunette.

Luke released the bull from the squeeze pen that had held the animal still while he and Josh examined the wound, and he walked the animal back to the main corral where the other bulls were munching dinner out of a long trough. He cast inquisitive glances toward the front drive, where Nina and the visitor chatted brightly, then embraced again. Nina's guest was well dressed, even though her car had seen better days. Another contradiction that tickled Luke's gut.

When Josh reached them, Nina motioned between her boss and the guest, obviously introducing them. Although curiosity about the attractive woman and her contradictions bit him hard, Luke kept his stride resolutely aimed for the stable. The lady was Nina's friend and none of his business. The whisper of a memory tingled down his spine. Sharon. A call at midnight that he'd ignored. *Hell.*

Luke pushed the disturbing thought aside and quickened his pace. He had ranch business to take care of, a bull with an abscess to treat and no time to wallow in the past.

A shrill whistle snagged his attention, and he jerked his head toward the source of the sound. Josh motioned to him from beside Nina's friend. "Hey, Luke, c'mere! I want you to meet someone."

Luke ground his back teeth together. If Josh was playing matchmaker, even in the most lighthearted, teasing way...

But then Nina faced Luke, as well, and waved him over, a bright smile lighting her face. "Yeah, come over here! I want you to meet my friend."

Resigned, yet also intrigued, Luke set his course toward the front drive, studying the new arrival as he crossed the ranch yard. Nina's friend lowered her gaze and leaned close to Nina, muttering something to her. Nina waved her hand in a dismissive manner and wrapped her arm around the brunette's shoulders in a sideways hug. For encouragement?

The clanging in his brain grew louder as he watched the woman shift her weight from one leg to another and draw a deep breath before raising her chin. The smile that twitched her lips didn't reach her eyes, and shadows dimmed her aqua gaze. As he neared the threesome, plastering a welcoming smile on his own face, he became increasingly aware of the contrast between his six-foot-three height and her diminutive size. So, it seemed, did she. Her gaze widened as it traveled up, up, up to meet his. Vulnerability and doubt seemed to vibrate from her in waves.

"Luke Wright," Nina said as he drew within earshot, "I'd like you to meet my high school friend Carrie French."

He extended a hand for Carrie to shake and smiled more broadly. "Carrie. Welcome."

She squared her shoulders, and her face brightened as she offered her thin hand. "Nice to meet you, Luke."

His hand engulfed her frail fingers, but to her credit,

she returned a firm shake. He added another tick mark to the contradictions column. "Likewise."

"What brings you to town, Carrie?" Josh asked.

Nina scoffed and tightened her side hold on her friend's shoulders. "What? She needs another reason besides visiting me?"

Josh's mouth opened and closed like a fish out of water. "I, uh, only meant—"

Carrie laughed softly, and Luke imagined he heard a nervous tremor as well. Or was it simply that he viewed every woman he met through his warped lens? Would he always look for cracks in every facade? She raised her left hand to tuck a wisp of hair that had escaped her ponytail behind her ear. No wedding ring, he noticed. And why was he even looking? His first impressions of her nervousness and all her contradictions should have been enough to warn him away from this woman. And yet his blood warmed as he drank in her delicate features, her seductive curves, the glint of moisture on her full lips. Clearly, his brain and his libido were not on the same wavelength. He needed to check his gut-level response to her and rein in his attraction. He'd gone down this path before and was still living with the repercussions of his failure. His best bet was to steer far away from Nina's friend for his own peace of mind.

"Nina invited me to come," Carrie said, drawing him from his thoughts. "I'm taking some personal time to unwind and refresh. She suggested I join you on your next adventure trip. Is that all right?"

Luke stiffened. She was staying at the ranch? Going on the adventure tour with them? He gritted his back teeth, working hard to show no outward reaction to this news.

Meanwhile, Josh's face lit with enthusiasm. "Heck,

yeah! You'll love it! We have a group arriving in two days. We'd love to have you! I'll even give you the friends and family discount, meaning no charge, since you're an old high school pal of Nina's."

"Hey, I said we were friends in high school. I never mentioned anything about us being old!" Nina said with a laugh.

"Why don't you let me and Luke get you settled in the guesthouse while you ladies catch up?" Josh hooked a thumb toward the rear of the car.

Wiping his hands on the legs of his jeans, Luke stepped to the rear of her car and patted the trunk lid. "Are your bags in here?"

"Oh, um…" Carrie hedged.

"Wait, Luke," Nina said. "Carrie, why don't you stay with me at my house until the rest of the tour group arrives?" Nina laid a hand on her friend's arm, and Luke caught the minute flinch and the shiver that rolled through Carrie.

A knot balled in Luke's gut, recognizing the indications of her inner stress. But what had Carrie so wound up? Was it just a case of overwork at her office? A family argument? Trouble with a boyfriend or lover?

He curled his hand into a fist inside his pocket. Carrie's story was none of his business, and he intended to keep it that way.

Carrie glanced from one face to the next. All well-meaning, all friendly and smiling, all…suffocating. Until she glanced at Luke. He'd remained silent, but his incisive stare was perhaps more unnerving than the kind but subtle pressure from Nina and Josh.

"I think I'd rather stay here at the ranch, if that's all

right? Get settled before the rest of the group arrives."
And not needlessly put you and Steve in the line of fire.

Nina cocked her head to the side. "Are you sure?"

"It's perfectly fine as far as I'm concerned." Josh added a charming smile to reinforce his assurance. "The guesthouse is all cleaned, stocked and ready for occupants."

Carrie's gaze darted to Luke's. Would Luke and the other hands be close by over the next few days…just in case?

"Yes, I'm sure." She set her shoulders and brightened her grin to reflect more confidence in her choice. "Thank you, Josh."

Luke slid his hands in his jeans pockets, and he chewed the corner of his chapped lip as he studied her. Under his scrutiny, she felt a bit like the frog she'd had to dissect in Mr. Bolling's biology class—pinned down, being picked apart and analyzed. His attention caused a prickling sensation to skitter over her skin. The feeling wasn't unpleasant. Just…weird. Awkward. She hadn't missed the fact that Luke Wright was ruggedly handsome.

His pale gray eyes reminded her of a wolf's, while his rumpled tawny hair she likened more to a lion's. But the predator analogies didn't carry any further than that. She saw kindness in his expression, along with curiosity. Luke was also tall, well muscled and clearly physically fit. Because of his size and obvious strength, he could easily overpower her, crush her. Break her. And while that knowledge stirred a quiver in her belly, his stature didn't frighten her the way, maybe, it should. Luke had a presence about him that was oddly soothing and completely inexplicable. Of all people, she should know appearances were deceiving. Perhaps that was why she trusted her gut reaction to him over the story his large size told. A curl of warmth had wrapped around her trembling heart when he'd greeted her, his bear-paw-size hand gentle and reassuring, his grip confident without being domineering. His smile had been genuine and kind, not calculating. He opened her trunk and, finding nothing but her spare tire, he closed the lid again. "No bags?"

She dragged her small canvas duffel from the front seat. "Just this one. I learned to travel light when my family used to travel to Europe every summer."

"Europe." Luke's eyebrows rose as he strolled toward her. "Wow. Sounds great."

"It was." She gave him a genuine smile, remembering her trips with her parents and brother.

He slid his hand around the handle of her bag and tugged lightly. "I'll get that for you."

His fingers brushed hers, and a strange warmth rushed through her veins. Her head spun as if she'd just stepped off the teacup ride at the fair, and she had to brace her legs not to wobble.

Avoiding his unnerving gaze, she shook her head and tightened her grip. Having anyone else handle her few possessions unsettled her. If anyone took the few things she'd escaped her home with, she'd have nothing. No resources for survival. No mementos of her parents. No building blocks for starting over. "I can get it."

"I don't mind—" he began, but she pulled the bag from his grasp.

"Okay. I'll show you the way, then," Luke said, motioning toward the guesthouse. "Show you the setup in there."

Carrie glanced to Nina, prepared to ask her friend to

replace Luke. But her friend's cell phone rang at that moment, and Nina frowned when she glanced at the caller ID. "Sorry, I need to take this. I'm so glad you're here, Carrie. I'll catch up with you in a few minutes. Okay?" Nina raised the phone to her ear as she turned, saying, "Hi, what's wrong?"

"You ready?" Luke asked, giving his head a side jerk toward the guesthouse.

Holding her duffel against her chest, she fell in step behind Luke. She studied his back as they walked. His broad shoulders. The shape and definition of his muscled arms. Whether because of his work as a hand, good genetics or hours in a gym, Luke had the body of a man who spent more hours in physical labor than sitting behind a desk.

Joseph sits behind a desk every day, and he still has the strength to hurt you in numerous disturbing ways.

"The front room is a common area for all the tour guests," Luke explained, casting a look over his shoulder.

He was definitely bigger than Joseph both in height and general build. If Joseph showed up here, Luke would have the advantage, would be able to defend her. If he chose to get involved. If she was willing to drag someone else into her personal problems and expose them to the danger Joseph posed. Guilt plucked at her. Why had she come here? She didn't want to put anyone else in harm's way, whether they were physically capable of overpowering Joseph or not.

"There's a kitchenette stocked with snacks and cold drinks, but once the other tour guests arrive, all your meals will be prepared by the ranch staff." Another glance back to where she lagged behind him, and his pace slowed.

Luke and the other hands at the ranch were not her personal security force, and she had no right to expect anything from them. Just the same, she dragged her gaze over Luke's wide back and lean hips once more and took selfish comfort in knowing someone like him would be nearby. If needed. But the heat that spun through her with her appraisal couldn't correctly be called comfort. In fact, the quivering in her belly was decidedly flustering. She hadn't ogled a man in *that* way for years, so a moment passed before she recognized the fluttery heat for attraction.

Stop it, Carrie. Now was not the time for such distractions. She had no room in her life for anything but survival. She had to apply all of her focus and energy on foiling whatever uncanny method Joseph had of tracking her.

He stopped and faced her, holding out his hands. "You sure I can't carry that for you? You're kinda dragging."

She shook her head. "I'm fine. I just have short legs compared to yours."

His mouth crooked in a grin that glowed as much from his pale gray eyes as his lips. "Yeah, I've been told I walk too fast before. My sister used to say she had to take two steps for every one of mine to keep up."

She returned a smile. "Your sister was right."

"Sorry. I spend most of my time around other guys with long legs and with lots to get done while the sun's up." He motioned that he was waiting for her to precede him to the guesthouse.

"What about Nina?" Carrie strode past him up the concrete steps to the lodge door. "Does she keep up with you guys?"

His brow furrowed as he considered her question.

"Yeah. She does. She's doing a great job as a hand. She's more skilled on a horse than most of us, too—which is humbling. Guess it was her years with the rodeo."

"She was a champion barrel racer," Carrie said, her chest swelling with pride for her friend.

"I know. I've seen the videos of her competing. She was a badass."

"Before the car accident."

His mouth twisted into a frown. "Yeah." He angled his head as he joined her on the small landing and stuck a key in the doorknob. "You knew her then? When she had the accident?"

Carrie nodded, a sharp pain lancing her chest when she recalled the moment she'd heard the news Nina was in the ICU. "The accident wasn't her fault."

He unlocked the door and pushed it open. One light brown eyebrow arched. "I didn't say it was."

Her pulse kicked, and she took a step back. Oh God. Did he think she'd challenged him?

"Sorry," she said quickly, dropping her gaze to the ground. "I guess I...still feel protective of her. She was in such bad shape for so long."

"No apology needed. Ironic, huh, that she'd end up engaged to Steve? Fate has a strange sense of humor."

Carrie shot Luke a confused look. "What does that mean?"

She edged past him into the front room of the guesthouse, where a grouping of couches and comfy-looking chairs faced a stone fireplace. *Homey* was the word that came to mind as she scanned the country-themed decor and wood paneling.

"She didn't tell you?" Luke asked, holding the door

key out to her. "Steve was the guy driving the car that caused her accident all those years ago."

Carrie blinked. Replayed his words in her head. Surely she'd misunderstood, being distracted by the warm ambience of the guest quarters. "What?"

"I know. Fate is strange, huh?"

"Um." She ran her fingers through her hair as she shoved loose strands back from her face. "She said something about not regretting her accidents, including a more recent one, because they brought her and Steve together."

"Well," Luke said, jiggling the keys on a clip he held, until she extended a hand to take it from him. "I'm sure she'll fill you in on the details later." He walked to the hallway and flipped on a light. "The guest rooms are all pretty much the same. The second key on that ring goes to room two."

She peered down the corridor, where several doors stood half-open.

"As the first to arrive, you get first pick, however. If you prefer a different room—"

"No." She waved off further explanation. "No, I'm sure room two is fine."

He stared at her a moment with those unusually pale gray eyes holding hers before nodding slowly and turning for the door. "In that case, I'll leave you to unpack." He paused at the threshold, though, adding, "Speaking of accidents, I couldn't help but notice the large crack in your windshield."

Carrie tensed, remembering the vitriol in Joseph's tone and the nerve-shattering moment when Joseph had smashed the front window of her getaway car. Her narrow escape as he'd jerked on the door handle.

She forced a light laugh. "Oh, it's nothing. A rock hit it while I was driving down here."

"Must've been a big rock. That break's pretty big and looks like it's getting bigger. Any little bump or pebble could make it blow out, cave in on you. It needs to be replaced. Right away."

And just how am I supposed to pay for the repair? she wanted to ask. Her frustration roiled inside her, and she squeezed the handle of her duffel tighter. She couldn't use a credit card, and her emergency cash was dwindling to nothing. Using an ATM was out, as well. Joseph could track her location through such a transaction. And yet… she hadn't done either, hadn't kept her old cell phone, hadn't done any of the obviously traceable things, but he'd still found her.

"I'll see what I can do," she said.

He rubbed a hand on his chin as he angled his gaze out the open door toward her car. "I have a friend who works at the body shop in town. Why don't I set up an appointment for tomorrow? I can drive you to town to drop it off, and I bet it will be ready before we even hike out on Friday."

"Oh, uh…" Damn it! Why was he forcing the issue? "You don't have to do that."

"Maybe not. But I'm happy to. And—" his eyes narrowed on her as he lifted that expressive eyebrow again "—it really does need to be taken care of. It's not safe as it is."

Safe. The term, she'd learned, was relative. Her stomach clenched. She could repair the windshield, but it wouldn't really make her safe. Only freeing herself from Joseph would do that.

But with Luke's piercing eyes trained on her, her paper-thin willpower was crumpling. His high-pressure tactics, well-meant though they may be, reminded her too much of the way Joseph had controlled every aspect of their marriage. What money they spent. What food they bought. What TV they watched. Who she could or could not socialize with. And she'd caved to his wishes for the simple reason that bucking him, disagreeing with him, challenging him was not worth the price. On a good day, he'd yell, tell her she was stupid and didn't know what she was talking about. Her ideas, her opinions, her suggestions were all worthless.

On a bad day, he reinforced his position of control with scalding water, cracked ribs or well-placed bruises that her hair or her clothes would hide. Carrie shuddered and tried to block the memories of lying balled on the bathroom floor, trying to protect her head from his hard-soled shoes. She'd learned not to retreat to the bathroom. The tile floor hurt more than the carpet in the living room, and the marble sink and bathtub were a more brutal landing than the cushions of the couch. And forget door locks. They were flimsy at best and angered him more.

A worry line dented his forehead as he angled his head. "You all right?"

Carrie held her breath. What had her face revealed? She'd thought she'd mastered the art of hiding her emotions, keeping her face impassive, but clearly Luke had seen something. Rather than a bald-faced lie, this time she put him off with a partial truth. "Just tired. And I have a headache. I'll be okay as soon as I can rest in a dark, quiet room for a while."

Luke grimaced. "Oh. My mom gets bad migraines. They could take her out for days at a time." He hitched a thumb toward the hall. "You go rest. I'll handle getting your windshield repair set up. Feel better, okay?"

Before he left, he gave her a wink and a warm smile, his silver eyes bright with concern and a dimple softening the hard line of his cheekbones.

She opened her mouth to call him back, to protest, but how could she turn down his offer without explaining she had no extra money for such a repair? At least, not with her. She had bank accounts back in Aurora with more than enough to pay for any car repair she needed. Enough to buy a new car. Enough to fund the lavish lifestyle she and Joseph lived. The lifestyle Joseph knew he'd lose, along with his seat on the board of directors at French Industries, if she exposed him. If she divorced him. But she couldn't get to those funds without sending up a flare that told Joseph where she was.

Tossing the duffel on one of the stuffed chairs, she dropped weakly onto the couch. Where was she going to get the money to repair her windshield? She'd confessed her secret to Nina. Maybe her friend would loan her the money until…

Carrie gritted her teeth so hard her jaw popped. She hated the idea of borrowing money, of dragging Nina any further into her melodrama, of admitting how deeply in trouble she was. Shame bore down on her, and she bent her head, covering her face with her hands as she fought to keep the tears at bay. She'd cried enough tears. They did no good.

She tried to remember what she'd read about spousal abuse on the websites she'd looked up in recent weeks using the computers in public libraries. The statistics had stunned her…and strangely—selfishly—comforted her, knowing she wasn't the only one suffering through a marriage like hers and Joseph's. What little she'd known about abusive relationships before meeting Joseph had been superficial and naive. She'd worn blinders about a truth that was all too real for too many women…and men.

But now, armed with more information, she recognized her shame and guilt and sense of futility for what they were—a product of Joseph's manipulation, disrespect and demeaning cruelty. Understanding her feelings and shedding the weight of those emotions, though, were two different animals. Carrie sighed and glanced around the rustic guesthouse. Tonight she'd sleep in bed number twelve—no, thirteen—in seven weeks. While logically she knew she was safe here tonight, she still imagined she felt Joseph's breath on the back of her neck. He'd sworn he'd keep hunting her until he brought her back to their Aurora home and made her pay for her attempt to leave him.

And she believed him.

Chapter 3

"Oh, Carrie," Nina said, her eyes full of tears after Carrie finished telling her the whole sordid history of her relationship with Joseph. "I wish I'd known sooner. I wish I'd been there for you, that I could've done something to help." Her friend squeezed her hand, her dark expression saying how overwhelmed she was by the ugliness of Carrie's full story.

She and Nina sat on a bench made of hand-hewn wood, under a shade tree on a hill that overlooked the Double M Ranch. The sun was sinking low behind the rolling foothills of the Rockies and casting a golden glow over the fields, corrals and buildings below them. The tranquil scene helped soothe the jittery, ragged sensations that tore at her as she explained herself to Nina.

Carrie bowed her head. "You wouldn't have known, even if we'd done a better job keeping in touch. He made sure I didn't talk about it. Not that I would have. I'm ashamed of how I've let him treat me, that I'd believe him when he said he was sorry, that I'd allow fear to keep me bound to him."

"It's called battered woman syndrome. Everything you did and felt is typical of a woman living with domestic violence." Nina stroked Carrie's arm sympathetically.

Carrie chuffed an ill-humored breath. "Yeah. It's crazy to think there's a whole clinical definition for it. I learned the term when I started reading articles on the internet about how to escape. I saw myself in every line of every blog post and article, and it made me want to cry. Not for myself but for the other women going through the same pain."

"And men. Domestic violence isn't restricted to women. Or any social class or race. It happens throughout society."

Carrie nodded sadly.

Nina sat taller and squared her shoulders. "But you did the right thing. You left, and I will help you make a fresh start. I'm proud of you, Carrie. I know it was hard."

Swallowing hard, Carrie said, "It's not over. He keeps finding me. I don't know how. He's sworn to keep coming after me, to drag me back home with him, to—"

"He won't. Not this time. We'll protect you. We'll figure it out together."

Carrie wished she could believe Nina. Experience was hard to ignore. And in her experience, Joseph always knew, always found her, always won.

Yet after she'd laid out all of the ugly details of her life to Nina, Carrie's soul felt lighter. A ray of hope twinkled for her like the first star on a clear night. She inhaled the fresh air and forced a smile for her friend. "Thank you,

Nina. You can't begin to know how much I appreciate your help."

Nina rose from the bench and tugged on Carrie's hand. "Come on. Let's head back. Melissa said she was going to make homemade ice cream for dessert. I know you don't want to miss out on that."

Carrie hadn't had much appetite in weeks, but she humored Nina. "Definitely." She walked beside her friend as they headed down the hill to the ranch yard, where they met Luke as he came out of the barn.

"Evening, ladies." He touched the brim of his hat and graced them with a pleasant smile, and his step fell in with theirs.

"You checking on that bull again?" Nina asked.

"Yup. Wound is looking better already. Not as inflamed."

Nina bobbed a nod. "That's good news."

Luke angled his head to glance past his coworker. "So how do you like ranch life so far, Carrie?"

Nina laughed. "She's been here all of six hours, Luke."

He shrugged. "Just being friendly."

Carrie returned a smile. "It has been a very nice six hours, thank you. Everyone has been so warm and welcoming. And the setting is beautiful. So peaceful."

"Peaceful," he repeated, and seemed to ruminate on the word. "I guess I can see that. Around about daybreak, when the animals are all asking for breakfast and the dogs are yapping and excited and the hands are all shouting to each other across the corral, you may not think it's so peaceful, but in the evening, when the sun is setting over the mountains—" he pointed in the direction of the rose and orange sunset that currently lit the western sky "—and the animals are settling in for the night, this place is a little piece of heaven. It's…healing."

His expression was contemplative for a moment, as if he was mindfully soaking in a needed dose of the quiet beauty. His eyes seemed so intense as he gazed at the sinking sun that Carrie wondered what past trouble or pain Luke might be remembering, if he needed the quiet to mend his soul or if he'd simply been speaking rhetorically. Either way, his countenance, bathed in the golden light, caused a stir in her chest. The evening glow highlighted the masculine cut of his jaw and shimmered in his sweat-darkened blond hair.

Carrie caught herself staring at him. And Nina caught her, as well. Her friend gave her a knowing grin and a nudge that Carrie dismissed with a subtle head shake.

"Want to join us, Luke?" Nina asked, her twinkling gaze on Carrie for another moment before facing the other hand. "We're on our way to grab a bowl of that ice cream Melissa mentioned at dinner. Homemade strawberry?"

"You bet. That's where I was headed."

Carrie hooked her arm through Nina's to slow her pace and said brightly, "We'll be there in a second, Luke. Save us some."

He hesitated a minute. "Don't be too long. Melissa's ice cream doesn't last long around a crew of hot and tired ranchers."

Carrie watched him stride toward the family's house, his dusty jeans hugging his hips and muscled thighs, and his shirtsleeves rolled up to expose work-honed biceps. No doubt, Luke was a handsome man. But—

"I know what you're doing," she whispered to Nina.

"And the answer is no. Don't try to play matchmaker for me."

"You could do a lot worse than Luke." Nina cringed, clearly realizing how her comment sounded. "What I mean is—"

"I know what you mean. But the answer is still no. I don't want or need another man in my life. I'm not even officially divorced from Joseph yet."

"But that's just a matter of time," Nina said, then with a playful grin she added, "You may not be buying, but you can still window-shop."

"No. Not even looking." Carrie sighed heavily. "I need time to just be me for a while. To get my life straight. So, while I admit he's quite easy on the eyes—" her gaze cut to the cowboy crossing the yard, and her pulse bucked "—don't push me at him tonight. Okay?"

Nina twisted her mouth in a moue of concession. "Fine. But for what it's worth, Luke is a prince among men. All the guys on the ranch are, but he's the only one who's unattached. He's kind and trustworthy and would treat you with the respect you deserve."

"That I deserve?" She shook her head. "That sounds rather…entitled."

"Hell, yes, you deserve it." Nina faced her, her hands on her hips. "Every person is entitled to respect and love and kindness. *You* deserve it." She poked Carrie lightly on the collarbone. "Don't give up on men because the one you married failed to treat you right."

Carrie raked hair back from her face and glanced away, unable to hold Nina's determined stare. "Maybe one day. I don't know."

Placing a hand on Carrie's shoulder, Nina sighed. "All right. I won't push. But promise me this much?"

Carrie met Nina's eyes with a wary gaze. "What?"

"Watch Luke. Talk to him. Don't avoid him. Allow yourself to see how a good man treats a woman. Luke is the kind of man you should be with, the kind of man you deserve."

With a slow exhale, Carrie gave a small nod to appease Nina, but she was a long way from ready to entertain thoughts of a new man in her life. Even one as devastatingly handsome as Luke Wright.

The next morning dawned with bright sunshine and a clear blue sky, and with a good night's sleep to restore her, Carrie's mood lifted. For the first time in a long time, she felt her ragged nerves calm, and she drew an easy breath. As she stepped out of the guesthouse, she lifted her face to the bright August sun, inhaling the fresh air—only to wrinkle her nose and laugh at herself. The ranch air was scented with manure and other fetid smells inherent to animal husbandry. Not the worst smells in the world, but she was still unaccustomed to the overwhelming odors.

"Morning!" a male voice called to her, and she turned to see Josh headed toward her from the stable, two black-and-white cattle dogs trotting along at his feet.

No. Not Josh. Or was it? She squinted against the sun and shielded her eyes with one hand.

"Morning," she returned to the handsome cowboy who closed the distance between them and offered his hand.

"You must be Nina's friend. I'm Zane. Welcome to the Double M." His grip was firm as he greeted her, and she introduced herself. He must have recognized her confusion, because he added, "I'm Josh's identical twin."

Carrie laughed and rubbed the head of one of the dogs

when it sniffed her hand. "That explains it. I thought I was losing my mind."

His rich laugh reverberated in the ranch yard. "You're not crazy. My wife and I were in Denver last night for a concert, so we missed your welcome dinner. If you're looking for Nina, she's in the stable. If you're looking for breakfast, follow me. I'm headed in to eat, and you're more than welcome to join us."

"No, thank you. I had some tea already." She motioned to the dogs. "Australian shepherds?"

"Close. Blue heelers. And feeling frisky this morning." Zane ruffled the ears of the dog closest to him.

"They're sweet. I love dogs." With a nod toward the stable, Carrie asked, "Is it okay for me to go in there? I won't be in the way?"

One of the blue heelers put its front paws on her hip, and Zane whistled at it. "Checkers, down." Directing his attention to her again, he answered, "No, you won't be in the way. But Nina'll be headed to the house for her breakfast in a minute. Sure you won't come with me? Breakfast is the most important meal of the day, you know."

She gave him a soft, amused snort. "So I hear. I, um…" Carrie glanced toward the stable then back to Zane's warm grin. "Okay. If you're sure I'm not imposing."

"The more the merrier."

As she hustled to keep up with him, Carrie sent an encompassing gaze around the grounds. She'd been road weary and rather shell-shocked yesterday when she arrived, so she saw the ranch with new eyes this morning. The outbuildings looked freshly painted, and the large corral, where several horses stood swatting flies with their tails, conjured images of old Western films. Though she'd never spent more than the length of an elementary school field trip on a ranch, the Double M looked… homey. Inviting. *Peaceful.*

The word she'd used when speaking to Luke resurfaced in her mind, as did an image of Luke's chiseled face and pensive eyes as he'd studied the horizon.

Healing, he'd said. And, Lord, did she need some peace and healing in her life, even if only for a few days. Time enough to figure out her next move.

"Breakfast is a big deal around here," Zane said, interrupting her thoughts. "Everyone eats a big meal together after the early-morning work—checking and feeding the animals—is done and before we head into the pastures. Years ago, we used to feed everyone, hands and family, in the bunkhouse before we converted it into guest housing. But that was back when we were a much bigger operation. We lost a lot of our help a couple years ago and only recently started rebuilding our staff."

"How many people work here now?" She tried to recall the names and faces she'd met since her arrival.

"We're back up to three hands and are looking to hire a cook. My mom, my wife and my sister-in-law have been doing all of the cooking for the last several months, and while they don't really mind cooking for the horde every day, they all have outside interests and careers they'd prefer to pursue."

He held the front door to the main house for her, and as she stepped inside, much more appetizing aromas greeted her. Bacon, coffee, a hint of cinnamon. She turned to comment to Zane about the delicious scents when something brown and another something black streaked from the large front room down the hall behind her with the thunderous pounding of small feet.

She gasped in surprise and chuckled. "What was that?"

Zane groaned and rolled his eyes. "*That* is what happens when you add my sister-in-law's little cat to my mom's crazy cat. As if this house didn't have enough chaos."

"Oh, hello," a cheery voice said, and Carrie turned to see an attractive woman with long, curling dark hair at the entry to the front room.

Carrie flashed a smile and watched as Zane gave the woman a kiss before introducing the brunette as his wife, Erin.

The women exchanged greetings, and Erin led the way into the house. "Breakfast is ready. Come get it while it's hot. Are the others on their way?"

"Soon," Zane said.

Carrie followed Erin through the comfy-looking living room into a large dining room, where a long walnut table with a dozen places set took center stage. Josh was already at the table with family patriarch Michael, whom she'd met at dinner the night before along with most of the McCall clan. Beside Michael, she noticed a brown-haired cowboy, whose hat was hung on a spindle of the back of his chair. She smiled at the men, and they nodded amiably.

"Howdy. I'm Dave," said the hand, rising from his seat to offer Carrie a hand to shake.

"Nice to meet you. Thank you all for including me. It smells terrific." The sound of more cat races called her attention to the living room, where the brown cat and a smaller black one had returned and now rolled on the floor, kicking and tussling with each other. "Oh gosh. Should you break that up?"

Erin shook her head. "They're not really fighting. That's how Zeke and Sadie play. They actually love each other."

Carrie watched the smaller black cat break free of the brown cat's wrestler's hold and, after backing up a step, tackle the brown cat again.

Matriarch Melissa and Josh's wife, Kate, emerged from the connecting room, presumably the kitchen since they each carried a platter of food, and Josh stood and pulled out a chair next to him for her.

As she sat, Josh then helped her scoot her chair up to the table, and she wondered idly if the gentlemanly manners were brought out especially for her as their guest. But seeing Zane show a similar kindness to his wife as she took her seat, she decided the gesture was habit for the family. And she experienced a prick of jealousy for the McCall women.

Joseph had shown her that kind of courtesy when they'd been dating. He still did when they went to dinner with business associates he wanted to impress. But more recently, simple kindness and manners in her marriage had become few and far between. She shoved away the pang that twisted in her gut thinking about all she'd lacked in her marriage. She didn't want to spoil this pretty day, these few moments around kind, caring people, dwelling on her past.

"Eggs?" Michael asked, passing her a platter loaded with scrambled eggs.

"Thank you."

"How long have you known our Nina?" Melissa asked, helping herself to bacon and toast before passing that platter to Erin.

Our Nina. Carrie smiled, liking how the McCall matriarch used the inclusive term. She thought about Nina's assertion that the McCalls were her second family, and a fuzzy warmth swelled in her chest. "Long time. We went to junior and high school together."

Josh made a low rumbling sound in his throat. "So you're another Bulldog?"

Carrie stilled, the disapproving tone in his voice waking her danger instincts—until he lifted a corner of his mouth and flashed a teasing grin.

She released the breath she held and relaxed her tensed muscles. Nodding in response to his question regarding her high school's mascot, she said, "I am."

"And you realize this family all went to Boyd Valley High?" His lopsided smile had a wry edge.

Boyd Valley High was her school's cross-town rival. She took the plate of bacon and toast as it reached her and cut a side glance and a wink to Josh. "I do, but I won't hold it against you."

He tipped his head toward her as a round of chuckles circulated around the table. "Likewise."

The sound of a back door opening and closing preceded Nina and Luke's appearance through the kitchen door.

Nina took the time to give Carrie a hug from behind before taking her seat. "How'd you sleep? You get settled okay?"

"Yes. Slept better than I have in months," Carrie said quietly.

"You saved me some bacon, didn't you?" Luke asked, taking the chair directly opposite Carrie.

"Yes, but you better hurry...oops! There goes the last of it," Zane teased, dumping all of the bacon on his plate.

"Zane!" his mother said with an eye roll. To Luke, she said, "There's more ready in the kitchen."

Nina took the empty bacon platter from Zane. "I'll go get the refill."

"Kidding!" Zane took several slices of bacon from his plate and said, "Catch."

The bacon flew across the table, and Luke snagged it from the air. Josh laughed at his brother, and Erin groaned.

"Really?" Melissa said, shaking her head. "We have company. She's going to think I didn't teach you basic table etiquette, son."

"Did you?" Josh asked, giving his mouth an exaggerated wipe with his sleeve and grinning devilishly. Melissa shot him a withering glance.

"Excuse my boys, Carrie," Michael said. "They think they're funny."

She smiled at the ranch owner, while privately acknowledging how much more she liked the twins' antics over the tense, appetite-killing atmosphere she'd known eating with Joseph.

"The toast is burned. Can't you even get that right?"

"Oatmeal again?" Joseph dumped the contents of his bowl on the floor. "What do I have to do to get a real breakfast around here?"

She gripped her fork harder, wishing she could quiet the echoes in her head. Would she ever be free of those haunting memories?

Nina returned with the refilled bacon plate and took her seat. "So, Carrie, want to ride out into the pastures with us today? We're checking the fence and moving the herd to an upper grazing area."

She met her friend's gaze. "By ride, do you mean a horse?"

"Do you know how?" Luke asked.

She shifted her gaze to Luke and was struck anew by how penetrating his light gray eyes were. He had yet to shave this morning, and with the day-old stubble dusting his square jaw, he was even more handsome than yesterday. For a moment she got lost, staring into his silver gaze and admiring the strong cut of his cheekbones and slightly crooked Grecian nose.

"'Cause I'd be happy to give you a few pointers if you want," he said, rousing her from her perusal.

"Oh, uh… I've ridden once or twice, but—" she motioned toward her friend "—I'm sure Nina can help me figure things out."

"Happy to if you want me, but—" Nina jerked her head toward the other hand "—Luke is actually the one who'll be instructing you for the adventure tour. You could get a head start on the rest of the group with him today."

She cut Nina an I-said-no-matchmaking side-eye, but her friend only shrugged and returned a faux-innocent grin.

From the living room, the cats launched into another race down the hall. Several heads turned to watch the felines disappear, and Zane chuckled. "Crazy animals."

Erin laughed. "Poor Scout doesn't know what to make of those two."

"Who's Scout?" Carrie asked.

Zane's wife pointed under an extra chair in the corner of the room near the opening to the living room. Beneath the chair, a chubby brown tabby with legs too small for her round belly sat peering out with a wary gaze.

"Scout was my mom's until a month ago. She moved to assisted living where no pets are allowed, so I took her. She'd prefer to be an only cat, seeing as she's an introvert personality, but while Zane and I finish the construction on our house, we're living here, and Scout spends her time trying to stay out of the way of the rowdy duo."

Carrie leaned to the side to get a better look at the cat. A longing she'd locked away years ago nudged her heart, a love of animals and desire to have a furry companion. But while she'd been with Joseph, she hadn't dared to adopt the pet she craved. He'd made violent threats concerning the neighbors' dog when it got in their trash, ones she had no doubt he'd carry out, and she'd witnessed his inhumane treatment of other small creatures—from frogs and squirrels to butterflies—to know that no cat or dog would be safe in their house.

"Hi, Scout. Aren't you sweet?" she cooed to the brown tabby, who stared back with big green eyes that reminded her of the wide eyes of a Disney character.

Zane snorted. "*Sweet* is not the word I'd use. She hisses at me more often than not."

"She is sweet!" Erin countered with a scowl for her husband. "She's just out of sorts in this new place. She's sweet to me and purrs when I rub her belly."

"She slept on my lap while I was reading last night," Melissa said, smiling at Erin.

"See?" Erin said to her husband.

Michael sighed loudly. "Some days I wonder if we've gone from a ranch to a zoo. Three-hundred-plus heads of cattle, nine horses, three dogs, three cats…and now Piper has those chickens at her place."

"Chickens?" Carrie asked.

"Yep," Josh said, leaning toward her with a conspiratorial glint in his eyes. "Dolly, Holly, Molly and Polly."

Carrie blinked and chuckled. "Well, golly!"

Her reply earned a laugh from her hosts.

Luke poked Nina with his elbow. "Hey, you didn't tell us your friend was so witty."

Nina gave the other ranch hand a broad grin. "Oh, she's witty and so much more."

"I like her." Luke's warm grin reached across the table and wrapped around her like a soft sweater. Comforting. Inviting.

Something about him drew her inexorably in. A magnet to steel. Before she'd married Joseph and had her soul battered, she might have pursued the attraction she felt toward the rugged cowboy. But as she'd told Nina, she had no place in her life for a man. After taking such risks to get free of Joseph, why would she want to tie herself to another man? Her freedom had been hard earned, and she wasn't about to give that up.

"By the way, I talked to my friend, like I promised, and got you an appointment to have your windshield replaced," Luke said. "I can take you to drop off your car this afternoon. They said they'd get to it first thing tomorrow."

She sent him a startled glance. "Oh. I, uh…" A rebuke rose to her tongue, but she'd learned to swallow argumentative words, had the desire to correct or disagree beaten out of her. A ball of resentment curled in her belly. She hadn't asked for his help, hadn't wanted to spend valuable funds on her car. But how could she say no? Especially in front of the man's bosses and friends. While Luke wasn't Joseph, she still didn't dare. The seed of fear and humility, of deferral and doubt, was deeply planted.

When she said nothing for several seconds, the conversation moved on. Only Nina still watched her from across the table. Her friend's eyes asked, *Are you okay?*

Carrie forced a limp smile and shoveled another bite of eggs on her fork. She chewed the bite but had trouble swallowing, her appetite gone, her throat choked with worry. If she let Luke bully her into replacing the windshield, how would she pay for the repair? What would happen to her if she stood her ground? Should she flee again? Run from the ranch and this host of kind, well-meaning people?

And when would she ever regain enough inner strength and self-confidence to stand her ground? To fight for herself? To take back control over her life?

Not today, apparently, because a few hours later she was in her car, following Luke into the small town of Boyd Valley.

Boyd Valley. Joseph studied the blinking dot on his computer screen and grunted. The small town was only around a ninety-minute drive from Aurora. Only ten minutes or so from the area where Carrie had grown up. Did that mean she'd run to an old friend for shelter? To the best of his knowledge, Carrie hadn't been in touch with her high school friends in years. He'd monitored her social calendar, her Facebook posts, her cell-phone records to stay on top of any dubious communications behind his back. He rocked back in his desk chair and pursed his lips as he thought. He could dig out her old yearbooks to see who appeared to be her closest friends and most trusted allies back then. The blinking light moved along one of the main streets in the small town then stopped. When he zoomed in, the address shown appeared to be in a business zone, not a residence. Could she be at a motel? Was Boyd Valley big enough for a motel or bed-and-breakfast? What was she up to?

A knock sounded on his office door, and before he could answer to grant the person permission to come in, his door opened.

Bill Fredericks, the head of accounting at French Industries, marched in. "Hey, Joseph. You got a minute?"

Joseph closed the lid of his laptop and gave his co-worker a tight smile. He had to remember that Carrie was just a means to an end—holding on to his position on the board at her family's business, French Industries. Toward that goal, keeping the other senior management on his side, supportive of his place at the table, was just as important. "Sure. What's up?"

Bill launched into a wordy explanation of some recent inconsistencies in the books, and Joseph refocused his energies on business affairs. He'd worked too hard for too long to rise to where he was today. As a poor kid, scraping by with his alcoholic mother and too many siblings, working back-breaking hours on the factory floor, he'd never dreamed he'd come so far. The position, power and wealth he enjoyed as a senior vice president were the product of fifteen years of blood, sweat and carefully managed opportunities. Only someone of his ambition and people skills could have advanced from line worker to floor manager to accounting grunt to department head to vice president to senior vice president as quickly as he had. Of course, finagling a meet with the owner's daughter and romancing his way into nepotism as Carrie's husband had gone a long way toward his mission for a seat of power.

And now Carrie stood to ruin everything he'd worked for. The bitch.

"So if you have a few minutes to look at the numbers, I'd appreciate your feedback. Nick wants a report on the account by the end of the week," Bill said, finally wrapping up his droning inquiry.

Joseph nodded. "Leave it there." He pointed to a tall stack of files. "I'll take a look before I leave the office tonight."

"Thanks, buddy." Bill dropped the thick report on his desk and gave a wave as he hurried out.

Buddy. Yeah, just remember who your buddy is if Carrie manages to get the divorce she wants. If his ties to the French family were severed, if Carrie made public her claims of being mistreated in their marriage, his job could go away.

Joseph scrubbed a hand over his face. *Not if I can help it.*

He opened his laptop again and stared at the blinking dot on the map. He knew where Carrie was now and needed to head down to Boyd Valley first thing tomorrow. He was running out of excuses for being gone from the office to hunt Carrie down. He had to bring her back home sooner rather than later. But as long as he had his secret weapon, Carrie wouldn't go anywhere without him knowing. He'd catch her unaware before long and bring her back where she belonged. It was just a matter of time.

Chapter 4

When they reached the body shop, Carrie pulled in next to Luke's truck and cut the engine. She still couldn't believe she'd let every opportunity to say no to this repair pass her by, even though she didn't have the ready assets to pay for the glass replacement. She sighed, frustrated with herself and her spinelessness. But Joseph had ingrained in her a fear of resistance. She'd bowed to his will to keep the peace and to mollify his temper so many times, she really didn't know what standing up for herself looked like anymore.

She sat, gripping the steering wheel with both hands, staring at the obscene crack Joseph had left on the window as she'd fled the last motel. She heard his angry shouts reverberating in her mind. *Give up, Carrie! I will always find you!*

A knock on her side window jolted her out of her daze.

Carrie clapped a hand to her chest, where her heart stuttered and stumbled.

Luke opened her door and, ducking his head to peer in at her, sent her an apologetic grin. "Sorry. Did I startle you?"

She tried to laugh off her nerves. "A little. I just got lost in thought and…"

Gathering her purse from the passenger seat, she climbed out and followed Luke inside the small body shop. Luke called a greeting to a short, stocky man wearing blue coveralls, and the man met them at the end of the garage bay.

Luke introduced her to Greg Beal, the shop owner, and Carrie shook the man's hand. "Thank you for fitting me into your schedule."

"No problem," Greg said. "You're parked around at the side? Let's take a look, see what we've got."

After one look at the damaged windshield, Greg agreed it needed to be replaced, echoing Luke's assertions about how dangerous it was to risk having it cave in. "See how the crack goes all the way to the edge? That's a problem. But I can get you fixed up. Not many BMWs around these parts, but I called around and found a replacement glass at Walter's in Denver. Should be here in a couple hours."

Greg led them back into the building and to his desk. Carrie shifted her weight and rubbed her hands on her arms, deciding how to broach the topic she had to discuss. "About payment…"

"All I need now is a deposit of a hundred dollars. We take all forms of credit card, checks and, of course, cash. Are you filing an insurance claim?"

"Uh," Carrie stammered, playing that scenario out in

her head. The insurance company calling the house in Aurora with follow-up questions, Joseph answering the phone, learning where the car was being repaired. Ice filled her veins. "No. No insurance." When Greg's eyebrows lifted, she clarified. "I have insurance, of course. I just mean…"

"No claim. I get it. For something as small as a windshield, I don't blame you. Whole repair shouldn't be more than three hundred, three fifty, and we'll apply the deposit to that total."

Her gut pitched. "Can I…break that into payments? I'm rather cash poor at the moment, but…"

Luke sent her a concerned look. "Geez, Carrie. I'm sorry. I didn't realize… And here I pushed you to do the repair, not realizing—"

She touched his arm and shook her head. "It's not that I can't pay. I have the money…or I can get it, anyway." *I hope.* "I just didn't bring my credit cards on my trip, and I wrote my last check a couple weeks ago and haven't ordered more." The lies rolled off far too easily, bitter on her tongue.

Pressing a hand to his chest, Luke turned to Greg. "I'll cover the charge. Just do the work, and I'll settle up with you when we pick the car up."

Embarrassment stung Carrie's cheeks. "No. Luke, I can't possibly…"

"Sure, you can. I don't mind." He pulled a slim wallet from his back pocket and handed Greg a credit card.

As much as she appreciated his generosity, Luke's high-handedness chafed a raw spot inside her. She'd worked too hard, come too far, sacrificed too much to get away from a controlling man to allow another one to take charge of her life, her decisions.

"No!" she said sharply, stopping Greg as he was about to slide Luke's card through the card reader. Dear God, where had that come from? Her insides tensed as if readying for a blow, but Luke only looked startled. A staggering heartbeat later, when nothing bad happened to her, she seized the tenuous stand she'd made, and she grabbed the charge card from Greg. As she thrust it back toward Luke, her hand and voice shook. "I'll take care of my own bills."

Luke shot her an uneasy look. "Okay. Sorry. Just trying to he—"

"Did I ask for your help?" she barked. Now that she'd cracked the dam of emotions she'd suppressed for years, bitterness spewed out in a stream she couldn't stop. "Did I ask for the new glass or for you to swoop in and play hero? I don't need to be rescued! And I sure don't want someone telling me what to do or micromanaging my life!"

In the awkward silence that followed her tirade, tears stung her eyes, and her gut soured. Why was she berating the one person, besides Nina, who'd shown the most concern and interest in helping her? Luke had been nothing but kind, and this was how she paid him back? With bitterness? Cutting him off at his knees? She hated the shrewish sound of her voice, the echoes of her diatribe still ringing in her ears. Her heart sank, and she shook her head. "I'm sorry. That was harsh. I…"

Luke turned up his hands and shrugged casually in dismissal.

Sorting her thoughts as quickly as she could, Carrie slid off the ruby ring she wore on her right hand, a gift from her parents when she'd turned sixteen, and slapped it on the desk in front of Greg. She hated to part with it, but she'd already sold her wedding band and engagement ring a couple weeks earlier in Omaha when her cash had started running low. "Here. You can pawn this. It's real. Twenty-four-karat gold and a ruby. You should be able to get at least five hundred for it."

Greg sent her an uneasy look.

"Carrie..." Luke's tone pleaded with her. "Don't. Let me loan you the money. Please."

She squared her shoulders, even though inside she was shriveling, aching. "No."

Greg picked up the ring, stared at it a moment, then divided a look between Luke and Carrie. "Tell you what. I'll hold on to this, put it in my safe, call it collateral, and you two can figure out between you who's gonna pay. Meanwhile, I'll get the boys to work on that windshield. All right?"

Carrie dragged in a deep breath. She could think of a lot of ways she'd rather spend the money from pawning her ring than buying a windshield. Eating in the weeks to come, for example. Having a roof over her head. Gas in her tank in case she had to flee again on a moment's notice. But if Joseph continued tracking her—God only knew how—she'd eventually have to borrow money from friends. Or sell others of the few treasured possessions she'd left home with. She gave Greg a nod, then turned on her heel and hurried out of the garage bay before she shed tears.

The ride back to the ranch was silent for the first several minutes. Carrie stared out the side window, avoiding Luke's gaze, though she sensed his attention. She owed him an apology for her waspish reaction to his offer to help. But apologies could lead to questions, and she wasn't prepared to explain herself. Maybe it was better if he thought her a churlish and ungrateful woman instead of allowing him to become any more enmeshed in her life. If Joseph should track her down again—or rather *when* Joseph tracked her down again—she didn't want any of the owners or well-meaning ranch hands at the Double M to find themselves caught in Joseph's wrath. And why shouldn't she believe that however Joseph had found her before would work again?

A dull pain lodged in her chest. Fighting the sense of futility and despondency grew harder each time Joseph caught up to her. Each narrow escape warned that *next time* she might not be alert to his arrival and might not get away. *Next time* he might vent his spleen and kill her.

"Does the ring have sentimental value to you?" Luke asked, drawing her out of her macabre musing.

She hazarded a glance at him and was struck again by how captivating and incisive his pale gray eyes were. How heartbreakingly handsome he was.

"Yes." She owed him at least a morsel of honesty.

"Is it a family heirloom?"

"No. It's not that old."

"Hmm." He twisted his mouth and shook his head. "I just hate for you to give it up when I can help you. Call it a loan. Take however long you need to pay me back."

She scowled at him. "You barely know me. Why would you give me money?"

He lifted a shoulder. "I know Nina. You're her friend. And…you seem to be at wit's end. In a bind. I want to help."

In a bind. That put it mildly. She considered his offer. Was her pride worth putting herself in deeper constraints?

"A loan, huh?" she muttered, and his face brightened.

"I'll even charge you interest if it makes you feel better." He sent her a wry grin, and Carrie chuckled.

"Oh, yes. More debt is sure to cheer me up," she quipped.

Luke lifted a palm in invitation. "You pick the terms, then."

"Me?"

"Sure. If you don't want the money as a gift, what terms will ease your mind?"

She sighed and turned back to the side window. Carrie couldn't remember ever being given the opportunity, the permission to decide something for herself. Joseph had told her what would be. Had dictated. Had savagely controlled every aspect of their marriage, from social invitations to finances. Every purchase she made, every lunch date she accepted, every meal she prepared had to have his stamp of approval. Or else...

Her gut soured realizing how much of herself she'd sacrificed to appease Joseph's temper. If her parents had lived to see her marriage, they'd have been appalled. Shame filled her for the cowering woman she'd allowed herself to become. Self-preservation had become her guiding principle, to the detriment of the confident woman she'd once been.

Crossing her arms over her chest, she angled her body toward him. "Okay. Zero percent interest and forty years to pay it off."

One blond eyebrow shot up. "Forty years?"

"You said I could pick the terms."

He snorted with humor. "That I did." Luke sent her a smile that stirred a pleasant quiver in her belly. "Okay. You have a deal."

She frowned. "Are you nuts? Those are terrible terms for you!"

His rich laugh filled the truck cab and resounded deep inside her. The baritone notes washed her soul and left her spirits lighter. "Considering I was willing to give you the money with no strings, I think I'm getting a good deal. This way, about the time I'm ready to retire, I can use the payments I've banked for a weekend trip or to have a splurge night on the town." He continued grinning as he returned his attention to the road. "You are good for it, right? I can count on steady payments for the next forty years?"

Carrie studied him. He was an enigma to her, and that bothered her. She didn't like, didn't trust, anything she couldn't understand. At least with Joseph, she knew what to expect, knew what made him tick, scary as that was.

"Why?" She narrowed her eyes on him. "Why are you doing any of this? What's in it for you?"

Luke cut his eyes toward her again, and she could tell that, when he saw her serious expression, the glib answer he'd planned died on his lips. After a beat, he said, "Why does there have to be anything in it for me?"

"In my experience, men always have ulterior motives."

His eyebrows quirked upward. "You need to expand your circle of male acquaintances, then."

Watch Luke. Talk to him. Luke is the kind of man you should be with, the kind of man you deserve.

Silencing Nina's voice in her head, she muttered under her breath, "I'd rather just eliminate men from my life altogether."

"That would be unfortunate for the men of the world. You're a beautiful woman with a lot to offer. Your sense of humor, for one. Once this rough patch is behind you—"

"This rough patch?" She snapped her gaze to his. "You don't know anything about my life, what I'm dealing with, so just…stop." Shaking from the inside out, she faced the passenger window again, hating her churlish response and the shrewish woman she seemed to have become.

Another few moments of silence passed before Luke said softly, "I don't know why I want to help you. Some misplaced sense of chivalry? Maybe I'm trying to prove something to myself. That I can make a difference. That I have things to atone for."

Her pulse skipped. Atone for? What had Luke done that needed redemption?

"A voice in the back of my head is telling me to walk away, leave you alone. It'd be easier to not get involved, but…"

He paused, and she prodded, "But?"

"But I can't." He blew out a breath, and his lips buzzed with his frustration. "I left someone I cared about alone when she pushed me away once before, and it didn't end well."

Carrie curled her fingers into her palms and lowered her gaze to her lap. "I'm sorry for your friend, but I'm not her. And I'm not interested in being some charity case to ease your guilt over—"

"Whoa, whoa, whoa!" He stopped the car at a cross-road and shot her a scowl. "I never called you a charity case. That's not how I see you."

She shook her head and shrugged one shoulder. "Regardless, I don't want your money. I don't need your help. And… I really don't want to talk about this anymore." Belatedly, she added, "But thank you, Luke. For trying."

Seeing the frustration in his eyes, she reached for his arm and squeezed his wrist. Mistake. The contact sent crackling sensations to her core, as if she'd touched a live wire. She snatched her hand back, and as she rubbed the pad of her thumb over the tingles in her opposing palm, she gathered her composure. "I do appreciate the thought behind what you've done, what you've offered. But—" she shook her head harder "—my situation is not going away any time soon, and I have to start figuring out my future on my own."

A car behind them honked its horn, and Luke raised his gaze to his rearview mirror to frown at the impatient driver. After checking for traffic, he pulled onto the crossroad, and his brow beetled. "And the adventure trip? How does that figure into your situation?"

Carrie wet her lips. "Well, Nina suggested that. I guess she thought that making me face some physical challenges would help build my confidence in the other battles I was facing. For me, it's just an opportunity to… escape my situation for a few days. Hit Pause. Take a breath."

The muscles in his jaw flexed as he, apparently, meditated on her answer. Then, with a quick nod, he met her gaze again. "Then that's what it will be. I'll make sure these next few days are a relaxing, confidence-building escape for you. Okay?"

She exhaled heavily. *Escape.* The word taunted her. If only it could be a permanent one, instead of just a few days. But for now, a few days of safety would be a gift. "I like that deal."

Thank you, Luke. For trying. Carrie's words taunted Luke that evening as he worked, saddling his horse to meet Josh, Zane and Brady in the west pasture.

For *trying.* He had to do better than try or else he needed to walk away. Half an effort was never going to be enough for him. For Carrie. Playing at help was a recipe for later disaster and a future of regrets and guilt. His half-assed attempts to help Sharon were proof of that. Guilt that had lurked in the shadows in recent months crept out and bit him hard. He rubbed a hand on his chest where, deep in his core, his loss and sorrow were a physical pain.

The sound of a feminine laugh reached him, and he peeked around the corner of his horse's stall to find the McCalls' blue heelers, Ace and Checkers, dancing around Carrie, their tails wagging enthusiastically. She crouched to pat the dogs, and Ace bumped her so hard with his wiggling body that she fell over in the dusty yard. Carrie laughed harder, hugging the dog's neck and receiving a tongue bath on her face. The setting sun cast a warm light on the scene and caught gold highlights in Carrie's wheat-brown hair. Smiling as she was, without artifice or pretension, her face glowed, and Luke's breath hung in his chest.

Mesmerized, Luke leaned his hip against the wall of the horse stall and simply watched, enjoying the musical sound of her laughter. He didn't know what secret and hurts she was harboring, why she was financially strapped when everything about her clothes and luggage shouted "money," but he knew laughter was good for the soul. Hers and his. Dogs were first-class ambassadors of love and healing smiles, and he silently thanked the rowdy blue heelers for giving Carrie a moment of cheer and for fate granting him the opportunity to observe the unguarded moment.

The gentle tug in his chest should have concerned him. He didn't need to feel an attraction to the beautiful, vulnerable woman who was merely passing through.

But when it came to matters of the heart, Luke had never been wise or cautious. If he wanted to protect himself from his growing affection for Nina's friend, his best choice was avoidance.

And how likely was that to happen given his role as a guide on the adventure trip this weekend? He grunted and twisted his mouth wryly.

Carrie struggled back to a crouch and spoke in a soft voice to Checkers, who was practically in her lap. Ace shoved his way back in, looking for a share of the attention, and Carrie was knocked backward again. She yelped, and Luke chuckled.

"Carrie! Are you okay? I'm so sorry!" Michael hurried across the ranch yard from the back door of the family house and offered her a hand up as he shooed the zealous dogs away. "Down, Checkers. No! Ace, sit."

Still laughing as she wiped dog slobber from her cheeks, Carrie took Michael's hand and let him pull her to her feet. "I'm fine. I invited them in for a hug and a pat and got kisses, too. I love their enthusiasm."

Michael growled his disagreement. "We can't have them assaulting guests."

When the rancher reached for her, Carrie cringed and jerked back.

Luke straightened from his lean, surprised by her dramatic reaction.

"Whoa, easy!" Michael smiled and held his hands up as if surrendering. "Only reaching for that bit of straw on your sleeve."

"Oh." Carrie gave an embarrassed-sounding chuckle and plucked off the mentioned debris. "You just startled me."

With a more concerned expression, Michael asked, "You sure you're all right?"

The smile Carrie flashed Michael appeared strained to Luke, unlike the glow she'd had as she giggled with the affectionate and hyper dogs.

Or was he seeing things that weren't there to justify the odd intuition he had about Carrie? Despite her repeated assertions that she didn't need help, that she was fine, in truth, was she inches from a breakdown, on the cusp of a disaster?

Grunting his frustration and indecision, he whirled back into the stall and finished tightening the straps on his saddle. He had work to do, and worrying about imagined problems and a woman who'd clearly rejected his help was not the kind of distraction he needed.

Chapter 5

The next morning, the other guests who would be joining Carrie on the adventure trip arrived at the Double M.
Zane had left to pick up the first group from the Denver
airport before Carrie had finished her breakfast. Hearing
the lively conversations in the yard, however, Carrie took
her mug of coffee outside to greet the group.

"Carrie," Luke said, waving her over, "these are
your new roommates." He motioned to a woman in her
late fifties, whose bright smile and obvious excitement
for being at the ranch lit her whole face. "Lylah Grace
Douglas from Louisiana." Moving his hand to indicate a
clearly newlywed couple, he said, "And this is Summer
and Nolan Colton from South Texas."

Lylah Grace stepped forward, offering a hand to
shake. "Nice to meet you, Carrie. I hear you're going
solo on this trip, as well. I lost my husband last year and

decided rather than sit around and mope, I'd better get busy doing all the things I'd put off while I was raising my kiddos. Not getting any younger, right?"

Carrie grinned. "You're right." After Lylah Grace stepped back, Carrie greeted Summer and Nolan, wondering to herself if she and Joseph had ever looked so obviously in love.

She'd believed she loved Joseph when she agreed to marry him. But had it been love or just some romantic notion because of the way he'd swept her off her feet and dazzled her for the early months of their relationship?

"Once you folks get settled in," Zane said, "we'll serve lunch out on the back lawn and start with our first horseback lesson and roping demonstration this afternoon. Sound good?"

"Sounds great!" Lylah Grace said. "Bring it on!"

Zane showed the group into the guesthouse, and Carrie decided to stay out of the way while the new arrivals unpacked. When she hung back, Luke approached her and hitched his head toward the stable. "Want to get a head start picking out your horse and gear?"

She faced him, shielding her eyes from the sun with one hand. "Is that fair? Shouldn't we wait for the rest of the group?"

He shrugged. "I don't know that it matters, but if you'd rather wait, then…come keep me company while I get things set up for after lunch."

She hesitated, knowing time spent alone with Luke was asking for trouble. She didn't want to fall any harder for his kind smile and intriguing eyes.

"I want to explain myself," he added, "and this may be our last chance to talk alone before the group activities start full throttle."

"You don't need to explain anything."

His expression darkened. "But I want to." He held his hand out to her, and before she stopped to think what she was doing, she offered her own, allowing him to wrap his strong fingers around hers and tug her toward the out-buildings. A tingle chased through her, and she couldn't decide if it was good or a warning. Was her body reacting to his touch or the uncomfortable knowledge that she'd so easily caved to Luke's wishes? Or the fact that she hadn't really caved to anything, but had wanted to be alone with Luke, had wanted it much more than she should have?

"So here's the thing," he said as they strolled hand in hand to the fence surrounding the corral behind the stock barn. "Yesterday, when we left your car to be repaired, I said some cryptic things that I think offended you."

Her pulse cantered, the beat thumping against her ribs like plodding hooves. She didn't want to have this conversation again. Didn't want to skirt around the truth of her situation or feel she had to lie to Luke. "Don't worry about it. I overreacted and—"

"Carrie," he cut in. They'd reached the railing around the corral, and he pressed her hand between his as he faced her. "This isn't about your reaction as much as mine. You see, I had a friend…a *girlfriend* who killed herself a few years ago."

Her eyes widened, and a fist of shock gripped her chest. Whatever she'd been expecting from this conversation, it hadn't been *that*. "Luke, that's…awful. I'm so sorry. I—"

"The thing is, I knew she'd been struggling, depressed. I kept asking her how I could help, what I could do, and she always pushed me away. She said she was fine. She didn't need help. Didn't want help. So I'd back off. I was naive. Selfish. I mean, I didn't really know how to help her, so having her permission to step back made me feel less guilty about leaving her alone. Until she took her life, and I knew I'd—" he paused to swallow hard, take a breath, close his eyes "—failed her."

"Oh, Luke, no!" Carrie's heart broke for him, the grief in his tone, the stoop of his shoulders. She raised her free hand to cup his cheek, and his eyes fluttered open to lock with hers. "You can't blame yourself. Please don't blame yourself."

"That's what people keep telling me," he murmured, "but I don't see how not to. I knew she was hurting, knew she was off her meds, knew she needed help, and I chickened out when she told me to give her space. I was actually *relieved* when she told me she would be fine and to go home." His jaw tightened, and self-recrimination soured his countenance. "I was scared of the responsibility of trying to help her, so I did nothing."

"What about calling 911 or a suicide hotline?" Carrie imagined how lost and overwhelmed she might feel if someone she cared about was in a deep depression. What would she do?

Luke sighed heavily and covered the hand she'd put on his face with his own. Curling his fingers around hers, he moved her hand to his mouth and pressed a tender kiss to the sensitive skin of her palm. Cloudy emotions swirled in his pale gray eyes. "I did, that last day, when she sent me home. They told me to go back to her place and to call an ambulance for her."

He glanced away from her, drew another deep breath and cleared his throat, obviously struggling with the painful memories. She waited quietly, squeezing his hand while he gathered himself.

Finally, he shook his head. "It was too little, too late. She was already gone when I got there."

"Oh God, Luke. You found her?" The pain slicing her chest rent harder. "Honey…that's awful!" She didn't realize she'd used the endearment until his gaze darted back to hers. Curious. Tender. Needy.

Even though a quiver of reluctance shimmied through her, she decided now was not the time to quibble over offering the intimacy and caring that felt so right in the moment. He'd spilled his guts to her, felt compelled to share a tragic memory and open a raw wound to her. She owed him every loving kindness and heartfelt comfort that swelled instinctively and automatically inside her.

"Yeah, I found her," he rasped. His brow dented, and anguish filled his eyes.

Her own tears forming, Carrie threw her arms around Luke's neck and held him tight. "I'm so sorry. I can't imagine. Luke…"

He returned her hug, his breathing ragged. After a moment, he said quietly, "So that's why I said what I did the other day. It wasn't about you or your situation. I didn't mean to make you feel like you were a charity case, but—"

She pulled out of the embrace shaking her head. "No, forget it. No hard feelings."

"—I couldn't in good conscience turn my back on you when it seems clear there's something troubling you, something going on with you."

Carrie bit her bottom lip and dropped her gaze to her feet. Despite his heartbreaking confession, she wasn't prepared to give him the same openness. "Why—I mean…you barely know me. Why do you care?"

"I don't mean to be nosy or pushy." He huffed a humorless laugh. "I'm actually a little scared of getting involved with something I'm not skilled to deal with again. But any friend of Nina's is automatically worth my attention. And you…well, you're pretty obviously special in your own right. I'd have to be blind not to see that." He placed his hands on her shoulders, his thumbs stroking the sides of her throat. The gesture was soothing. Hypnotic. Especially when she dared to glance up and meet the concern in those piercing gray eyes. Her belly quivered, and yearning pooled in her core.

"Honestly, a voice in my head is saying 'back off.' But I'm more terrified of letting you down. Recognizing that there's something troubling you and not helping…" He shook his head. "I can't walk away. Please, Carrie. Tell me what's going on with you. If only to put my mind at rest, because I'm imagining all kinds of terrible scenarios."

What could she tell him? Her situation was horrid. Frightening. Desperate. And that was why she had to keep Luke out of it. She had to protect him from the ugliness that her life had become and the danger Joseph posed.

But he was standing there, all devastatingly handsome, earnest and worried about her. She had to tell him something. The lies she'd told friends for years to hide the truth tasted all the more sour as they formed on her tongue, so she discarded them for one that was more palatable.

"A few years back I made some…poor choices," she began slowly, picking her words carefully, "and I'm trying to correct those mistakes. Until I get my life back on track, my finances are going to be tight. But I can't make the fresh start I need to if I accept money from you or anyone else. I need to do this by myself. To be truly independent and self-sufficient."

"Poor choices, huh?" A hum rumbled from his throat, and he twisted his lips. "We all make those at some point in our lives, don't we?"

With his gaze still locked on her, he inched his palms from her shoulders to her neck, and his thumbs now reached the bottom edge of her chin. His work-roughened hands were paradoxically gentle. The skimming strokes of his callused fingers against her skin pooled a honeyed lethargy inside her. Reason told her to pull away, but some competing force inside her rooted her to the spot to bask in the tenderness she'd had far too little of in her adult life.

Luke is the kind of man you should be with, the kind of man you deserve.

Carrie let her eyes slide closed, remembering the loving touches shared by the newlywed couple that had just arrived. Treasuring the touch of the sweet man before her. Oh, but she could get used to having a caring man to cherish her and lavish her with soft caresses and comforting words.

A horse near them in the corral whinnied and snorted, calling her back to her surroundings. Her circumstances. Stark reality snatched away the fantasy and jammed a heavy dose of disappointment in its place.

She took a step back, lifting her hand to remove Luke's from her throat. "I should go. Before I make another poor choice." Seeing the sting of her words in his expression, she fumbled. "That came out wrong. You're not—" She sighed. "It's just that I can't—"

His lips curled in a lopsided grin. "It's okay. I just

wanted you to know that if you change your mind about my help, I'm here."

She tucked her hands in her pockets, pressing her fingernails into her palms, before she reached for him again. *Don't kiss him. Don't lose your head over a few tender moments and head down a dead-end path.*

Taking two more steps back, she aimed a tight grin of appreciation at him before turning away. Not in the mood to exchange pleasantries with her new housemates, she veered toward the stable. But Josh and Dave appeared in the alley door and, spotting her, gave a wave. She waved back and rerouted herself again. After the intimate, axis-tipping moments she'd just shared with Luke, she needed time to catch her breath. To examine her insane attraction to him and shove it firmly to a back shelf. She glanced around the ranch yard humming with activity, animals and sunshine. A normal person wouldn't be running from such a warm and inviting place. But such was Joseph's legacy. She prayed she wouldn't spend the rest of her life running from people who cared, hiding the truth. Missing out on real love.

She glanced back at Luke, and a sharp pang wrenched her heart. Regardless of what her view of the world looked like years from now, the bitter truth of her *now* remained. Until Joseph was out of her life for good, until she was safe, any man who dared to care for her would be in danger because of her cruel and jealous husband. For Luke's sake, she had to keep him at bay.

An hour later, Carrie heard a shout from across the ranch yard for the tour group to gather up. She'd found a shady spot under a tree by the barn where she'd pretended to be reading from her phone but had instead spent time scrolling through old family pictures she'd saved to an SD card.

Her parents had both died in recent years, and being an only child, she'd been the sole heir to their shares of French Industries. She was now the majority stockholder, a point that was of key importance to Joseph and his position on the board of directors. As much as she loved the family's business, founded by her great-grandfather, she also hated some of the things it represented. Her grandfather's death on the factory floor, the long hours her father spent away from her and her mother and the catalyst for Joseph's pursuit of her and fixation in the years since.

"Come on, Carrie! Time to learn to rope and ride!" Lylah Grace called from the guesthouse with a large grin.

The widow's enthusiasm nudged Carrie's soul, encouraged her to make the most of her current situation. As long as she was at the ranch, part of the adventure tour, surrounded by friendly faces, she ought to savor the moments. This was the kind of carefree life she craved, the freedom she was seeking, the reason she'd fled her marriage. Returning a wave, Carrie dusted off the seat of her jeans and headed over to join the group.

Lylah Grace looped her arm through Carrie's as the group assembled. "Looks like we're a team, being the only singles. What do you say, darlin'?"

"I say, go team!" Carrie gave a playful fist pump, and Lylah Grace hooted a laugh.

"That's the spirit!"

Once they were all assembled, Zane greeted the group again, welcoming them to the Double M Ranch and the McCall adventure tour. "Tomorrow when we head out on the first leg of the adventure trip, you'll ride your assigned horse to the top of Nall Mountain, where we'll zip-line across a gorge to the base camp for our first night on the trail."

Murmurs of excitement filtered through the participants, and Lylah Grace gave Carrie's arm a squeeze. She glanced to the widow, and Lylah Grace flashed a smile that was half anticipation, half anxiety.

Carrie patted the woman's hand and offered a reciprocal encouragement. "You've got this, Lylah Grace."

The widow thanked her with a wink and a nod.

Zane surveyed the group for their level of experience with a horse, and learning that Summer and Nolan Colton were well-versed equestrians, focused his attention on the remaining four adventurers. Luke and Josh stood at Zane's side as he explained horse etiquette and safety, and Carrie found it hard to concentrate on the lesson. Her attention kept straying to Luke, remembering his poignant confession, the gentle touch of his callused fingers against her skin and the concern that glinted in his quicksilver eyes.

Luke glanced her way several times as Zane covered the basics of mounting a horse, how to sit in the saddle and how to use the reins to guide the animal. Each time their eyes met, Carrie guiltily jerked her gaze away, her pulse stuttering. After the third time it happened, she scolded herself. Why did she feel shamed for watching Luke? She had no intention of pursuing her attraction to him, but she also didn't want to send him mixed messages. *Focus, French*, she told herself silently.

When he finished his intro speech, Zane signaled for everyone to take their place by their assigned horse. Luke waved her over to a dappled gray mare.

"This is Hazel," he said, stroking the mare's nose.

"She's a gentle, well-trained girl that I think you'll find a good rapport with."

Carrie moved to the fence where Hazel was tied off and offered her flat hand for the horse to sniff. When Hazel bumped her nose against Carrie's hand, Carrie cooed, "Good girl. Nice to meet you," and pressed both of her hands to the left side of Hazel's neck before patting and scratching Hazel in greeting.

"I'd say she likes you," Luke said and passed her Hazel's lead before moving on to help Lylah Grace with her horse.

One by one the guests who felt they needed a little help getting on their horses moved to the mounting block, and Carrie sized Hazel up.

"What do you think, girl? Will you be still and let me climb up without extra assistance?" she said softly to the mare.

Hazel tossed her head, rattling her bridle, and flicked her ears as a large fly buzzed by.

"Okay, then. Let's do this." Carrie patted the horse's neck again, grabbed the saddle horn and jammed her left foot in the stirrup. What happened next, Carrie couldn't say. Something upset the horse next to Hazel, and it reared up. Hazel shied away from the riled horse, and Carrie lost her balance and stumbled backward. She reached out to grab the closest thing to catch herself. The lower barbed wires of the fence.

A sharp pain sliced through her hand. Her bottom landed hard on the packed dirt, then her head. Air whooshed from her lungs, and she lay still, stunned and aching.

Chapter 6

"Carrie!" Luke was beside her in an instant. "Are you hurt?"

She moved her jaw, trying to answer, but the impact had left her winded. She struggled to suck in oxygen, to clear the ringing in her ears.

"Carrie?" Luke's brow creased as he studied her.

She nodded, wanting to reassure him that despite the evidence, she wasn't grievously injured. Certainly she'd suffered worse thanks to Joseph's temper. She sat up slowly, taking stock of her joints and limbs. Nothing broken. Just rattled. She shook her head and flashed a wobbly grin.

"You're bleeding." Luke took her wrist and turned up her hand.

Sure enough, a red gash seeped blood on the fleshy part of her palm. She frowned at the cut, remembering the pain when she'd grabbed at the fence. Angling her gaze, she discovered the end of a thick piece of barbed wire turned up slightly where it had been wound around another end.

Luke shifted his attention, following the path of her gaze and grumbled a curse word under his breath. "Geez, Carrie. I'm so sorry."

She gasped enough breath to sputter, "Not your fault."

"No way that wire should be poking up like that." He grimaced as he examined her palm again. "Have you had a tetanus shot recently?"

"I…no."

Serious gray eyes pinned hers. "You'll need one, then. I'll take you to the local clinic."

Luke offered her a hand to help her up as Zane appeared, wearing his own worried frown.

"Is she okay? Carrie?"

She sent an awkward smile and reassurances to the cluster of faces that had gathered around her and struggled to get up. Her hip ached, her head still swam muzzily, but she marshaled her composure. Joseph had taught her that showing pain meant showing weakness. Zane put an arm under hers to steady her, and Luke kept hold of her uninjured hand even after she'd gotten on her feet.

"I'm good," she told them both.

"Bless you, honey," Lylah Grace called. "I thought I was going to be the first to fall on my bumpkus! Are you all right?"

She gave a small wave and nod to the group. "Just practicing pratfalls for my gig as a rodeo clown."

Luke chuckled and put an arm around her shoulders. "Come on, Bonzo. Let's get your hand cleaned up." As he guided her out of the corral, he called to Zane, "Back after we get her a tetanus shot."

"There's a first-aid kit over the washing machine in the family house," Zane called, and Luke raised a hand in acknowledgment.

Luke kept his arm around her as they made their way to the McCall family's home. Carrie held her cut hand with her good hand while blood dripped from the wound in garish streaks, leaving a trail of droplets on the ranch yard. Luke ushered her through a side door, into a mudroom and to the kitchen, where he turned on the faucet at the sink. "Rinse it first while I go grab the medical kit."

"Thank you, Luke," she said and stuck her injured hand under the cool faucet stream. When she'd rinsed all the blood and dirt from her hand, she tore off a paper towel from the roll by the sink and carefully dried her palm. She could hear voices down the hall—Luke talking to Melissa McCall.

Turning, she leaned back against the counter to wait for Luke to return and felt something warm brush against her leg. She gasped, unaccustomed to the sensation, and glanced down to find Erin's chubby brown tabby, Scout, rubbing her cheek on Carrie's ankle.

Smiling at her own jumpiness, Carrie exhaled a cleansing breath and squatted, her sore muscles protesting, to pat Scout's soft fur with her uninjured hand. When the feline tipped her head, Carrie scratched the offered cheek, and Scout gave a soft, chirping meow. "You are a sweet thing, aren't you?" She chuckled to herself. "But that's what I thought about Hazel, and she threw me."

Luke returned, his boots thumping as he hurried into the kitchen, and Scout scuttled away to crouch under a small table in the corner of the kitchen.

"Aw, you scared her," Carrie said with a pout.

"Huh? Scared who?"

She pointed to the tabby, who peeked out with wide green eyes. "Scout. She let me pat her until you startled her." She sighed. "Startled animals seem to be my theme today."

Luke cast a glance toward the cat and tugged up a corner of his mouth. "Hey, getting a pat from her is pretty big. Erin would love to know that." He took a step toward the cat's hiding place. "Hi, Scout. Who's a good kitty?"

Scout gave a quiet hiss and seemed to withdraw further into herself.

With a wry laugh, Luke backed away from the feline. "Okay. So she doesn't like me."

But I do. Carrie bit the inside of her cheek to keep the words from spilling out.

As she studied Scout sitting under the perceived protection of the corner table, she felt a connection to the cat. Overwhelmed by her changed circumstances, wary of other people, wanting only to hide and protect herself. And giving impotent hisses to those she perceived as a threat.

"Right. So let's have a look." Luke wiggled his fingers, asking for her injured hand.

"I can do it myself." She reached for the kit he'd set on the counter.

He caught her wrist and shot her a withering look. "One-handed? Come on. Let me see."

Facing Luke, Carrie remembered her churlishness when he'd forced her hand and tried to pay for her new windshield. He'd been trying to help in his own way, and she'd hissed at him. A protective, defensive reaction, maybe. But uncalled for. Compunction poked her belly.

His grip gentled, and he slid his hand to cradle her injured one. The slide of his warm, callused palm against her skin sent tingles up her arm, and as he bent his head to examine the wound, she took the opportunity to study him.

His gold hair had been tousled by the wind and creased by his Stetson. His sun-kissed face bore tiny lines around his eyes. Laugh lines, she'd heard them called, and she could easily imagine Luke laughing his way through life. He had a good heart. A kindness and compassion that Joseph never—

She cut the thought off without finishing it. Comparisons were pointless. Despite Nina's advice to watch Luke, appraise his qualities, she wasn't sizing Luke up as a candidate to replace Joseph in her life. She was better off with no man. The last thing she should do is trade her submissiveness to a controlling monster for needy dependence on someone else. Independence, self-determination and peace of mind were what she had to find for herself.

Luke dabbed something on her wound that stung, and the sudden zing of pain drew her from her meditation with a gasp.

His gaze darted to hers. "Sorry. Should have warned you it would sting."

"No, it's fi—" Her words stuck in her throat as he raised her hand to blow a soft caress of breath through puckered lips.

Angling his silver eyes to her, he asked, "Better?"

She managed a nod, then whispered, "You have the most amazing eyes."

He blinked, and his head drew back slightly as if she'd caught him off guard. After a beat, a smile tugged one cheek. "Thanks. I think your eyes are pretty amazing, too."

Carrie furrowed her brow and shook her head in dismissal. "I wasn't digging for a compliment."

He chuckled quietly. "Maybe not. But you got one."

Luke brushed the loose hair away from her cheek, and her pulse spiraled. Sensations like startled butterflies filled her chest.

"I've never seen a prettier shade of blue green." His thumb stroked the sensitive spot beside her eye, and his smile brightened. "Pretty eyes for a pretty lady."

She frowned, not sure how to process what was happening.

"What?" He asked, "Too corny? You are very pretty, you know, even if I'm no poet."

She ducked her head and tried to compose herself. Difficult, considering the tender touch of his fingers was scattering her thoughts and stirring crazy feelings in her blood.

"I just…it's been a long time since anyone said something so nice to me. You, um…"

He nudged her chin up, his breathtaking eyes homed in on hers. "Seriously? Have you been living in a cave? No one's told you how attractive you are? How beautiful your smile is?"

"N-no," she rasped, wrenching memories assailing her. Quite the contrary…

"Take off that horrible lipstick. You look like a whore."

"You couldn't put any better effort in fixing your hair?" Joseph scrubbed his hands on her head, disrupting the upsweep she'd styled. "These are important people we're meeting, and your hair is a mess."

"You're getting fat. You're an embarrassment."

"Well, that's a crime," Luke murmured, and when she saw genuine regret shadow his countenance, a knot clogged her throat. "You deserve to hear good things said about you. Everyone does."

She sighed, pulled her cheek away from his grasp and tried to sidestep him. "I'm not a child. I don't need false cheer or patronizing platitudes to feed my self-esteem."

He moved his body to more fully block her escape, and her heart thudded faster. "I'm not talking about anything false or patronizing. I'm talking about the truth, Carrie." Framing her face with both hands, he angled her head to stare deeply into her eyes. "You *are* beautiful. I'm certain of your outward beauty and learning quickly about your inner beauty. Someone should tell you that every day. Because I'm getting the sense that you don't know it about yourself."

She sighed and closed her eyes. "Luke, don't."

As much as she appreciated his kindness, she couldn't encourage his flirting. Didn't want to hear taunting snippets from a life she had never had, could never have. No matter how much she wanted it…

"Don't what? Tell you the truth? *Carrie.*" His commanding tone of voice cut through her dizzy mental debate. When he gave her a gentle shake, she opened her eyes again. His silver gaze captured hers. "Don't you know I have feelings for you? I know I'm not supposed to, professionally speaking, you being a client and all. But we're being honest here, and the truth is I find you attractive. And intelligent. And funny. And kind."

"Kind?" She scoffed. "After the way I barked at you for your thoughtfulness and generous offer to pay for my windshield?"

"That was your bark?" He flashed a lopsided grin. "You were about as scary as a puppy yipping. No teeth to it. And understandable considering my pushiness." He sobered and searched her eyes. "I kinda thought the attraction was mutual. Was I wrong? Be honest. If you don't feel any of what I'm feeling, I'll back off. I'll understand."

Lowering her gaze, Carrie drew her bottom lip between her teeth and shook her head. He'd asked for honesty, and she couldn't deny the truth while looking into his magnetic eyes. But if she'd thought that was the end of it, he proved her wrong.

His hold on her cheeks firmed. "Say it. Look me in the eye and say the words."

Her heart jolted, and nervous tension corkscrewed inside her. As she searched for the courage to do what he'd asked, the air in her throat sawed in. Out. In.

"Carrie?" Her name was a sweet caress of his breath.

Finally, she lifted her chin and allowed the raw emotion in his gaze to seize hers. Yearning blossomed, the affection in his eyes like rain on a thirsty landscape. A tremor from her core rolled through her. When he took a step closer, aligning his body with hers, she curled her fingers in the shirt at his chest.

She should push him away. She ought to duck out of his embrace and make a statement that she was unavailable.

But she couldn't. Her feet stayed rooted. Her gaze remained locked with his. Her heart pattered with anticipation. With desire.

When she kept silent, he bent his head and brushed a delicate kiss across her lips. Sensation, pure and sweet, poured through her, and her head grew muzzy. A beat passed, and he kissed her again. A longer, deeper kiss that buckled her knees. Ignoring the tiny voice in her head that she should stop, that she was making a mistake,

Carrie slid her hands up to his shoulders, then looped her arms around his neck, canting closer.

Luke angled his head and captured her mouth more fully. His hands moved to her back, anchoring her against him as he explored with his lips. Teased with his tongue.

Carrie might have gone on kissing him endlessly, sinking deeper into the magic he was weaving, but the back door opened and slammed closed, breaking the spell.

She jerked away from him, pushed against his chest where she could feel the strong, steady thumping of his heart. He released her, disappointment etched in his brow, and he stepped back.

Nina appeared at the entry to the kitchen, her expression a mask of concern. "Carrie, are you okay? They told me you got hurt."

Carrie braced her good hand against the counter, fighting to find her equilibrium while her head continued spinning. "It's just a little cut." Her voice sounded thick, so she cleared her throat. "It's nothing."

Luke glanced over his shoulder to address Nina as he cleaned up the first-aid supplies he'd spread on the counter top. "I'm about to drive her to the town clinic for a tetanus shot. Can you take the group through the roping demonstration?"

Nina crossed the kitchen and lifted Carrie's hand to examine the wound for herself. "I can lead the group, but shouldn't I be the one to take Carrie for the shot? You're my guest."

"I, uh…" Her brain was still too foggy and confused from the kiss to think rationally.

Luke cast Carrie an inquiring glance. "Your choice. Would you rather Nina took you? I don't want to overstep again like I did with the windshield."

I want you, she almost blurted. She wanted more time. More touches. More kisses.

But somehow discretion and common sense prevailed, and she heard herself say, "Nina. It makes more sense for her to take me."

Was that disappointment she saw pass over his eyes before he bobbed his head once in agreement? "All right, then. See you when you get back."

Coward! a voice in her head shouted. The voice didn't lie. She readily admitted she was frightened by the idea of being alone with Luke, of growing closer to him, of letting her defenses down. The internal battle she already waged because of her confused feelings toward him were proof enough of why she had to avoid him. She had to keep a clear head. Stay focused on her true purpose, her real goal—escaping Joseph, once and for all.

"While we're in town, would you mind taking me by the body shop that has my car?" Carrie asked Nina as they left the small town medical clinic. She rubbed the sore place on her arm where she'd gotten the tetanus shot, mentally adding the cost of the injection to her growing pile of bills. "They promised it by five today, but it could be ready now. No sense making two trips to town." Retrieving her car now would also mean not facing the discussion over payment options with Luke again. She'd accepted the loss of her ring as the price for her continued freedom from Joseph and considered it a good trade.

Nina clicked her key fob to unlock her car's doors. "Absolutely. It's at Beal's?"

"Yeah." Carrie climbed in the passenger side and scrutinized the small town as they drove the few blocks to the auto shop. She searched every face, every car, every window, certain she'd see Joseph. And if she did? How would she escape this time? Nina would defend her...and probably end up hurt in the process.

"I wonder if there'll ever be a day I don't feel I have to keep looking over my shoulder to be safe," she mused aloud.

Nina sent her a sympathetic look as she reached over to squeeze Carrie's hand. "There will be. Have faith. You'll find your old self again and make a fresh start. I know you will."

"After five years of living with Joseph, I'm not sure how much of my old self still exists."

Nina turned in at the body shop parking lot, and as she cut the engine, she gave Carrie a worried look. "Don't give up, Carrie. Don't let him win. I'm here for you, and I won't let you quit."

Carrie grinned weakly, appreciating the fighting spirit that had helped Nina overcome dire odds after her car accident. "Thank you. I appreciate your support more than you could know." She opened the car door, and when Nina unbuckled her seat belt, Carrie added, "No need for you to come in. I'll just check to see if it's ready."

Nina leaned over to give her a hug before Carrie headed into the body shop.

"Hi there," Greg called to her as she entered the garage bay. "I was just about to call you. Got you all fixed up, but I also wanted to show you something."

Carrie furrowed her brow. "What?"

He led her over to her car and opened the driver's side door. "In addition to replacing the windshield, we always do a ten-point safety check. Belts, hoses, fluid levels, that sort of thing."

She waved a hand and shook her head. "I can't afford any more repairs or maintenance. If the car will run, I—"

"Naw, I'm not trying to sell you on anything—although you could use new belts pretty soon. I just wanted to ask you about something."

Carrie sighed, and her heart sank. If she was going to keep running and stay one step ahead of Joseph, she had to have an operational vehicle. She'd have to find the cash to keep her car running somehow.

"When I was looking for the lever to pop the hood," Greg said as he climbed in and stuck his head under the steering wheel, "I found something plugged in your OBD-II port."

"My what?"

"Onboard diagnostics port. It's a computer port under the driver's side dash connected to the car's electrical system. It monitors the car's speed, mileage, emissions and the repair warning system. All cars have them nowadays, and it's where mechanics can plug their machines in to determine what system repairs your car might need."

"So you're saying I need some electrical repairs?" Carrie asked.

"No. But I found this—" He reached under the dash and extracted a device that looked like a large USB flash drive.

She frowned. "And that's not supposed to be there?"

"Depends. Has your car insurance company asked you to plug this in to monitor your driving habits? They do that sometimes to justify safe driver discounts…or not."

"N-no." Her heart's rhythm picked up even without knowing for sure the full meaning behind Greg's discovery.

The mechanic grunted and turned the small device

over in his hand. "So do you know any other reason someone would be monitoring your car?"

Monitoring... A chill rolled down her spine. She drew a quavering breath and had to try twice to get her voice to work. "Could that thing...b-be used as a t-tracker?"

Greg lifted a shoulder. "Sure. It could easily include GPS. Rental car companies, trucking lines, worried parents use them to keep track of vehicles all the time."

Her mouth dried. So that was it. *That* was how Joseph had been finding her so easily.

Spots danced in her vision, and her legs turned to jelly. Carrie reached for the car door to steady herself, even as Greg surged toward her, catching her as she slumped.

"Hey, whoa." He eased her down to sit on the ground, and Carrie blinked as the garage bay spun around her. "Ma'am?"

She fought the blackness that edged in at the periphery of her vision. She could *not* pass out. She had to stay alert. Stay on task. "I...I'm all right."

He crouched beside her. "Are you diabetic? Did you eat this morning?"

"No," she rasped.

"Hey!" Greg shouted to one of his shop techs as he hustled to get a folding chair from across the bay. "Bring her a soda and some of the cookies in the break room. Hurry!"

She waved him off. "No. Really. I'm fine. I—" She dropped her gaze to the device in his hand as he helped her to the chair. "How do you turn it o-off?"

"Huh?"

She wiggled a finger at the tracker. "That thing. Turn it off. Smash it. I don't want it."

The body shop owner narrowed his eyes on her and

seemed to be thinking about more than the gadget he'd found. Speculating, she was sure, about her odd behavior. "Unplugging it should be enough. But I can crush it if you really want."

"I just…need it not to work anymore. Not to—" She faltered, shivering when she realized the gizmo had almost certainly tracked her to Boyd Valley.

"Not to track you anymore," Greg said. A statement, not a question. "You skipping out on parole? Running from the law? 'Cause I don't need any trouble, aiding and abetting."

Carrie jerked her chin up, a shocked scoff scraping from her throat. "No!"

"Then what?" he asked. "Or should I ask *who*?"

She only stared at him for several seconds, until the tech hustled to her with a Coca-Cola can and two cookies on a napkin. She forced a trembling smile for the young man and held her palm toward him. "No, thank you. I'm…okay."

The tech consulted Greg with a glance, and when Greg shrugged, the tech stepped back and shoved one of the cookies in his own mouth as he strolled away.

Run. Get away, a voice whispered in her head. Her neck prickled as if someone was watching her, and the need to flee swelled inside her like rising flood waters. Choking. Drowning.

She tried to stand but swayed.

Greg held out his hand to help Carrie rise. Although her legs were shaky, she'd regained some mental composure.

"If you need to sit a minute, it's okay." The shop owner eyed her warily.

"No. I need to go. Wh-what do I owe you?"

Greg told her the sum and aimed a finger to the car. "Your key is in the ignition. So what did you decide about payment?"

"If you're willing to take it, keep the ring I gave you. Get what you can from it."

He grunted and tipped his head. "I asked a jeweler about it. Your ring's worth a few hundred more than your glass replacement cost."

She considered asking him for the difference in cash but made a snap decision instead. She didn't have time for him to pawn the ring and bring back the cash. Learning how Joseph had been tracking her had fired a fresh urgency in her to disappear.

"Keep the change," she told Greg, and his eyebrows shot up. "As thanks for finding the tracker." She drew a deep breath and squared her shoulders. "And if a man comes in here asking about me or the car, you don't know anything. You have no idea where I am or where I was going next. Deal?"

The look in Greg's eyes softened with concern. "Ma'am, if you're in some kind of trouble, if some jerk is lookin' to hurt you, don't you think you should go to the cops?"

She balled her hands and closed her eyes. "I— No. Just…promise me? Don't tell him anything. Okay?"

Greg raised his hands, signaling surrender. "All right. You've got my word."

With a nod, Carrie headed back outside to update Nina and prayed Greg's word would be enough.

Chapter 7

"Way I see it is forewarned is forearmed." Nina sat across from Carrie at the small kitchenette table in the ranch's guesthouse and held both of her trembling hands. The rest of the tour group was outside, enjoying a steak dinner and dancing hosted by the McCalls, but Carrie had no appetite for food or revelry. The only reason she hadn't climbed behind the wheel and sped out of Colorado was Nina's arguments to stay where the McCall men and ranch hands surrounded her, providing a protective wall.

"He's coming. If he's not already in town, I know he'll be here soon." Carrie released a shuddering sigh. "I have to go…somewhere. Anywhere else."

"And you will tomorrow morning. You and the group will leave for the mountain wilderness, off the grid, away from here. He won't find you there."

"What if he comes here? To the ranch? My car was here briefly, so he—"

"We'll park it somewhere else. Somewhere you haven't been with the tracker hooked up. My house, for example. We'll put it in my garage."

Carrie shook her head. "No. If he goes to your house looking for me—"

"Why would he? How would he know to look there? The car was never there with the tracker, and the house is in Steve's name. Does he even know I'm your friend?"

After a bit more negotiating and rationalizing, Nina convinced Carrie of her plan's merit. Taking Carrie's car key so she could drive the BMW home, Nina gave Carrie a hug as she left the guesthouse. "I'll be here pretty early tomorrow and heading out to the pastures right at sunrise, so I don't know if I'll see you before you all leave for the adventure."

Carrie pulled a face, then forced a teasing note to her tone. "Rancher hours. Ugh. Better you than me."

Nina held her shoulders and said firmly, "Have fun. Relax. You'll be safe, so enjoy it. Okay?"

Safe. Carrie exhaled a tense breath, wishing she could believe that, and reassured her friend with a nod. Maybe the three-day trip into the Colorado wilds *was* her best chance to find a little peace. If she couldn't hide in the middle of nowhere from Joseph, she really did have a problem. The pressure in her chest eased. For the next three days, she'd be as safe as she'd been in years. She smiled at Nina. "Okay."

Luke was crossing the ranch yard, headed from the send-off dinner to the barn for a final check on the sick bull before calling it a night, when he spotted Nina leaving the guesthouse. He was disappointed that Carrie hadn't come to the steak dinner. He'd been looking forward to the informal event to get to talk with her in a more social setting. The first few days of her stay had been such a strange mix of awkward encounters, instant attraction, intimate confessions… Before they set out on the adventure trip, he'd have liked a conversation that approached normal with her. Yet she'd stayed in the guesthouse.

He lingered in the shadowed yard until Nina gave Carrie a hug and turned to walk away, then with a quick step to catch up to her, he asked, "Is Carrie all right? I missed her at the dinner."

Nina arched an eyebrow and gave a half smile. "Did you?"

He scowled and elbowed her playfully. "Don't get any ideas. It's not like that."

Liar, his conscience shouted. *It's exactly like that. Who are you kidding?* Not Nina, apparently, because her knowing grin stayed in place.

"You can't fool me, Wright. I've seen you watching her. And she is very pretty."

He tried a negligent shrug. "Whatever. So why'd she skip dinner?"

Nina twisted her mouth. "Just…tired, I think. She's got a lot going on in her life. That's why she's here for a break. A get-away-from-it-all vacation."

"I kinda got that sense. Any hint what kind of stuff she's getting away from?" He raised a hand. "I only ask because…well—"

"Because you *are* interested in her." Nina jabbed him with a finger. Her grin was smug.

"Okay, fine. Yes. I like her. So what?"

Nina stopped walking and faced Luke, her expression sobering. "So…be careful with her. I know you're a good guy. I know you'd never intentionally hurt her, but…go slow. Give her space if she needs it."

He sighed. "Right. Space. I got that impression from her, too."

"She'd kill me if she knew I was out here playing matchmaker again, but…she needs someone like you in her life, Luke," Nina said. "And she's worth your wait, so don't give up. Just…give her some more time. She'll explain everything to you when she's ready."

"Time? You do know she's leaving after the trip. That means I have, like, three days to make an impression."

Nina patted his shoulder and winked as she set out for the parking area again. "Oh, but I think you've already made an impression on her, my dear."

Luke was mulling that news when Nina stopped, turned. "Oh, one more thing." Her grin faded, and she scratched her cheek as she pressed her mouth in a thin line. "Do me a favor?"

"Yeah?" he replied, his tone voicing his skepticism.

"Keep an eye on Carrie during the trip. Look out for her."

"We look out for all the trip guests, Nina," he said lightly but sobered when her serious expression darkened further.

"I know you do. Just promise me you'll take extra good care of her. Keep her safe."

A tingle ran down his spine, and he glanced to the lone light glowing in the window of the guesthouse, then back to Nina. "What aren't you telling me? Is she in some particular danger? Is she sick?"

Nina hesitated. "I can't say. I promised her. Just please promise me you'll look out for her."

Foreboding shrieked in his head like a warning siren. Luke's chest constricted until he couldn't breathe. He saw Sharon's dead body, cold, pale and stiff, as it had been when he'd discovered her. Never again, he'd sworn then. No more crises. No more guilt or responsibility for another's death.

No! his head screamed.

But he heard his mouth tell Nina, "I promise."

The next morning, Joseph pulled up at the last address the GPS tracker had shown before it quit transmitting. A body shop. He grunted. Made more sense that a car mechanic had found the tracking device than that Carrie had. He cut his car's engine and climbed out, scanning the small town street and wondering how close Carrie might be at that moment. Without her vehicle, she couldn't have gone far.

"Howdy, what can I do for you, sir?" a young mechanic in coveralls shouted from the end of a garage bay. The man flicked a cigarette on the ground and crushed it with his shoe.

Joseph strolled closer, pulling out his cell phone and scrolling to a recent photo of Carrie. "I'm looking for someone."

The young man, whose coveralls bore a name patch that read Barry, wiped his hands on an already filthy towel and sauntered closer. "Well, if it's the shop owner you're looking for, you're out of luck. He's at lunch, then heading to the school to register his kid for kindergarten."

Joseph smiled. "Kindergarten, huh? Big day." He held

the phone with the screen toward Barry. "I'm actually looking for this woman. Has she been here?"

The other man squinted at the screen and nodded. "Oh, yeah. I remember her. We replaced her windshield."

Satisfaction pooled in Joseph's gut. "Great! When was this?"

Barry shrugged. "She picked the car up yesterday, I think. Pretty lady."

Joseph furrowed his eyebrows. "And my wife."

Barry raised both greasy hands. "I hear you, man. Just sayin'."

"Do you know where I could find her? Did she leave an address in town where she was staying or contact information?"

Twisting his mouth, Barry shook his head. "I don't have that info. It'd be in the paperwork in the office, and boss man locked his files up when he left for the day."

Joseph sighed and tucked his phone away. Pulling out his wallet, he peeled off a twenty-dollar bill. "Are you sure you can't access that info?"

Barry eyed the money, speculation bright in his gaze. "I can't. But for a hundred, I'll tell you who she came in with and where you can find them."

Joseph clenched his teeth and added fifty to the twenty. "Seventy. And I won't tell your boss you were smoking around flammable chemicals and petroleum products."

Barry's chin jerked up. He bounced lightly on the balls of his feet, his agitation amusing to Joseph. He knew he had the young mechanic by the balls, especially in light of the large no-smoking-on-premises sign on the garage bay wall.

"Fine. Seventy." Barry stuck his hand out, and Joseph held the money just out of his reach.

"Who was she with?"

"Luke Wright, when she came in, but Nina Abshire brought her in to pick the car up."

Joseph set his jaw. "And who are these people?"

"They're both hands out at the McCall place. The Double M Ranch. They have an adventure tours thing out there, too. I assumed she was one of the folks doing the trip this weekend."

Cocking his head, Joseph eyed Barry. "Adventure tours?" That didn't sound like Carrie. She was too meek and fond of creature comforts to willingly go on some glorified cowboy trail ride.

"Yeah, they take groups out to someplace in the mountains and hike and raft and rock climb. That sort of thing." Barry wiggled his fingers. "Okay. I told you what you wanted. Hand it over."

Joseph flashed the money, asking, "Double M Ranch, you say? Here in town?"

"More or less. Outside town about ten miles. Big spread just off the state highway." Barry snatched for the money, but Joseph anticipated the move.

"One last thing. If anyone asks, I was never here. Got it, Barry?"

The young man gave him a leery look but finally bobbed a nod.

Flashing a you-can-trust-me grin, Joseph handed over the cash, and as he returned to his car, he swiped his phone to do a search for the Double M Ranch and the adventure tours they offered. He was about to dial the office number listed when he hesitated.

Just off the state highway...

Showing up on the ranch's doorstep would only prompt Carrie to jump in her car and flee again. And he'd be surrounded by wranglers and other witnesses if he had to physically restrain his wife.

But if Carrie was, in fact, planning to go on this adventure thing out in the boonies…

He mulled over an idea, and the more he thought about it, the more he liked it. Out in the mountains. Nowhere to run. He could catch her unaware…

He thumbed the call icon and raised the phone to his ear. "Yeah, hi. I'm interested in learning more about your adventure tours. Is it too late to join the group going out this weekend?"

Chapter 8

The tour group was up and out early the next morning. Anticipation buzzed in Carrie's veins as she took the middle seat of the ranch's SUV, squeezed in between Lylah Grace and Luke for the drive to the start of their horseback ride up a mountain. Zane, who'd driven the horse trailer over ahead of them, met the group with smiles and already-saddled horses.

Carrie found Hazel, greeted the horse as she'd been taught and whispered, "Let's do this better than last time, huh? Nice and easy."

Luke appeared at her elbow and stroked Hazel's nose. "Can I give you a hand?"

She eyed Hazel. "I think Hazel and I have an understanding. But maybe help getting up?"

He moved closer as she stuck her foot in the stirrup, took a deep breath as she grabbed the saddle horn and hoisted herself up onto Hazel's back. Her injured hand gave a throb of protest, and she shook it a bit after she was settled in the saddle.

"How's the cut?" Luke asked with a nod to her bandaged hand.

"Scabbed over. No sign of infection this morning when I changed the bandage."

He nodded. "Good. Be careful to keep it as clean as you can on the trip."

"Way ahead of you, cowboy," she returned. "I've packed sterile gauze, antibiotic ointment and protective gloves the clinic gave me for just in case."

He winked. "Good deal."

As he strode over to Annie and Jonah Devereaux, the other couple who had joined the tour, Carrie drank in the sight of Luke in his black Stetson, white T-shirt and snug blue jeans. The only part of his attire that broke the traditional rancher mold was the hiking boots he wore instead of cowboy boots. They were clearly a better choice for the walking, climbing and wading that they'd do on the trip. Nina had loaned Carrie a pair of hiking boots that were a tad big for her, a minor issue she'd solved by wearing two pairs of thick socks.

Zane approached her with a small insulated bag. "Here you go, Carrie. Your lunch and extra water are in here. The rest of your supply pack for the trip, everything you're likely to need, will be waiting at the base camp when you get there this afternoon."

Carrie hung the bag around her neck and over one shoulder, and Zane moved on to hand a bag to Lylah Grace.

Josh, mounted on a handsome gelding with a black mane, trotted past her and motioned to the riders. "Everyone line up! I'll lead, Zane will ride the middle and Luke will bring up the rear. Stay single file, please. Some parts of the trail are narrow. Keep control of your horse. They'll want to stop and snack. Don't let them. You're the boss. Pull up on the reins and keep them moving."

Summer and Nolan Colton, the skilled riders of the group, hung back, allowing the newbies to go first. Lylah Grace gave a whoop of excitement as they set out, and Carrie snapped Hazel's reins. "Let's go, girl."

As they climbed, the mountain scenery grew increasingly breathtaking and scenic. Wildflowers bloomed along the trail, and rocky vistas populated with tall skinny pines and aspen trees greeted them around each turn. The path was steep at times, and Carrie clung to her saddle horn as Hazel picked her way up the mountain. Other times they meandered across grassy meadows where butterflies fluttered in the breeze, and Carrie marveled at the natural beauty. The landscape held her in thrall and kept her from dwelling on her situation, on Joseph. No small feat.

As they crested a rise, two hours into the ride, Josh waved an arm grandly toward a stout cable stretched across the ravine. "Here we are, friends! Your first challenge—zip-lining!"

An excited twitter passed through the group, and the married couples exchanged bright-eyed looks. After she dismounted and passed Hazel's reins to Zane, Carrie stepped closer to the edge of the ravine and sized up the challenge. The valley was deep. Really deep. And the distance they would zip-line seemed crazy far. A nervous flutter swooped through her stomach. Wiping sweaty palms on the seat of her jeans, she edged back toward the others. As Carrie surveyed the other members of the group, her gaze stopped on Luke. He shifted his gaze to her as if he'd felt her eyes on him and sent her a smile and a nod.

Josh launched into a demonstration of the apparatus and explanation of the safety rules, and the group huddled closer to see and hear.

Luke edged up next to Carrie and whispered, "Scared?"

"Should I be?"

"Naw. Since the accident a couple years ago, they've scoured this thing ten ways to Tuesday for any flaw. You won't find a safer zip line in the country. They exceed industry standards in every way."

Carrie knitted her brow and leaned close to Luke's ear. "Accident?"

He waved a dismissive hand. "Ancient history. It's all good."

"But…"

Annie cut a curious glance toward them, and Luke gave the woman a reassuring smile and nod. Then putting his mouth right in Carrie's ear, he whispered, "I'll explain later. Nothing to worry about now. You've got this."

What she *had* was a serious case of goose bumps after having his warm breath bathing her ear and the scent of him, leather and musk, tickling her nose and firing all the synapses in her brain. Having him place his wide palm on her shoulder and give her tensed muscles a squeeze didn't help calm the heady trill in her blood, either.

"All right. Who's first?" Josh shouted to the group.

"Me!" Lylah Grace called out, her hand shooting into the air. "Go big or go home. Am I right?" The enthusiastic woman wiggled through the cluster of bodies to present herself to Zane, who held out the harness and helmet she'd wear.

A general buzz of anticipation filled the air as the

tour group watched Josh make the first crossing with a loud whoop of joy. While she watched Zane buckle Lylah Grace into her harness and clip the straps to the trolley, Carrie gnawed her bottom lip, wondering what she'd gotten herself into.

Lylah Grace gave Zane's cheek a kiss, declaring it was for luck, then shrieked as he sent her off over the gorge. Annie edged closer to Jonah and raised an anxious, wide-eyed look to her husband. In return, Jonah leaned down to place a kiss on his wife's forehead. "No sweat."

A pluck of jealousy joined the other writhing emotions in Carrie's chest. How different her life would be now if Joseph had been the husband he'd vowed to be. One who supported her, loved her, encouraged her rather than demeaning, humiliating and wearing her down.

She gave her head a little shake. She didn't want to dwell on all of Joseph's wrongs. And at the moment, she *really* needed to pay attention to the task before her.

Nolan and Summer crossed next, sharing a steamy kiss before Summer launched. Annie mustered her courage and volunteer to go next, leaving Jonah to follow her.

Finally, Zane and Luke faced Carrie with expectant gazes.

"Okay, Carrie. You're up!" Zane called to her.

"You know," she said with a wry grin, "I think I left something important back at the ranch." She started backing toward the spot where the horses milled about grazing. As she flashed a teasing smile to Zane, she came up against a wall of muscle and warmth.

Luke caught her shoulders, and she felt the rumble of his chuckle as a vibration against her back. "Nice try, but no dice. Come on. I'll be right behind you."

Carrie steeled her nerves and headed toward the edge of the launch platform, where Zane held the carabiner clip ready to hook her harness to the trolley. Luke stayed right behind her, and as she stood with her arms out, allowing Zane to clip, test and double-check all her safety gear, Luke donned his harness.

"Imagine the ravine is whatever life hurdle you're currently facing back home," Luke said quietly in her ear. "Then as you fly over that ravine, know that whatever is blocking the way in your life can also be overcome, just like you're soaring over the ravine. Embrace the feeling of conquering your fear and taming the challenge."

Carrie caught the odd, cocked-eyebrow look that Zane sent Luke. Clearly, the inspirational pep talk was not standard practice, and Zane's expression said Luke was laying it on thick. Regardless, Carrie appreciated the sentiment and the kindness behind the motivational speech. She knew she couldn't write off the danger Joseph posed simply by rising to the challenge of the zip line. But maybe if she rebuilt some of the self-confidence Joseph had chipped away in recent years, she'd have a better chance of surviving whatever the coming months entailed.

Zane gave the cable to the trolley one last tug. "All set. Ready?"

Carrie's stomach flip-flopped. "Wait."

She turned to Luke and gave his forearm a squeeze, then leaned in to place a quick kiss on his cheek. "For luck."

Surprise and tender emotion flashed in his eyes before she pivoted back to Zane and gave a nod. "Ready."

And suddenly she was sailing across the expanse of the gorge, wind whipping her face and adrenaline rushing through her veins. After a few seconds of gripping fright, she forced her jaw to relax, her mind to quiet enough to take in the magnificent view. She dragged a breath into her tight lungs and tried to see the valley below the way Luke had spelled out. Pictured herself flying away from Joseph's clutching hands, hurdling over the mountains of stress and doubt, her current financial worries and bleak unknowns. She was *not* without power. She had friends like Nina and Steve. The McCall family. Luke.

She smiled, thinking of the impromptu kiss she'd given Luke. Chaste and quick, but something she'd not imagined herself doing even a few days ago. Following an impulse, being true to her heart. A small step, but an important one to her.

Suddenly a carefree laugh bubbled to the surface as she reveled in the freedom she felt soaring over the ravine, the sun on her face and the wind in her hair. The exhilaration lasted precious seconds before the landing platform zoomed toward her, and she had to brake or risk crashing into Josh and the terminus pole. Giving her hand brake a squeeze, she slowed and glided safely to a stop, her feet touching down on the landing deck.

The other tour guests gave a cheer for her as Josh helped her unbuckle.

"Great job, Carrie. You did it!" Josh said, his ebullient smile beaming at her.

She returned a shaky smile, adrenaline still making her woozy. "What do you know? I really did!"

"Woo-hoo! Way to go, Carrie!" The shout from below drew her attention to Lylah Grace, who raised two thumbs-up and a broad smile to Carrie.

"Thanks. You, too!" she called back.

Josh nudged her aside. "Clear the deck. Incoming."

She stepped to the right and turned to watch Luke glide smoothly in for a safe landing, then give Josh a fist bump. "That never gets old, man."

Josh laughed and nodded his agreement. "Right?"

Carrie studied the glow in Luke's face as he joked with Josh and discarded his safety gear. The self-assurance, good humor and life-affirming vibrancy that radiated from him were heady. Sexy as hell. Her body gave a low hum of approval. Three days. She had three whole days alone in this beautiful, rugged landscape with Luke.

Well, almost alone. The five other tour guests and Josh notwithstanding. She smiled to herself. Close enough.

Luke caught up with Carrie as she staggered toward the stairs leading down from the landing platform. Giving her a querying look, he put a supportive hand under her elbow. "You okay?"

She drew and exhaled a deep breath as she grinned up at him. "Yeah. Just…finding my sea legs. Adrenaline overload, you know?"

"I know." He matched her smile. "Exhilarating, huh?"

"That's, uh…one word for it." Good humor laced her tone, and she angled a smile toward him. "*Scary* also comes to mind."

"But you did it." He squeezed her elbow.

She stopped and, raking her hair back from her eyes with her fingers, raised wide eyes to his. "Yeah…oh my God! I can't believe I did that!" Carrie clapped a hand to her chest and rolled her eyes as she laughed.

Luke put an arm around Carrie's shoulders and laughed. "That's kinda the point of the adventure tours. To push you beyond your comfort zone and experience thrills and nature and grow your confidence in yourself."

She nodded, her hair sliding back into her face. When she flashed another brilliant smile at him, he had to shove down the urge to brush the loose hair from her face himself and steal a kiss from her plump, grinning lips.

"Oh," she said with an airy gasp, "and the view! You could see *so far* down the gorge. It was beautiful! Terrifying, but beautiful."

Terrifying but beautiful. Yep. That summed up his attraction to Carrie. Every fiber of his being told him Carrie had ghosts, a past that could return to bite him on the ass, but she stole his breath, muddled his brain, made him want to toss caution aside for a taste of her ripe-plum mouth.

"Beautiful it is," he murmured, holding her gaze. The laughter of another tour member shook him from the trance her aqua eyes put him in. Blinking, he hitched his head toward the campsite.

"Can you walk now, sailor?" he asked.

She stood taller, squared her shoulders and slanted a look at him. "Sure. Lead on."

They walked together to the campsite, where the tents they'd sleep in that night were set up in a circle around a firepit with split-log benches. Other members of the tour group were already selecting their tents and settling in.

"So pick a tent, any tent." He waved a hand to the available tents. "They're all the same. For the next hour or so, you're free to relax and do whatever you want. We'll get dinner started in just a bit."

"Thanks." Her smile burrowed deep inside him.

"You should do that more often," he said.

She blinked, and a small dent of confusion furrowed her brow. "Do what?"

"Smile. You have a really nice one. You should use it."

A flush stained her cheeks, and her lips twitched up in response. "Oh. Um, thanks."

As she took a backward step, then turned to select a tent, he replayed his comment in his head and mentally groaned. *Cheesy much?* No wonder she'd blushed. She was probably embarrassed for him. He pinched the bridge of his nose and gave his head a slight shake. He really hoped Josh hadn't overheard the comment. That was just the sort of thing his friend and boss would love to tease him about.

Grabbing a supply pack from the waiting stack of backpacks, Luke took one of the remaining tents and set up his sleeping bag, ate a snack bar and checked the procedures checklist Zane had created for the adventure trips. Check, check, check. They were right on schedule, everything rolling along according to plan. Firewood was next on the list. A supply of split logs was already stacked, ready to use, but so that the trip guests could feel more a part of the adventure, his next task was to organize a few people to gather tinder with him from the woods.

When he asked for volunteers, Annie, Jonah and Lylah Grace were quick to raise their hands. As they headed into the surrounding trees and scrub bushes, Luke hesitated.

Keep an eye on her. Nina's request made his neck prickle, and he second-guessed the notion of leaving Carrie alone in camp.

Well, not alone. Josh was there. And the Coltons. Summer and Nolan both seemed more than capable of handling anything that might come up while he was twig gathering with the others. In fact, Carrie was immersed in a conversation with Summer at the moment and appeared content. Happy, even. She chuckled and nodded at something Summer said, confirming that hypothesis.

She'll be fine, his conscience whispered, assuaging the tug of doubt. Half an hour later, when he and his tinder gatherers returned to camp, Josh was crouched by the firepit, getting a blaze started, and Nolan had joined the animated conversation between Summer and Carrie. All was well.

As Luke approached the firepit with an armload of small sticks, ready to assist however he could in the preparations for dinner, the growl of an all-terrain vehicle rumbled from the surrounding woods.

"That'll be Dave with the latecomer," Josh said, rising to his feet and dusting his hands.

"Latecomer?" Luke arched an eyebrow. They'd never had anyone join the tour group after they'd started before. But Josh and his family were the ones to make that call. If they were okay with latecomers, who was he to complain?

"Yeah. Zane radioed earlier about it." Josh bent to pick up the clipboard with the paperwork on all of the members of the tour group and flipped through the pages. "The guy arrived just minutes after we left this morning and was, apparently, really eager to join the group. Seeing as this is our last trip for the season and we had available spots, Zane gave the guy the option of joining us here. He'll be packing in his supplies."

"Huh." Luke squinted into the woods, where the fading sunlight cast the trees and rocks in long shadows. "I'll go see if I can help the guy unload."

Josh nodded his appreciation, and Luke headed into the woods, toward the narrow dirt road the ranch trucks used to bring equipment and supplies out to the base camp. He met Dave and the new arrival on the ATV about a quarter of a mile from the tent site and flagged them down. "Hi there. Welcome. Can I give you a hand with your backpack or anything?"

The latecomer climbed off the back of the ATV and introduced himself as he shook Luke's hand. "Sure. Glad I could catch up with you. I just have the backpack Zane provided and one bag with my clothes."

Luke assessed the guy in a glance as a city slicker who'd likely never camped or hiked a day in his life. His jeans—at least he was wearing jeans and not suit pants—appeared to have been ironed, judging from the crease down the front of the legs, and the hand that Luke shook was soft and perfectly groomed. He'd obviously used some kind of styling product to slick his dark hair back from his face in a way that accentuated his widow's peak and receding hairline. The waft of cologne that tickled Luke's nose also spoke of a man who preferred the board-room to the rugged outdoors. So why was the guy here? Midlife crisis? An attempt to shake up a staid existence?

"The camp is this way?" the new arrival asked, aiming a finger the direction Luke had come.

"Yep. Perfect timing. We just finished with the zip line, and everyone is settling in their tents." Luke hoisted the prepacked, tour-provided backpack over his shoulder from the back of the ATV. "We'll be having—"

Luke cut his explanation short when he turned to find that the man had marched off toward the camp without him. Leaving Luke to carry both bags. Like a bellhop. Luke angled a *can you believe this guy?* look at Dave, who shook his head and laughed.

"Yeah. Have fun with that one," Dave muttered under his breath and grinned wryly. "He thought we should de-liver him to the camp by helicopter." He paused a beat. *"Helicopter."*

Luke snorted and lifted the man's second bag, one more than campers typically brought, with his free hand. "Right. Because everyone has a helicopter at their disposal."

With a chortle, Dave gunned the ATV engine and nodded to Luke. "Be safe. See you in a couple days."

Jogging a few steps to catch up with the new tour guest, Luke reminded himself that the McCalls' motto was to provide the tour group members with "service, safety and a smile," no matter what. If McCall Adventures wanted to build a reputation for top-notch tours and grow their business, every customer was to be treated with professionalism and graciousness.

"So where are you from?" Luke asked, attempting to make small talk with the city slicker as they closed in on the campground.

"Isn't that information on the forms I filled out? God knows I filled out enough forms and liability waivers this morning to wallpaper my house." He swatted irritably at a bug that flew past his face.

Luke smiled patiently. "I'm sure it is on the forms, but I haven't had a chance to review the paperwork yet."

The newcomer slowed his pace and faced Luke with a sheepish grin. "Of course you haven't. Forgive me. Los Angeles originally."

Luke didn't bother to point out that "originally" wasn't what he'd been asking. Instead, he said, "Oh yeah? You a Lakers fan?"

His companion sent him a confused frown. "Pardon?"

"Are you a Lakers fan?"

The guy twisted his mouth and wrinkled his brow. "That's basketball, correct?"

"Uh...yeah." Luke tried to keep the "well, duh" tone out of his reply. *So...he's not a sports fan.*

Lifting an eyebrow, the new guy said, "No." Continuing toward the camp, he added, "I'm usually too busy to waste time watching sports."

Luke squeezed the straps of the backpack and travel case harder. "Oh. Right."

Must. Not. Make. Snarky. Reply. But, damn, he wanted to rebut the man's comment with one defending sports and how sports fans used their time. He chose to change the topic and explained about choosing a tent, the evening plans for dinner around the campfire and the hike out early the next morning to go white-water rafting.

His comments were acknowledged with a nod, and as they reached the campsite, the man's gaze fervently searched the area, moving from tent to tent, face to face. Finally, his attention snagged and held where the Coltons and Carrie had been joined by Lylah Grace in lively conversation. Beside them, Annie and Jonah were examining a columbine blossom Annie had picked while they gathered tinder. The new arrival's restless expression settled into one Luke could only call cat-who-ate-the-canary smug.

Though baffled by the man's behavior, Luke set the backpack and travel bag on the ground and called out, "Hey, everyone, we have a new member to our party. Everyone please give a warm welcome to Joseph Zimmerman."

Across the campsite, Carrie turned with a jerk. Her eyes widened, and all the color drained from her face. Her reaction to the new arrival sent a chill to Luke's marrow.

Chapter 9

Acid flooded Carrie's gut, and a tremor rolled through her as she stared at Joseph's gloating grin. It wasn't possible. She was in the freaking middle of nowhere!

Panic climbed her throat when she realized that, out here on this adventure trip, she couldn't just jump in her car and race away. To another motel, another hiding place, another seemingly random location where he'd find her regardless of how careful she was. She was stuck. Trapped. Cornered.

His ability to find her here didn't make sense… Except it did. Obviously he'd gotten a reading from the tracker before it was disabled. People had talked. Not Nina. She knew Nina would never have given her location away. But the rest of the McCall family and the ranch hands hadn't known her situation. Greg Beal, the auto-shop owner, had sworn not to say anything, but Joseph could be exceptionally persuasive when he wanted something. And other people in town had seen her. The nurses at the clinic. The auto shop mechanic.

When tears pricked her eyes, she blinked hard to fight them back. She couldn't raise any questions by letting the guides or other campers see her distress. *The others...*

A flicker of hope pushed through her despair. Joseph never showed his dark side around other people. He was a master of masquerading as an affable, career-minded guy whose assertiveness was only proof of his professional drive and determination to succeed. The people around her father's boardroom table appreciated and respected Joseph's take-charge demeanor. Because he was careful not to let anyone but her see his cruel side.

Her gaze darted from Joseph to Lylah Grace, to Josh, to Nolan. Maybe, as long as she was on this tour, surrounded by the rest of the tour group, she might be safe. She drew and released a deep, slow breath, scrabbling for the edges of her frayed composure. At least with these other people around her, she'd have some measure of safety until the tour ended. Wouldn't she?

Her attention shifted back to Joseph, who was still staring at her with a smirk tugging his cheek.

Don't look at him. Don't let the others see how he rattles you.

"Carrie?"

Her heart lurched when the male voice whispered in her ear.

"Are you all right?" Luke asked as he edged in to stand beside her.

She jerked her gaze up, fixing a trembling faux smile on her lips. "Luke. You startled me."

"I see that." He wrapped his fingers gently around her arm in a comforting gesture. "You're shaking."

"I'm just…cold."

He arched an eyebrow, clearly dubious of her claim. "It's, like…eighty degrees."

"What I mean is…I got a sudden chill, kinda like someone walking on my grave." She flashed a weak grin.

"Because of Joseph?"

Damn! So he *had* noticed. She was slipping if she hadn't hidden her reaction any better than that. "I, uh…"

"I saw how you looked at him. You went pale. Looked like you were in shock." Though Luke kept his voice low, she glanced around to see who might be in earshot, listening. Fortunately, most everyone had either walked over to greet Joseph or had returned to their previous conversations around the fire.

"Well, yeah." She mentally cast about for an explanation for her behavior. "Thing is, he looks a lot like someone I used to know, a guy I used to be involved with. So I was caught off guard." She gave a blasé shrug. "But it's not him, so…" She waved a dismissive hand.

Luke turned to look at Joseph before returning his piercing gray gaze to her. "Are you sure it's not him? He acted like he recognized you, too."

Her heart thumped harder. She wasn't sure why she had lied to Luke. Maybe because lying was habit. A survival skill. Lies came so easily to her now…because of the life she'd led, the role she'd played while living with Joseph. Maybe to protect Luke should he learn the truth and do something noble to protect her. What would she do if Joseph outed her lie? Would Joseph declare to everyone that they were man and wife? Doing so would certainly raise questions about why she'd arrived at the ranch and left on the adventure trip without him. Experience had taught her that the last thing Joseph wanted was for other people to question his control over his wife. He'd drilled that into her multiple times in multiple ways over the years. Appearances were everything. She couldn't give *anyone* reason to believe she was anything but a happy, doting wife and he a powerful and respected husband. Ever. Or she'd pay for her slip.

"No, it's not him. I—" She stopped, seeing Luke's eyes narrow with skepticism—or was it concern? She doth protest too much. Most of the time, the simplest thing was to say nothing. The less said, the better. Fewer words to analyze and catch her in a lie. Again she waved a hand to dismiss his inquiries and worries. She stretched her smile broader. "Never mind. I'm fine now. Really."

Her legs trembling, Carrie turned to go back to her tent, to escape both Luke's interrogation and Joseph's weighty stare. Though she'd become somewhat anesthetized to the guilt of lying in past months, deceiving Luke left her with a sick pit in her stomach. He'd been so kind to her over the past couple of days. Fibbing to him about Joseph felt like a betrayal. But why should lying to Luke feel any different than the dozens of other friends and family members she'd misled and hidden the truth from?

Maybe because in the days since arriving at the ranch, the numbness that had gripped her for years had begun to recede. She'd been regaining a sense of freedom, a morsel of humanity, a hint of her former self. And the ice around her heart had begun to thaw. She'd allowed herself to feel again. Not all at once, of course. You couldn't release five years of dammed-up emotions and not drown in the flood. But drips and trickles of remorse, happiness, shame and relief had seeped to the surface in recent days. The McCall family dogs that knocked her down and licked her face showing unconditional affection. Luke's tender ministrations as he cleaned her cut hand. The obvious love of the couples that had joined her on the trip. Nina's unwavering friendship and encouragement. Tantalizing glimpses of what could be, if only…

Squelching the sob that rose in her throat, she crouched at the entrance to her one-man tent to unzip the flaps and crawled inside. Hands shaking, she busied herself by unpacking her bedding from the supplies tucked in one corner of the tent. She spread out the sleep pad and was unknotting the ties on her sleeping bag when the hair on her nape rose like some innate warning system. She sensed, then heard, someone behind her. Carrie whirled around as she inhaled sharply.

"I'm sorry. Did I startle you?" Josh asked with an apologetic grin.

Carrie blew out the breath she'd caught and tried to laugh off her overreaction. "I was off in la-la land, thinking about the rafting tomorrow and—" With another chuckle and a shake of her head, she asked, "What can I do for you, Josh?"

"The question is, what can I do for you? Are all your supplies accounted for? Do you need a snack to tide you over until dinner?" He spread his hands. "If I can get you anything or do anything for you, please ask."

"No. Thanks. I'm fine." *I'm fine I'm fine I'm fine.* The words she'd uttered so often reverberated in her head like a gong. A discordant clang that made her teeth hurt and that sent vibrations to her bones. Huffing her frustration, she lifted a hand to her temple, where the start of a headache pulsed.

"Okay." Josh backed up, flashing a lopsided grin. "Let me know if you ch—"

"Actually," she blurted, "I'm getting a headache. Do you have any aspirin?"

"Not aspirin per se, but other painkillers. In fact, you have a small supply in your personal pack." He motioned to her preloaded backpack, ready for tomorrow's hike.

"Oh. Okay."

"But—" he held up a finger "—save those. You may want them for muscle aches after some of our trip challenges. I have a bigger supply in the camp first-aid kit. I'll be right back."

After Josh ducked out of her tent, she turned back to finish prepping her bed for the night. Maybe if she stayed in her tent the rest of the evening, she could avoid Joseph. Maybe if she—

Another rustle of tent flaps sounded behind her. "Thank you, Josh. That was qui—" Her words died on her lips as she met her husband's hard stare.

"Surprise," he said smugly. "Told you I'd find you." Joseph clamped his mouth in a thin line of disgust and irritation. His face, cast in shadows, appeared all the more angry-looking in the dimly lit tent.

Carrie's heart scampered like a frightened rabbit's. She'd seen the simmering rage that lit his eyes too many times before. Should she shout for help? Surely with so many people just outside the thin wall of the tent he wouldn't hurt her. Would he?

She tried to muster the same fortitude that had allowed her to break free from him weeks ago. Lifting her chin, she met his gaze and firmed her jaw.

He moved inside the small shelter, crowding her, and let the flaps fall closed behind him. "Bravo, dear. Very clever, joining this camping trip group to throw me off your scent." He kept his volume low, barely above a growling whisper. "But lucky for me, I caught your trail before you found the tracker. All it took then was a few questions to the right people and a story about how very much I wanted to be on this last adventure trip of the season. The folks at the ranch were so accommodating. I must thank them when we get back for their help finding you."

She swallowed hard. "Wh-who told you I was on the trip?"

Surely not Nina. Her friend would never betray her that way.

"I figured it out once I heard who'd taken you to the body shop. Then all I had to do was sweet-talk some cowboys. The ones who drove you out this morning were returning with the horse trailer when I got to the ranch."

Frustration and fear gnawed at her. "What…what are you going to do now? What will you tell the others?"

He pulled his face in a mock frown. "What's wrong, darling? Are you ashamed of me? Don't want people to know we're married? Why would that be?"

"Joseph, please…" She swallowed hard, not sure what she was begging for, only that he had her cornered. She was at his mercy.

He reached out to pinch her chin tightly between his fingers. "Joseph, please!" he mimicked in a falsetto voice. "Telling those yahoos the truth now would only raise questions. And if you were half as smart as you think you are, you'd know the last thing I want is people asking questions about our private business. But then this whole stupid divorce scheme of yours proves that you aren't smart. I've told you for years that the only way you'll be leaving this marriage is in a casket. I'll never give you a divorce and let you take away everything I've worked so hard for." He squeezed her chin harder and leaned close enough for her to smell old coffee on his breath as he snarled, *"Never."*

Her breath sawed from her as she debated her options. She considered and discarded each as if reviewing flash cards. Scream? Appease him? Fight back? She'd been through this scenario so many times and knew the pitfalls of every choice.

If she screamed or fought him, she'd draw Josh and Luke's attention. But to what end? Pulling them into a physical altercation with Joseph? She didn't want that, couldn't stand to see anyone hurt on her account.

If she called Joseph out, told everyone who he was, *what* he was, what did she expect the ranchers to do? Calling the police had never done any good in the past, and she knew the owners of McCall Adventures would be wary of calling the cops on a guest without substantial evidence of wrongdoing. Joseph could sue them. *Would* sue them. And would be sure they knew he would. Then, when they got back to town, Joseph would take his pound of flesh from Carrie. She shivered remembering his anger the last time she'd called the police, his deadly vow.

Releasing her chin, Joseph sat back on his heels and let his gaze rake over her, slowly. She could feel the menace as he appraised her. "But if the casket is your choice, so be it." He angled his head as he narrowed his eyes. "Just not yet. Not until you've secured my place in your family and with your family's business."

Bile rose in her throat. She knew what he intended. They'd had this conversation before. If she had Joseph's baby, as the child's father, he'd hold a seat of power as the executor over the child's inheritance and the child's rights to her share of French Industries. Her hand moved to her belly as that thought settled like a rock in her gut.

The notion of any child of hers growing up under Joseph's cruel control sickened her. She'd never let that happen, even if it meant giving her own life to protect her child.

"So…" Joseph cast a glance over his shoulder toward the flaps of her tent. "You be on your best behavior until I figure out how to get us away from this ridiculous camping trip. Understand?"

She said nothing, only glared at him while she fought to quell the tremors in her limbs, at her core.

He gritted his teeth, and he balled his hands.

Instinctively, Carrie tensed, waiting for a blow from his fist.

"Do you understand?" he repeated in a hiss.

She dipped her head in a tiny nod. A concession in the name of self-preservation. If she followed Joseph's lead, kept him as calm as possible, she could, at the least, buy herself more time to figure out a new plan.

"Good." His shoulders and facial muscles relaxed. "Tomorrow morning, you and I will tell the guides that we've changed our minds and want to leave the tour. If needed, you can tell them you're not feeling well, that you think you have a stomach virus. Nobody wants to be around someone who's barfing all the time, huh? And no one wants to risk catching something like that."

A stomach virus. Ironic, since, at the moment, the churn of acid in her gut made it a real possibility she could lose her lunch. She could make Luke and Josh believe she was ill without really trying. Carrie closed her eyes and inhaled slowly.

Joseph finally backed toward the end of the tent but paused before exiting, his mouth twisting and his expression full of disgust. "I have to say, I'm terribly disappointed in you, Carrie. After everything I've given you, done for you…this is how you repay me? Is a little loyalty and respect such a hard thing for you to give?"

Something hot and dangerously rebellious pricked her, and before she could catch the words, she whispered, "I'm happy to give my loyalty and respect to someone who deserves it."

Joseph lunged toward her, and she flinched. With his finger in her face, he ground out, "Be careful. You're in far too deep already."

Then with a huff, he scuttled backward and left her, alone and trembling. After a moment to fight down the clawing panic in her throat, she muttered, "I'm disappointed in me, too."

Because he'd found her again, despite all her precautions and best efforts to evade him. Maybe she wasn't smart enough.

Because she still cowered and submitted to Joseph, despite the strong and self-possessed woman she'd believed herself to be when she'd married him. She'd allowed him to break her spirit.

Because she lacked the courage to go to the board of directors at French Industries and tell them the kind of monster Joseph was. Would they believe her? Would they listen? He'd done such a good job fooling people for so long, and despite his horrible treatment of her, he was a good negotiator and skilled businessman.

She angled her gaze to the backpack of supplies waiting for her use tomorrow and the following day. Or not. She would be leaving the trip with Joseph in the morning. Going back to their home in Aurora. Assuming she couldn't find a way to get away from him before that.

She snorted. "Fat chance."

Joseph would watch her like a hawk, stay glued to her side until they got back to Aurora.

And even if she found a way to flee again, she had no doubt he'd find her. He'd track her down again. And again. A fist closed around her lungs, a hollow, sucking emptiness that drained all her hope into a black void.

"Here ya go!" a cheerful voice said as her tent flap was tossed aside.

She gasped her surprise as Josh poked his head in her tent and held out his hand. "Sorry if I spooked you. Here are the ibuprofen for your headache. Can I get you anything else?"

A new life? A new identity? She took the pills with trembling fingers and flashed a strained smile. "No. But thanks."

"Okay. Dinner will be ready soon. See you out there in a few?"

She bobbed a nod, and Josh ducked out of the tent.

Dinner was the last thing she wanted. Her stomach hurt, her head ached, her soul was battered. And sitting around a campfire eating s'mores and telling ghost stories while pretending Joseph's presence didn't freak her out would take more strength and energy than she had.

She had to get away from Joseph before she lost the chance. Before morning. If she could sneak away from the camp, find her way back to the highway and hitchhike out of the area before anyone woke up and found her missing...

Her pulse thumped. Was it possible?

Chapter 10

Carrie had no real idea where the campsite was located or which direction to go, but if she didn't at least try, she knew for certain that Joseph would drag her back home in the morning. He'd vent his wrath on her. He'd restrict her freedom to the point she'd be a prisoner in her own home.

When, after an hour she'd not emerged from her tent, Luke came to the flaps and called inside. "Carrie, you okay? Dinner's ready. Everybody's gettin' their grub on."

"I, um...I'm fine." Then, remembering Joseph's ploy for the morning, she decide it couldn't hurt to lay some groundwork. "I'm not hungry. My head and stomach hurt a bit." At least she wasn't lying to him this time. Her gut really was all tangled up, and she couldn't choke down food if she tried.

"Oh. Can I do anything?" His concerned tone both warmed her heart and warned her to tread lightly.

"Just those darn migraines, I think. I'm going to rest. But thanks."

He didn't respond at first, then with a worried-sounding grunt, he said, "If you need anything, anything at all, please let me know."

Tears pricked her eyes. Leaving the adventure trip would mean leaving Luke. She'd been looking forward to spending a precious few days in his company.

She'd have to cut out on Nina, too, and go into hiding, which felt like a betrayal to her friend after all the ways she'd helped Carrie. She worked a raspy reply past the knot in her throat. "I will."

"Feel better."

She heard him shuffle away from her tent, and it took all her strength not to call him back and weep in his arms.

Around the campfire that evening, the guests on the trip took turns telling stories about themselves, laughing amiably as they teased each other gently, and shared hot dogs and s'mores. The Coltons, private investigators, told how they'd caught a murderer and drug dealer in their small hometown last year and nearly died in the process. Annie and Jonah Devereaux shared the tale of how they'd met when he'd rescued her from attackers in an alley. Joseph Zimmerman charmed the group with his dry sense of humor and the story of how he'd risen out of poverty to sit on the board of directors for a top company in manufacturing. Lylah Grace shared funny tales of her grandchildren's antics and her years of teaching kindergarten. Despite their diverse backgrounds, the group bonded and, to Luke, it seemed they were enjoying each other's company. Good. That was the goal of the tour. Fun, fellowship and adventure in the outdoors.

For his part, though, Luke couldn't take his mind off the tent at the edge of the fire light where Carrie had been tucked away since before dinner. He resisted the urge to go back to her tent to check on her, knowing his mother had always wanted to be left undisturbed when she had a migraine. He prayed her migraine would improve so she could complete the trip and enjoy herself.

He wasn't the only one who seemed concerned by Carrie's absence around the fire. Josh had checked on Carrie once, and Lylah Grace mentioned her worry several times. Joseph, though he'd just arrived and hadn't met Carrie officially, kept glancing toward Carrie's tent as if waiting for her to emerge and join the group. Luke thought back to Joseph's arrival, how the businessman had stared at Carrie while sporting a strange grin. Was the guy simply attracted to Carrie? She was decidedly beautiful, and he couldn't blame the guy for being intrigued by her, even if the notion of another man competing for Carrie's affection did gnaw at Luke's gut.

Later that night, once they'd all retreated to their tents for bed, Luke lay with his hands stacked under his head. His mind swam with thoughts of the day's events and plans for tomorrow swimming in his head. And continued concern for Carrie.

She'd made plain her life had no room for a new relationship. She might be kind and intelligent with a sense of humor that she didn't give enough free rein. But she had secrets, too. That was clear. Secrets equaled complications, and he'd had enough of complicated and conflicted relationships.

Sure, he could be overreacting to what he perceived as tension in Carrie. Maybe it was just her headaches that had her mood swinging. Maybe she was just nervous about the challenges they'd be undertaking on the trip. Maybe he was seeing things that weren't there because of Sharon. Maybe—

Hearing a snapping noise, like a breaking twig, outside, he paused. He was always alert to the possibility that the scent of their dinner had attracted wild animals. As a light sleeper, he also took note when the guests left the camp at night to relieve themselves, and he didn't rest easy until said guest returned. The woods at night were dark, and even with a flashlight, an inexperienced camper could get disoriented, lost, injured.

Luke sat up and parted the edges of his window flap, which he'd left partially unzipped for ventilation. Peering out at the campsite, lit only by the nearly full moon and the last glow of campfire coals, he watched a dark figure in a light-colored T-shirt tiptoe past his tent and into the trees. Carrie.

Wariness jolted through him.

The soft rays of moonlight glimmered on her hair and cast her womanly shape in stark relief. She moved gracefully, like a panther stalking its night prey. She was enchanting, mysterious, beautiful.

But it was the backpack she carried with her and the fact she wasn't using a flashlight that sparked his curiosity. She certainly didn't need her backpack to go to the bathroom, especially when the tour company had provided sanitation packs with tissue paper and a small shovel in a zip-sealed bag. He considered stopping her and reminding her she didn't need to lug her full backpack with her, but she disappeared quickly into the woods beyond the circle of tents.

Then the quiet rasp of another tent zipper caught his attention. Across the campsite, Joseph emerged from his tent, flashlight in hand, and he crept past the campfire and followed Carrie into the woods.

Now a tingle of ill ease crawled up Luke's back. His instincts told him this was no coincidence. Joseph's focus seemed trained on the spot where Carrie had entered the trees, his movement focused on following her. Luke sensed ill intent on Joseph's part, though he couldn't say why.

He'd had a similar itchy feeling about Sharon in the days before he'd lost her, a feeling he'd ignored, talked himself out of. And she'd died. Killed herself. A death he might have prevented if he'd listened to his gut instead of worrying about being nosy or pushy or whether he was being manipulated by her drama.

He'd sworn then to stay far away from needy women. He'd had all the drama and guilt and conflict he wanted for this lifetime. And yet, as a tour guide, he was responsible for Carrie's safety. Because he'd vowed to Nina to keep an eye on Carrie, his responsibility extended beyond returning her to the ranch in one piece from the zip-lining and rappelling. It was personal.

He sighed, pinching the bridge of his nose as resignation washed through him and duty compelled him to follow. He dug in his supplies for his flashlight, unzipped the door of his tent and set out after them. Moving his flashlight beam in an arc, Luke searched the black night. The woods were filled with deep shadows, cast by the moon's light, and he saw no evidence of Joseph's flashlight. Either he'd turned it off or covered enough ground for the beam to be swallowed by the night.

Luke continued in the direction he'd seen the pair disappear for several minutes before deciding he'd veered from their trail and doubled back. Every few moments, he paused to listen, to scan his surroundings for signs Carrie or Joseph had passed that way. He'd only been a couple moments behind them. How could they have gotten so far ahead?

He nixed the idea of calling out to them, not wanting to wake the other guests or raise an alarm if none was needed. Luke pulled up short, and his pulse tripped when he considered the possibility that he'd read the situation wrong. Could Carrie and Joseph be having a late-night tryst? While it didn't seem likely, Josh had said adventure trip romances had happened before. The mental image of Joseph with Carrie caused a jealous burn in his veins, but if a tryst proved the case, he would sneak away as quietly as possible and leave the lovers to their covert affair. And put an end to any notion he had of a potential relationship with Carrie.

A mosquito buzzed in his ear, and he swatted at it, frustrated with himself. Then the low buzz came again, and he realized what he was hearing was low voices, not the hum of a bug. Luke perked his ear and turned slowly, trying to home in on where the voices were coming from. With his flashlight beam shielded and pointed low, he moved slowly toward the murmur. He eased through the deadfall and maze of branches as quietly as he could. So he could listen. So he wouldn't startle them.

As he homed in on their location, drawing closer, he picked up on subtleties he hadn't heard earlier. The tone of the voices. Joseph's hostile. Angry. Carrie's fearful. Broken. No midnight tryst, then. So what was going on?

The sound of a slap and a sharp cry of pain rolled through the chilly night air, and Luke stopped, stunned. *Hell!*

Forget slow and quiet. He barreled through the dark

woods as quickly as he could. He found Carrie and Joseph a short distance farther up the hillside. He had her backed against a tree, one hand holding her throat while he made threatening gestures with his other hand.

"Hey!" Luke shouted, focusing his flashlight beam on the pair. "Take your hands off her!"

Joseph whipped a startled glance toward him but made no move to free Carrie. "Butt out. This doesn't concern you."

"Oh, but it does. Anytime I see a guy manhandling a woman, hurting her, it becomes my business." Luke stalked closer. "Now, let her go."

"Get lost, pal."

Luke moved right up to Joseph and grabbed a fistful of Joseph's shirt near his throat. "I said get your hands off her! Now!"

"Luke, don't. Please…" Carrie's rasping plea stunned him. Don't? Don't what? Help her get free of the idiot strangling her?

Sharon had pushed him away, too. Told him she didn't want, didn't need his help. Hours before she'd taken a whole bottle of pills…

Joseph leaned forward, sticking his nose right in Luke's face. With his free hand, he gripped Luke's wrist below the hand clutching his shirt. "She's my wife, and I'll discipline her however I see fit."

A jolt like a hit from a cattle prod raced through Luke. *Wife?* His gaze darted to Carrie's. In the dim glow from the flashlight he'd dropped as he stormed up to Joseph, Carrie's aqua gaze filled with defeat, apology.

He swatted that revelation, and the curious stab of disappointment, aside, because Joseph's terminology was equally disturbing. An indication of the man's mental state. "Discipline? Geez, man, she's not some misbehaving child. What right do you have—?"

"I have every right!" Joseph barked, his grip biting harder on Luke's wrist. "Now you let go of me and get lost. Or I swear I'll—"

"What?" Luke snarled, tightening his grasp of Joseph's shirt, twisting it so that it cinched around his throat.

Joseph released his grip on Carrie's throat with a shove that sent her stumbling backward. As she fell, her head smacked the tree trunk.

"Damn it, man," Luke growled, giving Joseph a shove. Before Joseph could catch his balance, Luke landed a punch to Joseph's eye. "You're an ass, you know that?" Luke turned, squatting to check on Carrie. "Are you o—?"

Carrie's eyes were still fixed on Joseph, and they flared wide, terror filling her face. "Luke!"

He spun, tumbling to his butt as he jerked his attention back to Joseph.

The businessman had stepped back and reached under his shirttail. Joseph pulled out a handgun with a silencer, and Luke's heart rose to his throat.

"I told you to stay out of my business," Joseph said, his tone low and menacing.

"Joseph, please," Carrie cried. "Please, don't do this!"

Ice filled Luke's veins. He was in over his head, going up against an irrational, armed husband. But he would not, *would not* leave Carrie alone in the woods with the lunatic. He edged his body so that he was more fully between Carrie and the gun now aimed at them. While the moon and his dropped flashlight gave enough illumination for Luke to keep Joseph and his movements in focus, the light was too dim to determine what caliber gun it was. Any gun could be fatal, but some had less stopping power, lower accuracy. Not that he could put Carrie at risk by betting against the odds...

"I said I'd go home with you if—" her voice cracked as she continued pleading "—if you'll leave Luke and the others alone. No one needs to get hurt."

"What's your interest in my wife, anyway?" Joseph asked.

"She's a client. It's my job to keep her safe. That's all."

Joseph's expression pulled into a sneer. "What did you think when you followed us? That you'd come out here like some cowboy knight in shining armor to rescue her?"

"I only came out here because I was concerned for her. For both of you. It's easy to get lost in the woods at night and I—"

Joseph snorted loudly. "I bet you were hoping to screw her. Weren't you?"

Luke gritted his teeth as he flexed and balled his hand, itching to smash it into Joseph's crude mouth. "No. I was afraid you were going to hurt her. Looks like I was right. Huh, asswipe? You think you're tough when you mistreat a woman?"

In the glow from the flashlight, Luke saw Joseph's eyes flare hot as he flicked off the safety on the pistol and reaimed it at Luke.

Carrie whimpered fearfully and gasped, "Luke, please! Don't antagonize him. Joseph, I'll come with you. Just...don't hurt him."

Joseph cast a look of disgust at her before returning his attention to Luke. "Did she tell you she was pregnant?"

Chapter 11

Behind him, he heard Carrie's breath catch. But she didn't deny Joseph's assertion.

Pregnant? She'd had every opportunity to tell him she was carrying a baby, that she was married, but she hadn't. Even when he'd spilled his guts to her. Even when they'd kissed. Shock, disappointment and betrayal wound through him like cords wrapping around his throat. He choked on them, yet Luke forcibly shoved them down and schooled his face.

Stay on task. Don't let your emotions sidetrack you.

He heard shuffling behind him, felt her leg bump his ankle as Carrie shifted on the ground. Luke did his best to cover her movement by distracting Joseph with subtle actions. Picking up the flashlight, clearing his throat, taunting him. "A baby is just one more reason for her to get the hell away from you."

Joseph scoffed. "No, my friend. A baby is all the more reason why she's coming home with me. Tonight."

"I'm not your friend." He waved a finger, hoping the gesture would hold Joseph's attention. He didn't know what Carrie had in mind, but he'd give her every chance he could to succeed.

"I am Carrie's friend, though, and I won't let you hurt her again. So here's what's going to happen," Luke said with a calm he didn't feel. "You're going to put the gun down, step away from Carrie and return to the campsite with me, where we will call the police to sort this out."

Joseph arched an eyebrow and grunted. "No. What's going to happen is I'll keep my gun, to be sure you don't try anything stupid, and we're all going back to the camp long enough for my wife and me to get our things. Then, without the police or anyone at the camp being any the wiser, we're going to call a cab to meet us at the highway. I saw the satellite phone Josh had. You'll get it for me without alerting Josh. Then Carrie and I are going back home to await the birth of our child without any interference from you or anyone else. *Capisce?*"

Luke shook his head. "Not a chance. I won't leave her alone with you."

Joseph huffed, his lips tightening. "Enough of this. Get up, Carrie. We're going home." When she didn't move, he barked, "Now!"

"You won't get—"

A primal-sounding roar cut him off as Carrie lurched from behind Luke and surged toward Joseph. A muted pop sounded at the same instant something stung his ear. Ignoring the hot bite, he dropped to his haunches, ducking as the next bullet whizzed over his head.

With a feral snarl, Carrie clawed at Joseph like a wildcat. Joseph swept his arm across his body, knocking away her battering hands, then employed a reverse swipe to strike to her chin.

Luke seized the opportunity Carrie's distraction offered. He scrambled to his feet and rushed Joseph from behind. Hooking an arm around Joseph's throat, he squeezed his forearm against Joseph's windpipe, using the stranglehold to drag the man away from Carrie.

Joseph's free hand flew up to grab at Luke's arm while he twisted his body and bucked to get free. Carrie was panting, her fingers raised and curled, ready for her next attack. Tears soaked her face as she stood glaring at Joseph, trembling.

"Go, Carrie! Get out of here!" Luke shouted.

Anticipating his opponent's next move, Luke jerked his head to the side just in time to avoid Joseph's head smashing backward into his nose.

Joseph growled and raised the gun he still clutched. He angled the muzzle blindly over his shoulder and squeezed the trigger. Luckily the trajectory was wrong, and the bullet pocked a tree, splintering the bark rather than hitting Luke.

Apparently sensing the folly of shooting randomly behind him, Joseph, still gasping for breath past Luke's choke hold, trained the weapon on Carrie. She whimpered as she staggered back, shaking her head. "No... please."

Adrenaline spiked in Luke's blood, caused a buzzing in his ears. He had to disarm Joseph. As long as Joseph had that damn gun, things could turn tragic in a heartbeat.

Before Luke could make a play for the weapon, Joseph fired again, and Carrie screamed. Went down. Stayed down.

Horror slammed Luke like being kicked by a bull. But he had no time for more than that instant reaction. Joseph was still armed, still fighting to get free of Luke's stranglehold.

Using the skills he'd mastered to subdue a struggling calf, Luke shifted his weight abruptly and yanked Joseph to the ground. He went down with Joseph, releasing his arm's grip on the man's neck so he could lob a fist into Joseph's nose. Joseph's return punch had a savage strength and accuracy. Pain streaked from Luke's jaw to reverberate in his head.

Luke caught Joseph's wrist as the next blow came at him, and he used his size advantage and position to wrestle his opponent's arms over his head and pin Joseph's legs with his own. With his fingers digging into Joseph's wrist, he slammed the hand holding the gun against the ground, again and again, until it slipped from Joseph's grip.

When he released one of Joseph's arms so he could grab the handgun, Joseph reacted instantly, shoving his hand into Luke's face. Gouging. Pushing. Joseph's braced arm jammed Luke's head back so that he couldn't see, couldn't reach the gun. Worse, his hold on Joseph was slipping. Joseph was regaining his mobility by inches.

With a sudden buck and twist, Joseph rolled Luke off him and reversed their positions, trapping Luke beneath him. Joseph reared his arm back, and Luke turned his head aside to avoid the impact of his opponent's fist. He twisted, fighting to free his hands, then a leg. Rocks, roots and thorns dug into his back and scraped his head as they traded punches, jabs, scratches. At last he wrenched away from Joseph's restraining grip. Luke hadn't forgotten the gun, though in their tussling, he'd lost track of where the weapon was.

They continued in a savage back-and-forth wrestling match for several minutes—or maybe weeks or a few seconds. Time became a blur as Luke fought for his life. Because it quickly became apparent Joseph's anger had turned to bloodlust. He wouldn't let Luke walk away from this battle alive.

A sharp throbbing woke Carrie. She roused slowly, her mind fuzzy. Confused.

It was dark. She was cold. She was lying on stabbing sticks, damp earth and uncomfortable rock. Over the chirp of crickets and the lonely call of an owl, the sound of animalistic grunts and growls reached her. Rustling noises. Her pulse jumped at the thought of wolves or bears prowling the night.

But as she sat up, pressing a hand to the pounding pain at the back of her head, movement drew her attention to an even more terrifying tableau. And memory returned in a tidal wave of shock and panic. Joseph. The woods. A gun. She'd tripped. Hit her head.

And Luke. He'd found them—her and Joseph. Heard and seen…and stepped into the maelstrom.

With her heart in her throat, she squinted to watch the men, two dark forms grappling, hitting, circling each other like rabid dogs in a territorial standoff.

Because of her. Because she'd run. Because she'd brought this danger to the Double M. To the adventure tour.

Guilt squeezed her chest, and hot tears burned her eyes. She had to do something, had to help Luke.

When she staggered to her feet, her head spun, and she wobbled. She paused to brace a hand against a tree. Swiping her face to dry her tears, she sucked in deep breaths, needing to regain her composure. Clear her mind. Find her equilibrium. Resurrect the courage that had set her on her flight to freedom.

Her first task had to be minimizing the danger Luke was in. But how? Help him fight Joseph? Call the focus of her husband's wrath back to her, giving Luke time to escape?

A pang wrenched inside her. Luke wouldn't take the chance to run, even if she provided it. In just the few days she'd known him, she'd learned that much about the kind cowboy with the piercing eyes that saw and understood too much. He was stubborn. A fierce protector. Honorable.

The kind of man she wished she'd found before she'd allowed herself to be duped by Joseph's suave facade and emotional manipulation.

In the eerie glow from a flashlight on the ground behind the men, she watched Luke plant a foot in Joseph's stomach and send him reeling back several steps. In the precious seconds he'd bought, free of Joseph's battering hands, Luke bent to rake his hands through the detritus of the forest floor. As if searching for something. What—

The gun! If Joseph was no longer brandishing it, threatening Luke with it, he must have dropped it, lost it. She gasped at the realization, and Luke's gaze flew to her.

"Carrie, run!" he yelled.

But like Luke, she would not abandon her new friend.

Luke's shout drew Joseph's attention to her, and he seemed stunned for a moment before taking a long stride toward her.

"No!" Luke tackled him, knocking him to the dirt.

Carrie rushed forward and began searching the ground, raking through dead leaves, tiny twigs and gravel, hunting for the pistol. She searched, crawling on her hands and knees, frantically looking for the weapon that would put an end to this nightmarish standoff.

But Joseph's gloating laugh put an end to her hopes. Raising her head, the chilling sight that greeted her confirmed her fear. Joseph had recovered the gun. With the pistol aimed at Luke and with blood dripping from his swollen nose, Joseph dragged himself to his feet to hover over Luke's prone form.

"You sorry son of a bitch," Joseph growled, panting from exertion.

Carrie didn't analyze. Didn't hesitate. She simply saw Luke in danger and acted. Lowering one shoulder, she charged Joseph, knocking into him and ruining his shot. Even muffled by the silencer, the sound of the gun firing jolted through Carrie.

One upward swing of his arm was all Joseph needed to send her stumbling back, her jaw stinging and pain blurring her vision. As she blinked, the dark outline of the man she'd married came into focus again. In her peripheral vision, Luke made only small, slow movements. He didn't get up.

"You ingrate." Joseph took aim at her with a two-handed grip on the gun.

Fear streaked through her anew, and the acid bite of bile burned her throat. "If you kill me," she cried, raising both hands, desperate to stop him, "you'll kill our baby. Your child. Your link to the company."

She thought she saw Joseph flinch, a twitch of his cheek. He huffed and hissed, obviously physically spent and frustrated. He muttered a foul curse word. "You put our baby at risk coming out here on this pointless trip in the godforsaken middle of nowhere. How could you be so stupid?"

"To hear you tell it, stupid is par for the course for me," she said quietly.

"And you just keep proving my point. Don't you?"

The clatter of gravel and a fast-moving shadow were the only warnings before Luke surged toward Joseph and swung something large and dark at Joseph's head. Joseph howled in pain and crumpled on the ground.

"Go, Carrie!" Luke yelled. "For God's sake, run! Get outta here!"

More muted pops told her Joseph had fired the gun again, each low blast sending ripples of terror like waves of electricity coursing through her. As long as she stayed and fought, Luke would stay and fight. Maybe running was the best way to protect him.

When something smacked the tree beside her and sent splinters flying, her flight response kicked into high gear. Adrenaline fueled her legs as she turned to scramble away from the dangerous scene. But the path was dark, the trees blocking most of the bright moon and casting the landscape in demonic-looking shadows. Still she ran.

Her feet slipped and skidded in loose gravel and dried leaves. Her toes tripped over roots and rocks. Low branches slapped and grabbed at her as she raced down the mountain. Weaving between trees and pale boulders scattered over the hillside like gravestones, Carrie panted, her heart thrashing in her chest, as she stumbled forward. All she wanted was to put distance between her and the nightmare behind her. The pain, the danger, the evil.

Only when her foot skidded out from under her and she landed hard on her bottom did she slow down to consider what she was doing, where she was going. She gulped in air as the metallic taste of blood filled her mouth. The sting on her tongue told her she'd bitten it when she'd thudded onto the hard dirt and rock. She took precious seconds to catch her breath and squint into the night, deciding her best path. A larger rock formation blocked her path a couple dozen yards ahead, the pale gray of the granite face reflecting the moon.

Pale gray…like Luke's eyes.

She clamped her lips together to stifle the moan of remorse that welled in her throat. She'd fled without a glance back, leaving Luke alone with her irate husband. Luke, whose intervention in the dark woods had probably saved her life. Luke, who'd been nothing but kind and concerned for her well-being from the moment she'd arrived at the Double M. Luke, whose smiles and gentle touch had unmistakably stirred something dormant in her soul. Regret nudged her. In a different reality, where she'd never known Joseph or experienced his brand of control, she would have pursued her feelings for someone like Luke. But now…

Now. She had to focus on her current crisis. She shook herself back to the present as the urgency to get moving again pressed down on her.

Suppressing the groan that welled in her throat as she hoisted herself back onto her feet, she turned away from the rock wall blocking her path and angled her path up-hill. Carrie continued in the general direction she believed would take her away from Joseph, away from the camp, just…*away* as quickly as possible.

Distance was the key at the moment. Making herself hard to find. Come daylight, she'd worry about getting to a road or finding an inhabited house or business. In her initial attempt to flee Joseph, she'd lost her backpack.

Though she knew she'd miss the supplies in the pack, she couldn't regret having dumped the extra weight slowing her when Joseph had given chase.

Carrie trudged uphill as fast as she could given the incline and the darkness. Her saddle-sore legs trembled, and her chest heaved. Her head, her jaw throbbed where Joseph had smacked her. But exhaustion and exertion were untenable reasons to quit. Not when Joseph had made clear how he planned to punish her for her desertion. Giving up was not an option.

As she wove through the shadowed forest, tripping along the uneven ground and dodging branches, she cringed every time her foot broke a twig or disturbed a rock. Sound was her enemy. Night-blind but for the moonlight, as she was, too, Joseph would follow the noises she made to track her.

She stilled when the truth struck her. Was her best tactic to stop? To find some sheltering cave or deadfall tree to hide behind and simply lie low and keep quiet?

Her oxygen-deprived lungs and tired legs liked that idea, but the flight instinct inside her screamed for more distance. The farther, the better. The farther, the safer...

She cast her gaze around the blackness-encased woods, the sound of her own breathing harsh to her ears. Squinting, Carrie searched for evidence of a place she could hide. Anywhere that the landscape could provide cover if Joseph made it this far. As her breathing calmed, she grew more conscious of the sounds of the night. The murmur of leaves when a light breeze blew. The chirp of crickets and some night bird. And—she strained to listen—the low rumble of rushing water. A waterfall? Or was that the river the tour group was supposed to raft tomorrow?

That gave her pause. If she was near where the group

would travel in the morning, they could find her. Her pulse skipped. Being spotted meant risking being thrust back into Joseph's presence. Would Joseph have returned to the campsite after losing track of her? Not if Luke was still alive to report him.

If Luke was still alive…

Her gut soured, and bile rose in her throat. Had she cost Luke his life? How could she live with herself knowing her actions had gotten him killed?

A whimper escaped her throat, and when her knees buckled, she braced her back against the nearest tree. While she battled to keep what remained of her lunch in her stomach, a new sound filtered through the darkness. A rhythmic crunching, stones rolling, sticks cracking. Footsteps. She froze. Held her breath. Listened, trying to discern which direction the noise was coming from. Was it Joseph? An animal?

A beam of light strobed over the trees near her. Not an animal, then. Something far more dangerous to her. Frustration, terror and panic roiled inside her. The additional surge of acid in her gut brought up her stomach contents in a violent gush. Heaving, coughing, spitting. There was no way to vomit silently.

The flashlight beam swung toward her, blinding her.

"Carrie?" a male voice called in a stage whisper.

Pushing away from the tree, she stumbled up the hill on rubbery legs. Buzzing filled her ears as her adrenaline surged anew. She pumped her legs as fast as she could make them move. Away. She had to get away. He'd kill her if he caught her.

After staggering uphill a short distance, she veered from that path to angle down the mountain slope. Faster. She used the downhill momentum she'd gained to push harder. She could hear, could sense her pursuer gaining on her.

Go, go, go! her brain screamed. She'd come too far to get caught now. She had to—

A large, hard body tackled her from behind. She fell to the ground with a jarring thump. Rocks scraping, sticks poking, her lungs aching.

"Nooo!" she wailed.

And rolled to her back to fight.

Chapter 12

"Carrie!" Luke shouted as he battled her flailing hands and battering fists. He tried to pin her arms down, to calm her, to reassure her he meant her no harm, but she fought like a trapped wildcat. Fingernails raking, legs thrashing, teeth bared as she growled and shrieked.

When he finally got control of her pummeling hands, he gave her a gentle shake. "It's Luke, Carrie! Stop fighting me. I won't hurt you."

Carrie gasped and stilled, though her chest rose and fell as she gasped in air.

He, too, was winded and sucked oxygen into his lungs. He was exhausted after chasing her through the woods, searching. He'd dropped his flashlight beside him when he'd grabbed her, and the beam's glow cast a dim sphere of light around them from the ground.

"Luke?" Her breathy whisper cracked with emotion, and something deep inside him twisted.

"Yeah, it's Luke. You're safe." Slowly he released his grip on her, and she flung her arms around his neck, wrapping him in an embrace that startled him. Moved him.

Damn it, he'd never wanted to feel this way again! He'd never wanted to be torn between a sense of duty and protection and his own emotional survival. Sharon's death had wrecked him. Pulling himself together had taken months and cost him the college degree he'd only been a few classes short of completing.

But kneeling there in the pitch-darkness with Carrie trembling as she clutched him, he put his arms around her and held her close. Stroked her back. Soothed her as best he could.

"It's okay now. I got you. I won't let him hurt you," he crooned.

He heard her swallow hard, then she levered back to study his face at close range. Her aqua eyes, full of tears, glinted in the moonlight. Dirt—or was it blood?—smudged her cheeks and chin. Carrie lifted a hand to his face and carefully touched his swollen lip. His aching eye and throbbing ear. When she drew her fingers back from her stinging ear, they were stained with blood. "He hurt you."

"I'll be all right." He wrapped his hand around hers and kissed her scraped and dirty palms. "How are you? Are you injured?"

She closed her eyes, sending tears down her cheeks as she inhaled slowly and released a shuddering sigh. "No. Not…not really. I mean…" Her eyelids fluttered open again, and her chin quivered as she met his gaze. "Oh, God, I'm so s-sorry. I n-never wanted anyone else to g-get hurt. I just…had to get away from him. I—"

"Shh." He pulled her close again, squeezing her tighter, trying to absorb the shivers that racked her body. "You're okay."

Her fingers curled into the shirt on his back. "J-Joseph?"

He gritted his teeth. When he'd left Joseph, he hadn't been sure what condition the man was in, only that he had stopped fighting back long enough for Luke to bolt away and follow Carrie. His first concern had been to find her, keep her safe.

When he didn't respond, Carrie pulled away again, moistening her lips nervously before she pressed, "What happened...with Joseph? Is he—?"

"I don't know," Luke muttered. "I just...took the opportunity to get away when I got it and came after you."

She jerked her head toward the dark forest, her gaze darting back and forth. "So...h-he could still be coming? I...I have to go. I have to keep moving."

When she tried to pull free of his grasp, Luke gripped her more tightly. "Carrie, wait. Stay put. I won't let him get you."

Her eyes were wide and wild as she continued scanning the woods. "If he finds me—"

"Then I'll be here with you. I won't let him touch you."

She swiped a hand across her nose as she sniffled and shook her head. "I can't let you get hurt again. I should never have put you at risk. I n-never wanted—"

"Shh. Take a breath. I know you didn't." He stroked his hand down her cheek, and when his hand glided over her jaw, she winced. Remembering the backhanded smack Joseph had delivered to her chin, Luke frowned. "Are you sure you're okay? He hit you pretty hard."

"I'm used to it," she mumbled, then turning away, she scooted out of his embrace. Drawing her knees to her chest, she held her legs close and put her head down. "I've had worse."

When he thought of Joseph mistreating Carrie, battering her, rage roiled in Luke's gut. He fisted his bruised hands, ignoring the sting of his raw knuckles and wishing he could choke Joseph the way the bastard had been choking Carrie when he'd come upon them. Expelling a cleansing breath, he cupped her cheek gently and held her gaze. "Why didn't you tell me you were escaping a bad marriage?"

She snorted derisively. "Are you kidding? My friends and family don't even know how volatile Joseph is. It's not something you tell."

"Why not? Didn't you trust your family to help you?"

"I knew they'd try. That's the main reason I couldn't tell them. Joseph would have done something to keep them quiet, to intimidate them if they tried to help me. I couldn't put anyone else at risk."

"Maybe he would, but maybe not. He couldn't—"

"He did."

"Sorry?"

She shook her head. "Never mind."

Luke huffed a sigh. "Does Nina know?"

Carrie stiffened, and her head jerked back up. "Oh God. Nina! If he found me, he may have figured out Nina helped me. What if he goes after her?"

"He'll have to go through Steve to hurt Nina. And if she's at the ranch, she'll have a whole lot of other people protecting her, too."

"But…I have to warn her! I—"

"We will. When we get back with the tour group, we can use the satellite phone to call the ranch…and the police."

Carrie shook her head. "No. That could be too late. We have to tell her now! God only knows what Joseph's next move will be. If he gets back to the ranch before us—"

Luke sighed. "How?"

"What?"

"How are we supposed to warn her? Even if we had a cell phone—which I don't. Do you?"

She shook her head. "I lost my backpack when Joseph showed up and chased me."

"Well, no signal out here anyway, so a mobile phone would be useless. And if we try to find our way back to camp tonight—"

She shook her head again. "No."

"No?"

"I'm not going back to the camp. Not joining the tour group again. It'd be too easy for Joseph to find me. He may have already rejoined them and told them some lie to explain our absence. I have to—I don't know—find a way back to civilization on my own. Disappear." Her face crumpled as she added in a croak, "Again."

Luke grunted. "Seriously? That's your plan? To keep running?"

"It's all I *can* do!"

"You can stand your ground and call the cops on him!"

She gave a sarcastic laugh. "They're no help. Besides, Joseph swore to kill me if I ever—"

"Geez, Carrie! Do you hear yourself? He said that to scare you. To control you."

"Well, it worked. Because I am scared. And I've lived with him long enough to believe he meant what he said. He's come close to killing me before. It wouldn't take much extra effort on his part."

The horrible truth was, Luke believed it, too. He didn't have personal experience with spousal abuse, but he'd read enough in the news, seen pamphlets in doctor's offices and heard about cases through the grapevine to know some general statistics. Grave statistics.

In a nutshell, far too many men were hurting their wives and girlfriends, killing the people they'd said they loved. And getting away with it because friends and neighbors turned a blind eye.

Guilt bit hard. He'd probably ignored warning signs in the past himself—especially after he'd hardened his heart to deal with losing Sharon. If he didn't get involved, he couldn't be blamed when disaster happened. Right? Better to walk away than to get involved and carry the burden of guilt. Luke swallowed the bile that rose in his throat, acknowledging how selfish and ignorant his defense mechanism had been.

How many times had he ignored the guy yelling at his girlfriend in a parking lot? The easily dismissed bruises on a friend's arm? The excuses, withdrawal and sudden changes in a loved one's mood and behavior? In protecting himself from more of the pain and guilt that had been Sharon's legacy, he'd likely left others to suffer in silence.

Until Carrie's abuse had been thrown in his face. Carrie, whom he'd grown to care about in a few short days. Carrie, who was married, pregnant and desperate to escape her abuser. No matter the cost to him personally, he had to see this through. He had to help Carrie, had to defend her, had to show her the truth about herself and her situation.

"Look," he said calmly, trying not to escalate her worry, "we'll sleep here tonight. If we try to find our way back to the base camp tonight, in the dark, we're just as likely to end up getting lost."

"We aren't lost already?"

"We—" He'd intended to reassure her he knew exactly where they were and how to get them back to camp, but he hesitated. Truth was he had no idea how far they'd come in the dark woods and how much they'd veered from a straight path. He'd heard it said that studies showed a person lost in the wilderness without a compass, trying to walk in strictly one direction, will actually go in circles. And Carrie had veered off at sharp angles, specifically trying to lose her tail. If not for her light-colored T-shirt and the sounds of her being sick, he might have walked right past her. "Maybe. I'll know more in the morning when I can see landmarks. For now, we need to stay here until first light."

She bobbed her head. "I'd just decided the same about the time you found me. I figured still and silent in the darkness was the best way to stay hidden from Joseph if he made it this far looking for me."

"Hmm. Good point." He scrubbed a hand over his face. "So it's decided? We sleep here tonight and head back to the base camp in the morning?"

Carrie bit her bottom lip and cast a glance around them. "Is it safe? What about wild animals?"

"Do you have any food on you?"

"Food?" Her eyes found his again and widened. "No. Why?"

"Because food is the main thing that would attract animals. I doubt they'll bother us if there's nothing in it for them."

"So *we* aren't food? For, say, bears or mountain lions?"

"Generally, no." The moonlight was just enough illumination to see the skeptical dent that puckered her brow, telling him his answer wasn't conclusive enough to allay her concerns. He stroked a hand down her arm and gave her a reassuring smile. "We'll be fine. Trust me, okay?"

Trust him? Trust was one thing Carrie was wary to give. Joseph had betrayed her, his vow to honor and protect her, so badly for years that he'd tarnished the term. He'd made clear the price of her trusting anyone else with her dark secret, as well, so that trust had become a rare commodity for her.

When she didn't respond to Luke's request for her faith in him, he twisted his mouth in disappointment and ducked his chin as he sighed. In the dim glow of the flashlight, she could already see dark bruises forming around his left eye and on his cheek. Blood from his nose smeared his upper lip. Guilt tugged her chest. He'd sacrificed his body, putting himself in Joseph's line of fire for her. But was that reason enough to trust him?

A tender ache throbbed at her core, knowing all the ways he'd been there for her in just a few days. He'd shown nothing but care and concern for her since she arrived at the ranch. Her windshield, the cut on her hand… now this. Whatever this was. A late-night dash in the dark. A botched attempt to escape. If he didn't deserve her trust, no one did.

Pushing to his feet with a pained groan, Luke aimed the flashlight around them on the ground, walking a few steps each direction until he stooped to pick up a fallen branch. Tucking the minilight under his arm, he stripped off a few smaller branches then smacked the limb on his hand. "This should work."

"For what?"

"A defensive weapon." He paused and shrugged. "Should we need one."

"Against animals...or Joseph?"

He inhaled deeply, then winced and rubbed his ribs. As he carefully lowered himself to the ground, he shot her a wry grin. "Yes."

Raking his fingers over the forest floor, he cleared away small rocks and uprooted spindly plants and brushed aside dead leaves. He removed his jacket and rolled it before placing it at the top of the cleared area. "Your bed, my lady."

When she frowned at him, he lifted a dark blond eyebrow. "Those tents and sleeping bags aren't looking so bad about now, are they?"

"I wasn't complaining," she said, settling beside him. "I was just thinking that you barely know me, yet you look out for me as if you were my brother. I don't know that I deserve this. I wasn't completely honest with you. I got you embroiled in this—" she waved a hand, searching for the right word "—disaster."

He angled his head and held her gaze. "First of all, you deserve every bit as much care and protection as anyone else. I don't know where that came from." He growled, then added, "Well, I guess I do. But still..." He placed a gentle hand on her cheek and thumbed away a spot of dirt. "As far as that brother bit? I'm not sure what I feel toward you is brotherly. I'd have thought our kiss the other day told you that much. Obviously, since you're married, I'll back off. But I still care what happens to you. I'm your friend, Carrie, no matter how few days we've known each other."

Luke scooted closer, wrapping an arm around her, then tugged her with him as he lay back on the mountain floor. "Now, try to sleep. I'll make sure nothing and no one hurts you."

Nestled against him, his warm body chasing away the night chill and squelching the last of her tremors, Carrie stared up through the canopy of branches to the millions of stars that lit the sky. She marveled at the brilliant display of twinkling diamonds, typically hidden from her view by the lights of civilization. Only by traveling far beyond her comfort zone did this miraculous view reveal itself.

And only by digging deep within herself and finding the courage and strength to break free of Joseph's control over her had she met the kind and handsome cowboy beside her. Her champion. Her defender.

Moisture filled her eyes, blurring the stars. For once, though, her tears were not born of pain, but from the sweet joy she'd found, even if for a few precious days. The starry sky, Nina's friendship, Luke's caring comfort were beacons that gave her hope.

Chapter 13

The next morning, a gasp woke Luke.

When Carrie screamed, his eyes flew open—just in time to see Joseph hovering above him...with a large rock raised above his head.

Instant adrenaline shot through Luke. He juked to the left, narrowly avoiding the blow.

Carrie scrambled backward, whimpering her fear. "Joseph, no!"

Her husband raised the large stone again, shifting toward Luke to take aim a second time.

Luke tried to roll farther out of harm's way but came up against a stand of saplings and net of thorny weeds. As Joseph's arm swung down, Luke shoved upward with one foot and planted his other boot in his attacker's stomach. And pushed. Joseph tumbled back, dropping the rock.

Luke scrabbled to his feet, snatching up the hardwood

limb he'd placed beside him before settling in last night. Bracing his legs in a partial crouch, he prepared to feint whichever direction he needed.

As Joseph recovered his balance, eyeing Luke, his lip curled in a sneer. His gazed darted briefly to Carrie as he growled, "Want to tell me now that there's nothing going on between you and this cowboy?"

"There's not!" Carrie insisted.

Joseph grunted. "Why should I believe you? And why shouldn't I just kill him now? Kill both of you?"

"Because you're not a murderer." Carrie's voice was remarkably calm, though Luke could hear the shaky undertones.

"I can make sure it looks like an accident. Way out here in the middle of nowhere...accidents happen all the time, I bet." When Joseph took a step toward Carrie, Luke edged sideways to place himself between her and Joseph.

"Carrie, go," Luke said quietly. He didn't dare take his eyes off the threat her husband posed, but the lack of retreating footsteps, the continued sound of her panicked breathing behind him told him she'd ignored his advice. "Carrie, go! Run!"

Then Joseph lunged toward him, and his focus narrowed to his opponent. And the rock again clutched in his fist. And the possibility that Joseph could still produce the gun from under his clothing.

Luke answered every move Joseph made with a swipe of the branch, his goal being to keep Joseph at enough distance that he couldn't smack him in the head with the large stone. After a few strikes from Luke's branch, Joseph dropped the rock and used his free hand to clutch the thick stick and grapple for control of it.

Luke was sizing up how best to defend under these

conditions when a figure moved from his peripheral view, behind Joseph.

Carrie. With her own rock. A smaller one than Joseph had wielded, but effective in its own way. She crashed it against her husband's skull, and he dropped the branch to shield his head. Hunching his shoulders, Joseph turned toward the new attack, growling his rage.

"Damn it, Carrie! Run!" Luke shouted now. He gripped the branch with two hands, then whipped it over Joseph's head and pressed it against his throat. While he restrained Joseph, Carrie fled.

Joseph clawed at the branch that choked him, finally managing to twist his head and body so that his airway wasn't compressed. With a fresh gulp of oxygen to fuel him, Joseph thrashed hard enough to unbalance Luke. A tug-of-war for control of the thick branch ensued. Luke knew he had to make a decisive move soon to get away and catch up to Carrie. Joseph had shown he had no compunction over inflicting grave harm. Luke accepted that he might have to be just as brutal to even the odds in this battle. Digging deep, Luke mustered every ounce of strength he had and spun, adding his body weight to the pull, to wrench the branch from Joseph. In the same motion, he completed the full turn and swung the limb at Joseph's head. He heard the thwack of wood meeting flesh. Watched Joseph grab at his temple, growling in pain. When his opponent's knees buckled, Luke seized his chance. Dropping the limb, he bolted up the hill after Carrie.

She'd made it surprisingly far in the brief time he'd needed to incapacitate Joseph. But then, she wasn't starting out winded from hand-to-hand combat. He resisted the urge to call out to her. When Joseph recovered his senses, he could use the sound of their shouts to track them. So he plowed on through the trees until he reached the top of the incline. Here, the trees were much sparser, and he had a good view of the surrounding terrain. Almost immediately, he spotted her pink T-shirt moving through the obstacle of scrub and rock below him on the lee side of the mountain. He charged after her, swatting low limbs out of his face and leaping over deadfall and half-buried boulders.

Ahead of him, Carrie tripped and fell. She was slow to get up, and he reached her in a matter of seconds. His lungs heaving, he bent at the waist and braced his hands on his thighs. "Are you…okay?"

She glanced up from examining a skinned knee and nodded. Shifting her troubled gaze up the hillside, she rasped, "Joseph—"

"Could follow…any minute." He offered her a hand to help her to her feet. "Gotta…keep moving."

Carrie's shoulders slumped, and she stared at his hand. The dejection and defeat that filled her eyes raked Luke's heart. He'd only just encountered the evil that was her husband, but Carrie had been trying to escape Joseph for weeks, months, years. Joseph had been a relentless storm that stayed right behind her no matter how hard she fought to outmaneuver him. He couldn't imagine how demoralizing such constant stress and plaguing pursuit had to be.

Luke gritted his back teeth, breathing hard through his nose, as he set his mind on one goal—seeing Carrie free of the cruel man pursing her, once and for all. But the first step meant getting them out of the wilderness and back to the ranch in one piece.

Joseph would be on their heels soon. Time to move.

He pulled off his navy blue jacket and handed it to her. "Put this on. Your shirt is too easily visible in this setting."

Silently, she took his coat and slipped it on, zipping the front.

"I know you're tired. I know you're frustrated. But we need to keep going. I promise to keep you safe, if you'll trust me." He shoved his hand closer to her. "Come on, Carrie."

With a heavy sigh, she wrapped her fingers around his palm and shoved to her feet. From over the crest of the mountain, the low grumble of a male voice warned them Joseph was on the move, headed their way.

Fear flared in her gaze. With an encouraging tug, Luke guided her downhill. Although this morning he hadn't seen the gun Joseph had used last night, that didn't mean their tail didn't still have the weapon. With or without the gun, though, Joseph was dangerous. He and Carrie had no supplies, no means of communication with Josh or the police, no weapon to defend themselves. They needed distance. Staying out of Joseph's reach was their only tool.

They were now far from the part of the McCall property he was familiar with. He knew wandering farther from the camp would make finding their way out harder. Would make finding them more difficult for a search party. But as long as Joseph stayed behind them, tracking them, he had to keep urging Carrie forward.

And he would do everything he could to protect her.

Carrie couldn't be sure how long they'd been walking, but the sun had risen above the mountaintops and hovered in the sky with unforgiving heat and burning rays. Though they stayed largely under the protection of the trees' cooling shade, the rocky terrain meant they spent a good bit of time crossing more arid, exposed areas.

As she plodded behind Luke, feeling the sun sting her cheeks and nose, she thought back to elementary school days when her mother had told her to stay in one place if she ever got separated from the family. Good advice for a little girl in a department store, but what about a woman being hunted in the wilderness by a vengeful husband? She had no doubt Joseph was still searching for her. He wasn't the type to give up or admit defeat. He had to be right all the time. Had to enforce his will. Had to get his way.

Luke had assured her they were going the right direction to reach the state highway, where they could flag down a motorist, but she couldn't help feeling they were walking in circles. Her energy flagged and her hunger grew. Not having eaten dinner the night before or breakfast that morning, what little strength she'd possessed had been depleted a couple hours into their hike. And dehydration was a serious danger. She knew they needed to find potable water soon, sweating the way she was.

But a time or two, she'd thought she'd seen or heard Joseph nearby, and her sense of urgency would spike anew, shoving aside all thoughts of stopping for rest or water.

After several hours of trudging through the hilly terrain, Luke stopped at the top of a ridge, and bracing his hands on his hips, he surveyed their surroundings. "Okay. This is the point where, if we were in civilization driving around aimlessly, I'd admit we were lost and stop to ask directions."

Carrie, who'd been stretching the muscles in her back, jerked her attention to Luke. "We're lost? I thought you were taking us to the highway."

"That was the plan, but…" His sheepish expression and hesitant head shake shot panic to her core.

"So…now what do we do?"

He stepped closer to her and placed his hands on her shoulders. "I'll tell you what we're not going to do. We're not going to panic. By now, I'm certain Josh has reported us missing and search crews are headed out looking for us. We'll hunker down somewhere safe—"

She caught her breath. She hated the idea of giving Joseph any chance to catch up to them.

Luke squeezed her shoulders and pinned a steady gaze on hers. "Somewhere *safe*," he repeated. "I won't let anything happen to you, Carrie. I promise."

She closed her eyes and choked down the cloying sense of impending danger. "I do trust you. It's just…" Opening her eyes again, she cast a glance to the path they'd just climbed. "I have this creepy sensation that he's right behind us. Watching us. That we're in the sights of his gun and he could pick us off any second." Vocalizing her fears made them more real, and her breath sawed from her lungs in unsteady pants.

"Hey, stop." Luke stroked the side of her face and cupped her chin. "Imagining the worst doesn't help anything." He pulled her close and hugged her tightly. "Believe me. I know about playing the what-if game. Regrets and guilt and fearing the most awful scenarios were how I lived my life for months after Sharon died. Getting out of that rut has been an uphill battle. We are not, repeat, *not* in a worst-case situation here. It's just a matter of time before the SAR team finds us and we're back at the ranch drinking a cold brew and taking a hot shower." He paused, and his lips twitched in a lopsided grin. "Just not at the same time, 'cause you don't want to dilute a good beer with shower water. Right?"

The spark of teasing in his eyes, the absolute absurdity of the comment—and perhaps a tad of hysteria—goaded a chuckle from her. But that small concession to humor lifted her spirits, and she realized how fortunate she was to have Luke at her side, despite the dire circumstances. She laughed a little harder, winning a full-fledged smile from Luke that set her heart pattering. Oh Lord…what a crazy mess she was in! Running from a violent man, lost in the Rocky Mountains, and falling head over heels for a man she had no right falling for. All she could give Luke was more heartache, a trainload of baggage and an ex-husband who would always be a threat to her peace.

Setting aside those depressing thoughts, she asked, "So…what safe place did you have in mind?"

He pressed his mouth in a taut line and rolled his shoulders. Giving their surroundings another encompassing scrutiny, he flipped up one hand. "Maybe we'll come across a cave or a fallen tree that we can add cut branches to so we can camouflage ourselves. Honestly, Carrie, I'm making this up as we go. I'm not a stranger to the outdoors, but wilderness survival is a little beyond my pay grade. That's Josh's gig."

She swatted a gnat out of her face and nodded. "Okay. But we're smart. Common sense goes a long way, doesn't it?"

"It does. What specifically were you thinking?"

"We're going to need water eventually, assuming we've got at least a few more hours before we're found. And it could be tomorrow or—" She didn't finish the thought. That was the worst-case thinking he wanted to avoid. For now. "Water runs downhill." When he raised an eyebrow as if to say, "Obviously," she added, "So it follows that we should head downhill. Summits are good for views and perspective on the terrain, but a creek or stream will be at the bottom of the mountain, in a valley."

He drew a slow breath and narrowed his eyes. "You know that we can't drink from a stream or river, right? Giardia is only one of a few nasty bacteria that could be lurking in even the clearest-looking water."

She chewed her bottom lip as she thought. "So how do we sanitize it?"

"Without a pan for boiling or a lighter to start a fire? Without the iodine tablets that were with our camping supplies?" He contorted his face. "I don't think we do."

Her chest tightened with an all-too-familiar dread. Her mouth was already feeling dry and her leg muscles achy. "Dehydration will happen more quickly if we keep sweating. So your camouflage idea, low exertion and shade, sounds pretty good."

Luke bobbed his head in agreement and motioned for her to precede him down the slope toward the least underbrush-snarled path.

"What exactly is giardia, and what happens if we drink it?" she asked as she set out.

"It's bacteria pretty commonly found in untreated waterways that causes…" He paused to grunt. "How to put it politely? Extreme intestinal distress. It can last for weeks."

"Oh." She snorted. "Extreme intestinal distress is not something I want to deal with. Especially out here without indoor plumbing." Her foot slipped on some scree, and he caught her elbow, steadying her.

"Well, on the bright side, if you can call it that, the symptoms don't generally show up for a couple weeks after exposure to the germs. We'll have bigger problems than giardia if we're still stranded out here in two weeks."

"Two weeks?" She picked her way more carefully across the field of small rocks as she processed this new fact. "What's the treatment? Or is there one?"

"Antibiotics, I think. It's definitely survivable. Just really unpleasant."

"So if push came to shove, drinking contaminated water is better than suffering dehydration?" she postulated.

He hummed warily. "Maybe. Let's put a pin in that idea for now. Keep your eyes open for wild berries or edible plants. We can get some moisture from those, as well as vitamins."

She chuckled. "Luke, you're talking to a homebody. I wouldn't know an edible plant if it bit me on the tush."

He chuckled. "In that case, don't eat anything without pointing it out to me first. Although there are plenty of things out here we can eat, there are also deadly threats. Things like the death camas might look like wild onion, but even touching it can cause convulsions, coma and vomiting blood before it kills you. Nasty stuff."

Carrie shuddered and deadpanned, "Lovely."

"Well, I can—"

A loud crack sounded near them.

Carrie gasped and dropped to her haunches.

Chapter 14

Luke hurried to her. "Are you okay?"

"What was that?" She scanned the area around them with quick, sweeping glances. "It sounded like a gun."

"It did. Sorta. More likely a big branch breaking and falling or a chunk of rock hitting more rock."

Carrie stood slowly, her heartbeat still scampering, and dusted off her knees. She'd skinned one on the scree, and it stung, but considering how much worse she'd suffered at Joseph's hands, it was easy to ignore the pain and forge ahead. "Sorry. I'm just jumpy as hell."

"Rightfully so. And better safe than sorry." Luke put a hand at the base of her spine as he walked beside her. He, too, looked left, right, back and front as they crossed the rocky area where they were exposed. Apparently she wasn't the only one still jittery about Joseph finding them. "Let's try to get back in the cover of the trees as soon as we can," he said, confirming her theory.

Her legs were tired from the climbing they'd been doing, and she would have thought heading downhill would be easier. She would have been wrong. While gravity did make the descent easier in one sense, gravity also wanted to carry her down the hill at the speed of a falling object…until terminal velocity. She wasn't clear on all the physics, but she knew a misstep could prove fatal. Her weakened legs trembled as she tried to slow and steady the tug of momentum as they stepped, slid and traipsed down the rocky slope.

She spent half of her time watching her step, trying not to fall and end up tumbling head over tail down the embankment, and the rest of her time watching for signs of Joseph. She glanced at the plants and shrubs they passed, wondering which might be edible and which would kill them in a protracted, humiliating and painful fashion. But the more she thought about what they would eat, where they'd find clean water and how they'd survive until a rescue team found them, the hungrier and thirstier she became. With a shake of her head, she refocused her attention on the majesty of the peaks around her, on the lush, flowering meadows and shaded woodlands of Colorado. *Stay positive. Keep moving forward.*

But her ears were perked to every faint twig snap, rustling leaf and startled bird squawk. Joseph was out there, somewhere. Searching. Stalking her like a tiger. Waiting like a snake coiled in the rocks, ready to strike.

After several tiring and tense moments trekking downhill, Carrie paused to catch her breath, and between raspy gasps, she heard a new sound that lifted her spirits.

"Luke."

He turned and, seeing her bent at the waist, holding a

sapling trunk for support, he frowned and hurried back to her. "What's wrong?"

She held up a finger. "Listen."

He tipped his head as if straining his ears to hear what she'd heard. After a moment, he asked, "What am I listening for?"

"I thought…" She paused to gulp a breath. "I heard water. Like a lot…falling…rushing."

"The river?" His expression brightened.

She shrugged. "I just…think I hear water."

He stretched his back and rolled his shoulders as he turned slowly, listening. When he came full circle, he met her gaze again. "If we can intercept the river where the group was rafting today, we might find Josh and the others. Or, at least, be on the right track to walk down to the extraction site. It can be done. Josh and Kate did it."

At her puzzled look, he waved a hand. "A long story for another day. But I say we find the source of the water you hear. Can you tell which direction it's coming from?"

Good question. With the buzz of insects, the murmur of breeze, the sawing sound of her own lungs laboring for oxygen, isolating the distant noise was tricky.

"Not with certainty, but my best guess is that way." She pointed in the direction where she thought she heard the water.

Rerouting them in the direction she'd indicated, Luke led her on through the maze of boulders, tall grasses and scrub bush. When they reached a wooded area again, she welcomed the shade. She could already feel her cheeks and nose stinging from the sun. The babbling sound of water grew more distinct the farther they walked. The low rumble of water over rocks reminded her how long it had been since she'd had a satisfying drink. Or a shower.

Luke grumbled something beneath his breath.

She hurried a few steps to catch up to him. "Did you say something?"

"Nothing I should repeat in front of you." He waved a hand toward the waterfall. "I don't think it's the river. Just a side stream." Discouragement etched tiny lines around his mouth and eyes. A ping of disappointment poked her chest, as well.

As they hiked closer, Luke's suspicions were borne out. The waterfall they found was part of a fast-flowing stream. While the water source was welcome, assuming they figured out a way to disinfect some, it seemed their hopes of intercepting and rejoining the tour group were in vain. For now.

"Again," Carrie said, seeing Luke's shoulders slump, "I'm not much of an outdoorswoman, but common sense says this creek, running downhill, has to go—" she spread her hands "—somewhere. Maybe just a lake or pond, but maybe it flows into the river."

Luke lifted his chin. Nodded.

"It's as close to a map as we're likely to get. I suggest we follow the creek as best we can. See where it goes." She squared her shoulders, trying to project confidence, for his sake as well as her own. She'd grown skilled over the years at faking contentment, self-assurance and well-being to the public. Avoiding unwanted attention and questions had always been a priority. If people probed, they might catch her in a lie. They might look closer at her marriage and put the delicate balance she maintained in jeopardy. Joseph would blame her for drawing attention to their private life, and he hated when people judged or second-guessed him. She'd learned quickly to defer to him, no matter what she really thought. It spared her unwanted grief and conflict.

But now she had to relearn how to assert herself, how to make decisions and stand by them. "I mean, can we really get *more* lost?"

He chuffed a short laugh. "I suppose you're right."

"Is that even a thing?" She wrinkled her nose in thought. "There aren't really degrees of some conditions, are there? You can't be just a little pregnant or mostly dead."

His eyes darted to hers with a sharpness in his gaze that surprised her. What had she said that caused his strong reaction? Her heart tripped, and she took a step back. Habit. Self-preservation.

A muscle in his jaw twitched, and with a sigh and a hitch of his head, he turned to keep hiking. "Right. Let's go."

Carrie stared after him for a moment before following, rewinding her comments to figure out what had set him on edge. Her mention of death could have reminded him of the danger he'd put himself in for her. Or…pregnancy?

Recognition gut-kicked her. Joseph had talked about her pregnancy, their baby, last night, and Carrie had done nothing today to correct Luke's impression that she was carrying Joseph's child. He'd also been generally mute on the topic of her marriage. He was bound to have questions. Resentments. She'd kissed him at the ranch, let him believe they actually had half a chance to pursue the attraction between them. She could only imagine how hurt and angry he must be toward her. She owed him an explanation. She owed him facts and unvarnished truth and the ugly details she guessed he'd never ask for.

Soon. Not now. Kind of hard to hold a conversation

about something as sensitive and raw as her marriage when they were walking in tandem. Or was she just being a chicken, delaying the inevitable?

Her heart hurt as she stared at Luke's back. They hadn't said much to each other as they'd forged through the wilderness today, but the silence had a different timbre to it now. Another skill she had acquired while living with Joseph. Sensing tension in a quiet room, interpreting the mood of silence and stillness, reading subtleties of body language. She'd learned a lot of survival skills in the last few years. How those lessons would translate as she made a life for herself on her own, she had yet to see. Or would those habits prove liabilities? She could already tell that in this dog-eat-dog world, her learned deference to Joseph could mean she would get chewed up and spat out by society, as well.

Lost in her thoughts, she stumbled over a half-buried rock and had to grab a tree trunk to break her fall. Luke apparently heard her gasp and the change in the cadence of her footsteps, because he turned and rushed to her.

"You okay?"

His concern for her, despite all he was suffering because of her lies and misjudgments, touched her. "Just need to be more careful. I don't want to end up being *that* woman." When he furrowed his brow, she clarified. "You know, the one in movies who injures herself and slows the group down?"

He gave an ironic half grin. "Right." Placing a hand under her elbow, he steadied her as she pushed away from the tree. "Do you need a moment to rest?"

Her heart thumped wildly and her breath hitched, but she couldn't attribute her rattled state entirely to fatigue. Luke's strong grip and the kindness in his eyes were equally to blame. "No." She tugged her cheek up. "But if we get out of this alive—"

"*When.* We will get home."

She ducked her chin in assent. "When we get home, remind me I need to spend more time in the gym."

His smile brightened, and he touched her cheek before continuing down the hill toward the creek.

When. She wished she could be as positive as Luke. But she knew Joseph better than her companion did. Her husband did not like to lose and was ruthless about getting what he wanted. The only *when* she could count on was when Joseph found her again…

When. Luke mulled over the word and the inherent promise behind it. He had every intention of getting himself and Carrie back to the Double M in one piece, but her husband—he gritted his teeth—her *husband* was an unknown factor. Had he found the gun Luke had tossed away in the woods? Did he have another weapon with him?

He replayed the scene last night, the repeat that unfolded this morning, and his gut soured. He didn't want to be angry or hurt that she'd not mentioned she was married. And pregnant. Or that her husband was an abusive bastard. He didn't have any right to think she owed him anything. But after the kisses they'd shared, after he'd bared his soul to her about Sharon's death, he'd thought they were forming a bond. That there was something there worth exploring.

Apparently he'd been wrong. For the hundredth time that morning, he shoved down the irritation and uneasiness about the whole situation. If she wanted to talk, if she wanted to explain herself, she would. If not—he paused at the edge of a steep drop-off above the stream and let her catch up—he'd set aside his disappointment and move on. He'd help Carrie as much as she'd allow and return to his life knowing he'd done what he could.

When she stepped up beside him, he cast her a side glance. "The footing going down could be tricky. Slippery. Take it slow, okay?"

She jerked a nod, and they eased their way down the embankment. He pointed out good footholds to her, and when they reached the bank of the creek, she exhaled a relieved-sounding sigh. Surveying the stream, she said, "So we head downstream?"

He could see the longing in her eyes for a drink of the cold, clear stream that matched his own thirst. "Okay, here's what I'm thinking. And remember, I'm no expert at this stuff, but I say we have a drink here. It's fast moving, which I understand is safer than slow or ponded water. When we get back to the ranch, we'll go to a clinic and get antibiotics, just in case. But right now we need hydration. Agreed?"

Relief crossed her face, and she nodded. Kneeling, she scrubbed her hands together before scooping water up to her lips to drink. He did the same, savoring the cool drink on his dry throat and splashing some on his hot face.

They were both reaching their fill and catching their breath when he first heard it—the low, rhythmic drubbing that sounded like banging drums. Luke stilled, held his breath to listen, praying he wasn't imagining the sound.

Carrie frowned when she glanced at him. "Luke, what's wrong?"

He hushed her with a finger to his lips, then pointed up. "I think I hear a helicopter."

Her face brightened, and she tipped her head back,

searching the limited view of the sky peeking through the canopy of tree branches. "Rescue searchers?"

"Maybe. Could be a sightseeing tour. Hospital transport. Military drill."

She twisted her mouth as she clamped her lips tight in frustration. "They won't see us under all these trees."

"No. Not likely." He splashed one last handful of creek water on his neck, then shook the excess from his hands as he stood. "Let's see where this stream leads."

"But the helicopter—" She struggled to her feet, her wince clearly speaking for her fatigue and sore muscles. "Shouldn't we be trying to find a clearing where they can spot us?"

"If it is a search team, they'll circle back. And if this stream does meet up with the river, the riverbank is a good place to get seen."

She bit her bottom lip as if considering his suggestion before jerking a nod.

Luke found a thick branch lying half-submerged a few feet downstream and picked it up, tested its strength. Satisfied it wouldn't break, he handed it to Carrie. "Here. This will make a good walking stick. An added bit of stability while we hike down the bank. Loose stones, mud, moss, water. It's all slippery stuff. Don't get in a hurry and twist an ankle."

Carrie stabbed the ground a couple times, testing the walking stick herself. "Thanks."

As they picked their way down the edge of the stream, Luke kept his eyes out for another fallen limb he could use, for hazards like deep mud, snakes, bears—and Joseph. Always lurking near the surface of his thoughts was the reality that their greatest danger was Carrie's husband. Joseph was almost certainly still close behind them.

After about a half mile, by Luke's estimation, down the streambed, Luke pulled up short. A small group of mule deer stood at the water's edge sipping from the creek. He held up a hand to signal Carrie to stop, touched his lips to keep her quiet, then pointed to what was likely a family. Two does and a young buck.

A grin split Carrie's face as they watched the animals twitch their large ears and black-tipped tails. One of the does raised her head from drinking and spied the human intruders, pulled her ears back, then darted uphill out of sight. Alarmed by their companion's sudden departure, the other two deer yanked their heads up and bolted into the trees, following the first.

"Sorry," Carrie called quietly. "Didn't mean to disturb you."

Luke glanced at her and grinned. "Ever seen one this close before?"

"At a petting zoo. Not in the wild." She flashed him another smile full of wonder. "Pretty cool."

He nodded his agreement and set out again. Encountering deer was better than coming across a bear or mountain lion getting a drink, he mused, but didn't share the thought. He didn't want to worry Carrie unnecessarily. Besides, she was smart enough to know they were sharing the woods with more dangerous forms of wildlife.

Fifteen minutes later, give or take a few, the sound of a helicopter returned, buzzing almost directly overhead. Carrie stopped and looked up through the trees. "God, what I'd give for a flare right now."

"Well, the good news is, the helo's return makes me think it is a rescue bird. Problem with trying to signal them is we give away our position to Joseph, too."

The whump-whump-whump of the helicopter faded,

and Carrie squared her shoulders. "So we keep moving. We try to find a place where we'll be more visible without alerting Joseph."

The skepticism darkening her face told him she wasn't confident in the plan, but at the moment he didn't have a better one. He gave her a brief smile, hoping to buoy her mood. Her returned smile was dim, but as she set out again, she gave his wrist a squeeze.

After another thirty or forty minutes of hiking, they came to a spot where the stream emptied into a larger waterway. The banks along this stretch of water were wider, flatter and largely rocky.

"Is this the river we were supposed to raft down?" Carrie frowned at the shallow, mostly slow-moving current.

Luke shrugged. "I don't know. If it is, the launch site is a good bit farther downstream. This looks more like another feeder stream."

Carrie heaved a tired sigh full of frustration. "So we keep walking?"

Luke scrubbed a hand over his face. He wished he knew more about wilderness survival and how SAR teams operated. Give him a lost calf or a cow with a cracked hoof, and that he could handle. But he'd never imagined he'd be lost in the mountains without any supplies. For what it was worth, following the water seemed like a logical choice, but the wearier they became, the more energy and sweat they expended, the more likely they could injure themselves or become dehydrated.

"The stream here cuts a wide enough swath through the trees that, I think, a helicopter flying over would see us." He glanced at Carrie, who was settling down on a large flat boulder to rest. "I think it's time to take off my jacket. Let that pink shirt show again."

She lifted a hand to the zipper then hesitated, turning her attention to the tree line on both banks. "Maybe I should wait until we hear the helicopter again."

He nodded. "Suit yourself."

She shoved the sleeves up her arms and flapped the shirt at her neck. "I'll say this for the tree cover. It was cooler."

"You can wait in the shade if you want."

She mumbled something under her breath he didn't catch, then shucked the jacket and tossed it on the boulder beside her. Using the back of her hand, she swiped her forehead. "So we're staying put for now? Hoping the helicopter flies over again and spots us?"

"That's what I was planning. You okay with that?"

She blinked as if surprised he was consulting her. "My feet certainly are. I was starting to get blisters."

"We'll give it an hour or so, and if the helicopter doesn't return, we can move downstream. Deal?"

Her head bobbed in agreement, and she pulled her knees up to her chest, folding her arms over her bent legs.

While she rested, Luke stalked restlessly back and forth along the shore. He stopped every now and then to grab a stone and fling it into the water. Waiting for the rescue helicopter, giving Carrie the chance to rest might be the smart plan, but inaction didn't sit well with him. He wanted to do something. To act. To swing a sword and slay Carrie's dragons. This passive waiting gave him too much time to think…

His frustration gnawed at him, keeping him off balance, quietly seething. He replayed his encounter with Joseph from last night, from this morning. He had too many violent images and relentless questions plaguing his mind to know which end was up. For his peace of mind, he had to settle at least a few matters with Carrie. He glanced back at her, sitting with her legs tucked to her chest as she stared forlornly into the gurgling stream. He crunched over the loose rocks to her side and dropped onto his haunches beside her. He scratched his chin, trying his best to find a way to phrase the many questions he had for her. He wanted to be tactful, but he was also hurt. His heart stung. She'd lied to him, misled him at the least. But he ached for her, as well. And he was confused by her choices.

"Carrie, why—" He groaned as he cut himself off.

She lifted her blue-green eyes to his.

"I don't understand how—" Again he stopped. He didn't want to push her, wound her with his questions or sound like he was accusing her of anything. But where did he begin?

"I know you have questions," she said, her voice barely audible over the tumbling water. She sat straighter and rolled her shoulders, rubbed her neck muscles. "You don't need to dance around the truth or cushion your questions. You deserve the truth." She inhaled and compressed her lips before saying, "I'll answer you as best I can. I swear. Just…ask."

Still, he hedged, looking for a kind approach.

"Why did I kiss you if I'm married? Is that it?" Her eyes blazed with aqua fire. "Because I consider my marriage to be over. I'm sorry if I misled you. I did want to kiss you, but…yes, I'm still legally married. But I'm filing for divorce. Sure, he'll fight me on it. Hell, he might even kill me before he signs divorce papers, but in my mind, I've left him behind. I don't love him anymore!"

Yeah. That was one of his questions. "So you did love him once?"

She exhaled deeply. Her expression said she'd never considered the question.

"I don't know. Maybe."

"You don't know? How can you not know if you loved your husband?" Because he was tired, frustrated, itching to punch Joseph for the grief he'd caused Carrie, Luke's tone came out gruffer than he intended, and he saw an inkling of something—fear?—cross her face.

She swallowed hard and rubbed one thumb in the palm of her opposite hand. "Well, my memories now are muddled by what he proved to be, and…I question what I really felt. Was it love or did he manipulate me even then? Did I just give in when he pressured me to marry in order to make him happy?" She lifted one shoulder. "I can't say."

He took a breath and steeled himself before asking, "Are you really pregnant?"

Carrie licked her lips and shook her head. Moisture puddled in her eyes as she said, "I was…when I left him. But I lost the baby a few weeks ago."

"I'm sorry."

The first of her tears spilled from her eyes, and she looked away. "The baby was…" She paused when her voice cracked. "The baby was my wake-up call. When I thought of raising my child in our home, under his control and around his violent temper, I—" She shook her head and met his eyes again. "I couldn't do it. I couldn't put my baby in that kind of danger. I had to leave him."

"You did the right thing."

"Did I?" She sighed heavily and sniffed as she wiped her face. "I'm still not free of him. I've only made him madder than ever. Put you and other people in his path. I don't see myself getting out of this marriage alive."

He gripped her hand and drilled her with a hard stare. "Don't say that."

"It's true."

"No, it's not." He cupped a hand on the side of her face and held her chin up with his thumb, making sure she looked at him, listened to him. "There are resources out there to help you, to protect you. *I will protect you.*"

She met his gaze with a heartbroken weariness. "It's not your job to take care of me. I've already put your life in danger, gotten us lost. I won't be a burden. I won't let you put yourself at risk again for—"

"I want to do this," he interrupted, and he realized he meant it. He'd spent the last several years avoiding women with any hint of drama around them, yet he wanted to be a part of Carrie's life. Luke edged closer to her, rubbing a hand on his jaw, then wincing when he hit a tender spot, a reminder of Joseph's right hook. "Didn't you know what kind of person he was? Weren't there signs that warned you away?"

She snorted. "Believe me, I've asked myself that question a thousand times. What did I miss? Why didn't I see through his charm?" She sent him a direct look. "Because he *was* very charming and persuasive. He swept me off my feet and buttered me up from the day he set his sights on me."

He stilled, frowned at her. "That makes it sound like he targeted you for some reason."

She nodded. "He did."

Chapter 15

"He found out that I'm an heir to a major block of stock in my family's business. French Industries is a multimillion-dollar business started by my great-grandfather. The company has been kept under family control since day one. Joseph was working for French Industries, moving up the rank and file, because he truly is a talented businessman. But that wasn't enough for him. He wanted a seat on the board of directors. Something he knew he'd get as my husband. It wasn't so much that he wanted me as he wanted more voice in my family's business. He wanted voting rights. He wanted the financial benefits, too, of course. But mostly he wanted more power and control. That's the bottom line with Joseph in all aspects. Control."

"And you didn't see that before you married him?"

"I saw parts of it, but I called it confidence and purpose. I admired it. I saw his single-minded pursuit of me as flattering. He pulled out all the stops to keep my interest. Flowers, fine wine and the best tables at the best restaurants. He took me to Paris for Valentine's Day and proposed at the Eiffel Tower. We'd only been dating a few months, but he was so persuasive, so magnetic and charming, I got caught up in the romance of it. It's heady stuff, being the focus of someone's attention that way. Within weeks of our wedding, it was clear I was just a check mark on his path to the top. A tool to get what he wanted. And pretty quickly the romance and flowers became arguments and bruises."

"Why didn't you leave him the first time he hurt you?"

Her shoulders sagged, and she gave him a sad grin. "Because he apologized. Promised it would never happen again. At the time, it was an aberration. Sure, I knew he had a temper and liked to have the final word in disagreements, but I could live with that."

He frowned. "And when it happened again? I want to understand, Carrie, but not having been in your shoes it doesn't make sense to me."

She raised a hand as if confused. "I've asked myself the same thing. Of course he apologized. Again. And we'd only been married a few weeks, so he was still being smooth and charming most of the time. Who gives up on a marriage after only a couple months? Quitting would mean I'd failed. At least that's how he made me see it. He lashed out when I failed as a wife somehow. He convinced me it would be an embarrassment to the family, to French Industries if our marriage failed. I had to try to fix things. I thought if I did better, he'd go back to the suave and attentive man who'd laid the world at my feet and made me think I was his everything." She scoffed at her naïveté.

"What about the police?" he asked, clearly trying to tamp the frustration in his tone. "Why didn't the police help you?"

She snorted derisively. "The first time I called 911, Joseph convinced the cops I'd overreacted to a light scuffle between us, because I'd tripped and fallen and blamed him. They gave him a warning and left. He was royally ticked off that I'd *dared* to call the cops over a personal argument and hit me all the harder to teach me not to air our grievances publicly."

Luke grumbled a curse word under his breath.

"The next time I called the police, they took him in to the station to 'cool down' but didn't file any charges. Lord knows what story he told them, but no doubt he employed his winning charm and well-honed people skills to convince them he'd been falsely accused. When he got home, he ranted about how I could ruin his career by going 'crying to the cops' again. He swore if I ever filed another complaint against him, I'd not live to regret it. He'd find a way to make my death look like an accident. I believed him. I never dared to call the cops again. What good did it do except make Joseph madder at me?"

"A restraining order, then? Why not get—?"

He cut his question short when she shot him a dubious look. Finally she sighed and touched his hand. "I know it seems like I didn't try hard enough, like I gave up, gave in…but please understand. When you are inside the situation, everything looks and feels different than it does to outsiders. Reality is warped. What may be common sense to someone else is fraught with pitfalls and danger and tainted by bad previous experiences."

Luke exhaled harshly and closed his eyes as he tucked his chin toward his chest. "I don't mean to be judgmental.

I'd never want to criticize you for your choices. It just… sickens me to think of him hurting you, and—"

"It sickens me, too. Knowing how long I stayed, how much I accepted before I left… And the hard part is, he's still in my head. I'm still scared to death of him and what he'll do. Even if I get a divorce from him, which will be its own battle, he'll always be in the shadows. He'll always be a threat to my peace. He's not going to just let me walk away. Not when I'm the key to his position and power at French Industries." She hesitated and exhaled a defeated sigh. "That's why…I can't be with you. I can't let you tie yourself to someone who'll never—"

"Hey—" He flipped his hand over to lace his fingers with hers. "I'm not going to let him or your past scare me away from a relationship with you. I can handle him." He paused and frowned. "That is…if a relationship is what you want."

His tone was so heartbreakingly uncertain she wanted to cry. She'd never wanted anything more. But it was impossible. Longing and regret squeezed her heart so hard she couldn't get enough air in her lungs. "It doesn't matter what I want. I can't get anyone else involved in my plight. It's bad enough I put Nina at risk!"

"Nina's tough. She'll be fine." He tightened his grip on her hand to reinforce his statement. "And Steve would never let anyone hurt her."

"You don't know Joseph like I do. I told a friend about him once, about his temper, and she confronted him." The memory made her so sick to her stomach, she had to stop and draw a slow breath to force the bile back down her throat. "He killed her dog. And he got her fired from her job with our company." Her eyes lowered to her lap.

"After that, I swore never to involve anyone else in my problems."

He stared at her silently for a moment, his expression stricken. "He killed your friend's dog?"

"As best I can tell. He stole her dog from doggie day care, and Peanut was never found after that. As good as dead, anyway. He sent a very effective message to Hanna and to me. Our marriage was no one's business but ours."

Luke clenched his teeth so hard the muscles in his jaw flexed, and she'd swear she heard his jaw cracking. He raised his free hand to pinch the bridge of his nose and muttered another earthy curse word. "Carrie, I—"

"No." She pulled her hand free of his and scooted off the rock where they sat.

He shook his head. "No? No, what?"

She worked to pull oxygen into her constricting lungs. "Just…no. I don't want to talk about this anymore. You know the truth now, and I can't—" She raised her hands to warn him away when he made a move toward her. "I can't talk about it anymore, and I can't…I can't let myself fall in love with you. I'm sorry."

Luke stared after Carrie as she strolled to the edge of the fast-flowing stream and folded her arms over her chest. He'd heard once that the crossed-arms position was a defensive one. Self-protecting. Since he knew she couldn't be cold in this summer sun, that left the body language option. Carrie…protecting herself from hurts, on constant guard against anything that could chip away the walls she'd had to erect around herself. Because of the man who'd vowed to love and care for her.

His gut burned with a deeper hatred for the man who'd battered Carrie and put the fear in her eyes. Who cast such a long shadow over her life that even now that she'd freed herself from him, he manipulated and intimidated her.

As she'd asked, he didn't question her any further about her marriage. He knew enough to keep his mind roiling as he watched the sky for the rescue copter to return. The point he would *not* let rest, however, was that of their relationship. Joseph had already robbed Carrie of enough. Luke couldn't stand the idea of her passing up a chance at real love, real happiness, real companionship going forward because Joseph had stolen her ability to trust and filled her with fear. Maybe he wouldn't be the one she eventually gave her heart to, but he wouldn't stop believing that if he was patient, if he kept showing her what real caring looked like, she would change her mind about him.

He scoffed at the irony of his line of thought. Him actively pursuing a woman with a whole graveyard of skeletons in her closet? With a living, breathing nightmare chasing her? When had he changed his tune about getting involved with such complications again?

He glanced at Carrie as she returned to sit beside him on the large, sunbaked rock, and he noticed the bruises darkening around her throat. With a grimace, he recalled his horror at finding Joseph choking her in the dark woods last night. Was that the moment his intentions had shifted? Or was it later, when she'd curled against him to sleep, trembling and heartbroken, and the aches and pain in his own body had faded to nothing in light of his determination to keep her from further harm? When he'd seen the spark of wonder and glimmer of joy light her eyes upon spotting the family of deer? When she'd furrowed her delicate eyebrows and analyzed their situation with the calm and common sense of someone with clear leadership capabilities? He compressed his mouth in frustration, knowing her inherent talents had been squashed under Joseph's dominance and need for control.

Next to him, Carrie lifted her face to the sky and followed the flight of an eagle swooping and soaring above them. Her lips twitched in a smile, and he lost another piece of his soul to her. That was how it had happened, he decided. He'd fallen for her not in one moment, but one smile, one kiss, one glimpse of her strength at a time. He saw a woman with so much potential, so much inner beauty, so much love and a guarded sense of humor. A woman with intelligence and kindness and…sunburn.

He shielded his eyes from the bright sun and studied Carrie's high cheekbones and narrow chin more closely. She was getting redder by the minute, and not from some innocent emotional blush. "You're frying to a crisp," he said and pushed off the rock where he'd been reclining. "We gotta get out of this sun."

Luke squinted against the glare of sunlight on the water and turned a full circle, searching for any amount of shade where they could wait until the search helicopter returned. Though he saw nothing in their vicinity, the nub of an overhanging rock gave him an idea. "I hate to ask it, but are you up to a bit more walking?"

Dread and fatigue flitted across Carrie's face, but she visibly marshaled her strength and set her shoulders. She licked her parched lips and gave him a confident nod. "I can be. What do you have in mind?"

"There's no good shade around here, but I'm thinking that farther downstream, we may find a rocky outcrop like that one—" he pointed to the nub of rock jutting from a wall of granite "—but bigger. Or maybe a cave.

Or some trees near the water's edge where we can dart out and be seen if we hear the helicopter."

"Lead on, Captain." She extended her hand to him, and he helped her to her feet. Before releasing her hand, he hauled her close and stroked a hand down the back of her head. With gentle persuasion, he nudged her closer and angled his head to kiss her lips.

A small noise escaped her throat. If he hadn't been holding her close, hadn't been so attuned to her, he'd probably have missed it, thanks to the rumble of the water and thrum of blood in his veins. He lifted his head, and before he could ask if she was all right, she muttered, "Luke, I said I couldn't do this. We can't—"

"I'm not giving up on you, Carrie. If you can look me in the eye and say you don't have feelings for me, I'll walk away. But I don't believe you can. And I'm not going to throw away a chance at happiness because of Joseph. If we do that, he wins."

She bowed her head, and a frustrated-sounding moan rose from her throat. Nudging her chin back up, he held her gaze. "Can you do it? Can you honestly say you don't feel a connection with me? That you don't want more? Don't you feel something between us, Carrie?"

"Then you don't hate me?"

He blinked. That was not the answer he'd expected. At all. "Hate you? Good God, my kissing skills are rustier than I thought!"

She twisted her mouth in a wry moue. "There's nothing wrong with your kisses. I mean…I figured you'd hate me for lying." She lowered her gaze and dented her brow. "By omission if not outright untruth. I kept the whole sordid truth from you, even when you were trying so hard to help me and be my friend."

A grunt of disbelief rumbled from his chest. "No, I don't hate you. I understand why you hid the truth." He traced a knuckle over her cheek, as hot to the touch as it looked. She'd be in pain this evening if not sooner. "And I'd like to be more than just your friend if you'll let me, Carrie. I will wait as long as I have to. I'll stand by you and protect you until your divorce is final. Until Joseph is out of your life for good."

Her eyes closed, and her shoulders drooped as if that was a future she couldn't believe would happen.

"Hey." He tweaked her chin. "Don't give up. You've already taken the hardest step."

A half grin flickered at the corner of her mouth. "Have I?"

He chuckled lightly. "Let's hope so, huh?" He dropped another quick kiss on her lips, adding, "But whatever happens, promise me you won't quit hoping, believing. That you'll keep fighting for yourself and the life you deserve."

She drew a long, slow breath, then bobbed her chin once. "I promise."

An expanding warmth filled his chest, and he captured her mouth again with another kiss. A deeper, longer kiss. A kiss that told her what his heart wasn't ready to share, words she wasn't ready to hear, but a truth she needed to know—just how much she'd come to mean to him.

Taking her by the hand, he headed nearer the edge of the water, where the rocks were smaller and the footing was better—provided they avoided the muddy or mossy spots. As he'd hoped, they found a place about a half mile downstream where a rock formation jutted out, creating a small pool of shade. After dousing themselves with stream water to cool themselves and wash the sticky sweat from their faces, they took refuge under the rock formation.

Luke kicked a few stones out of the way to smooth out a place for them to sit, and Carrie sank to her knees, raking her damp hair back from her face with both hands.

"When we get back to the ranch, I'm going to sleep for a week." She shifted to her bottom and leaned against the rock wall.

Luke rolled his stiff shoulders as he settled beside her. "Sounds great, but first I'm going to eat about three racks of smoked ribs, a whole casserole bowl full of Mrs. McCall's mac and cheese, and a gallon of butter pecan ice cream."

She groaned and slapped lightly at him. "Stop talking about food. Especially ice cream. God, what I'd give for some Ben and Jerry's right now!"

"Oh, yeah? What flavor?" he asked.

She slanted a frown at him.

"What flavor of Ben and Jerry's is your favorite?"

She made a mock growling sound. "You're still talking about food!" She made a slashing motion across her throat along with a "szzbbt" sound.

"All right. All right." He chuckled and stretched out his legs as he made himself more comfortable. As he settled in, he put an arm around Carrie's shoulders and tugged her closer. She needed little encouragement to curl against him and close her eyes. Staying alert for sounds of an approaching predator—human or wild—or the returning rescue team, Luke rested his eyes.

As far as beds went, this lumpy, hard, creek-side napping spot was less than ideal. But with the lulling rumble of rushing water in his ears, a gentle breeze bathing his skin and Carrie's soft body nestled against him, he decided his situation wasn't half-bad. When she placed her hand over his heart, her fingers relaxed, her palm warm through his damp shirt, he grew more sure this moment was a tiny slice of bliss, despite the circumstances. As the moments ticked by and Carrie's breathing slowed, deepened, Luke assumed she'd drifted to sleep—until she mumbled, "Phish Food. Definitely Phish Food."

And then he was quite certain. He was falling in love.

Something buzzed in her ear. Tickled her cheek.

Carrie tried to ignore it. She was so dadgum tired. And sore.

Something sharp was poking her hip. Moving took a monumental effort, but she tried to roll away from the jabbing offender. With a groan, she added stiff to her list of complaints when her muscles took extra effort to move.

"You okay?" a gentle voice asked, and her bed shifted.

She opened her eyes a crack and took a second to orient herself. Considering she was in a strange place and quite uncomfortable physically, she was surprised to realize that for the first time in many weeks, maybe months, an instant sense of danger, of fear, was *not* her initial reaction on waking.

She angled her sore neck and peered up at Luke.

Safe. Protected. Yes, that was her gut feeling as she groggily blinked the day into focus. She gave him a quick smile, then, with another moan to match the protest of her aching body, she sat up and stretched. "How long was I asleep?"

"Can't say for sure. The sun's a good bit closer to the top of that ridge, so maybe two hours or three? But that's a total guess. You were sleeping so soundly, I hated to wake you. Besides, the rescue helicopter hasn't been back, so..."

She hummed in acknowledgment and wiggled her tired toes. Blinked. "Did you take my shoes off me?"

He smirked. "Wasn't the cobbler's elf."

Her foggy brain took a moment to make sense of his joke. "Oh. Right. The fable." Smiling her appreciation of his humor—had she ever felt relaxed enough around Joseph to joke and tease?—she bent her knee to bring one foot in reach and rubbed deeply on the arch.

Luke patted his leg. "Here. Give 'em to me."

When she hesitated, he reached for her and dragged her foot into his lap. "Are you sure you want to do that? It's bound to be pretty stinky and—" The rest of her sentence was swallowed in a half moan, half sigh.

Luke chuckled. "I'm sorry. I didn't quite catch that."

"I said, don't you dare stop. That feels heavenly."

He dug his thumb into the meaty part of her heel and made small circles with each stroke. His fingers continued up her arch, then massaged the base of her toes. Though she'd been tired before, now she simply went limp with pleasure. When he hit another particularly stiff spot near her big toe, a happy sound, practically a purr, vibrated in her throat. "Ooohhh yeah."

His hands stopped, though he didn't release her foot, and Carrie opened one eye to peek at him. The hunger in his pale gray gaze startled her. Intrigued her. She'd seen so many emotions in his expressive and striking eyes, from raw grief when he told her about Sharon's suicide to cold rage when he'd confronted Joseph that morning. But this…this was lust, pure and simple.

She tried to swallow, but her mouth was dry. "Luke?"

His attention latched on her mouth, and his breathing grew rapid and shallow. His pupils dilated, filling the silver irises with dark pools of desire.

An answering heat filled her, prickling on her skin and tingling to her core. And when he cupped the back of her head and drew her close for a kiss, every reason she'd had to push Luke away fled her brain. A need that swelled from deep inside her clamored to the fore. She sank her fingers into his hair and curled her fingers around his nape as she returned his kiss and savored the sweet sensations flowing through her. Angling his mouth across hers, Luke groaned his satisfaction, whispered her name. The hypnotic caress of his thumb against her chin lulled her, while his lips, the tip of his tongue teased hers.

Carrie eased closer, straddling his lap so that the proof of his arousal pressed intimately against her most sensitive spot. When he trailed nibbling kisses down the curve of her throat, she tipped her head to give him better access. All of her nerve endings and most secret places seemed to be rousing from a slumber, reawakening to the heady and fulfilling promise of intimacy with someone you loved. The thought drifted lazily through her mind that there was something here she needed to examine, something that needed more attention, but she shut the nagging sense down. All that mattered in this moment was Luke. His kiss. His touch. The deep need to show him how she felt.

And when he slipped his hands under her shirt, the warm press of his callused palms sent dizzy pleasure skittering through her. She rocked her hips against his, and he issued a half hiss, half moan through his teeth and kissed her harder.

Carrie loved knowing her actions drew such a fevered response from him. She'd never had this kind of power during sex before. Had never enjoyed the act or anticipated the escalating heat so much.

When she sighed her approval of his touch on her skin, Luke moved his hands from her ribs to the clasp of her bra at her back. With deft fingers, he unhooked the bra, and anticipation sparked in her blood. Her nipples tightened, ready and aching for his touch. When he raised her shirt and pushed her clothes aside, his breath caught at the sight of her. But not in the way she'd hoped. He frowned and touched a dark spot on her ribs, a matching bruise below it.

"How long have you had these? Are they from last night?" he asked.

Suddenly self-conscious, she covered her breast with her hands. "Maybe. I—" She shook her head to refocus, clearing the haze of lust to answer him. "More likely from my fall when Hazel bucked." She sighed. "Honestly, I stopped keeping track of all my bumps and scars long ago."

Luke's jaw tightened, and he lowered her shirt and sat back. A sadness for the lost moment washed through her. "Luke?"

He gave her a half smile and stroked her cheek with his fingertips. "The moment isn't right." His eyes drilled into hers, and he whispered huskily, "When I do make love to you the first time, it will be in a bed, after a shower and a good meal. Not on a rocky creek bank, stinking to high heaven and covered in dirt and sweat. You deserve better than this." He waved his hand to indicate his disheveled state.

A knot formed in her throat, knowing she might not ever get the second chance to make love with him, much less the bed, shower and meal he promised. Swallowing hard, she rasped, "What I don't deserve is you. You're too good for me. And always so good to me. So—"

He silenced her with another kiss and cuddled her close to his body with a "shh."

Carrie leaned in, resting her head on his shoulder. After several minutes watching the water rushing over rocks in the stream, she asked, "Do you think we missed our chance of rescue? The helicopter hasn't been back."

He shrugged the shoulder her head rested on. "I'd just be guessing. They could have gone back to refuel or… who knows?"

The glint of sun off the rolling stream, the whoosh and gurgle of the tumbling water were mesmerizing, relaxing. But they also called Carrie's attention to another need she'd ignored for several hours. One she couldn't put off any longer.

Luke's eyes were closed, so she jostled him lightly. "I have to go." At his panicked expression, she grinned. "Nature calls," she said with a meaningful lift of her brow. "I'll be right back."

He seemed prepared to argue, to insist on accompanying her and turning his back for privacy, but she scuttled out from the shelter of the rock overhang and hurried off. She wouldn't go far. She wasn't looking for trouble.

And yet trouble found her, just as she was readjusting her clothes and preparing to head back to Luke.

"Carrie," Joseph said calmly, quietly, stepping out from behind a large scrub bush.

Her heart leaped to her throat as she weighed her options, studying him for clues to his mood and intentions.

His eye was swollen, and his lip cracked and sporting dried blood. "Honey, please…can we talk? Just talk?"

She took a step back and to the side, putting a knee-high boulder between them. Not much in the way of protection, but it would hinder his progress if he lunged toward her. Her body quaking, she squelched the urge to glance toward the path that led to Luke or to shout for Luke's help. She'd seen what happened when Joseph's fire and Luke's gunpowder met. And she recognized the apologetic and quasi-reasonable plea in her husband's eyes. This was the part of the cycle where he'd beg her forgiveness, promise her the moon and swear he'd never hurt her again.

He stepped forward, crunching on loose rocks and wild grasses. He held his hands out, palms out in false supplication and pseudo-concession. She knew Joseph well enough now to know he only appealed to her this way when he saw it as advancing his agenda. She'd fallen for his lies and promises too many times before. Because the sweet words he'd promise were what she wanted to hear, what she wanted to believe, what she needed to justify returning to their marriage. He knew that and had always used it against her.

"Things got out of hand before. I know that." He kept his voice low, his expression even. "I just get a little crazy when it comes to you. The thought of that guy taking you away, interfering in our marriage…" He shook his head as he paused and reached toward her. "It hurt me to think you could leave me for some yahoo like that."

A sour resentment curdled her gut, but she swallowed the desire to defend Luke, which would only anger Joseph. If she did nothing else until this mess was resolved, she would protect Luke in every way she knew, no matter the cost to herself.

"Look at us, Carrie. Out here in the middle of nowhere, getting eaten by bugs and stumbling around lost. This isn't us. We're better than this. Let's go home. We can fix this."

She shook her head and sighed. "You've said that before. Too many times. I'm through, Joseph. I'm finished with being your punching bag and taking the blame for every disappointment in your life."

He braced his hands on his hips and exhaled harshly. "Carrie, that's not fair. It's not true. I don't blame you for everything wrong with my life. But when you provoke me, knowing I have a short temper, you have to take at least some of the blame for what happens next."

At her soft grunt of disagreement, he raised his hands again. "Okay, okay, let's not play the blame game. The point is, I miss you. I want you to come home where you belong. I'll do better. We'll do better. Try harder. I need you, Carrie."

"No, you don't. All you want is the access to the board of directors our marriage affords you."

"Your running away *has* played havoc with my standing with the board. That's true," he said with a tight smile. "I've had to do a lot of covering for you and your disappearance." He drew in a deep breath. "But we can smooth things over. No one has to be any the wiser about where you've really been. Please, Carrie. Be reasonable. Give our marriage another chance."

"Be reasonable? Is it reasonable to go back to a situation where you know you'll be hurt? Beaten? Screamed at? Treated without respect?"

As soon as the words slipped from her mouth, she tensed. Why had she let the accusations, the bitterness escape, true though the words may be? She'd gotten too confident, spending time with Nina and Luke, allowing their pep talks to take root and change her perceptions. She watched Joseph carefully for indications she'd frayed his thin temper.

He shifted his weight from foot to foot, swatted irritably at a bug buzzing in his face, then sighed. "What do you want, Carrie? For me to get on my knees and beg? I'm your husband. Does that mean nothing to you?" After another long, heavy pause where he stared at her with confusion and frustration, he added, "I'm sorry I lost my temper before. It won't happen again. If you'll promise to meet me halfway, not to push my buttons and test me, I'll promise to work on my temper."

She blinked, stunned to hear him apologize. She'd heard his promises to rein in his temper before, his assurances that things would be different, but "sorry" had never crossed his lips. *Too little, too late.*

"Carrie?" Luke called through the trees from beside the stream. "You okay?"

Joseph's jaw tightened, and his dark gaze shifted in the direction Luke's voice had come.

"Yes. I'll be right back!" she shouted back, hoping to keep him from coming after her and confronting Joseph. To Joseph, she said in a stage whisper, "If you mean everything you just said, then walk away. Leave Luke alone. He only wanted to protect me."

Joseph's eyes narrowed with suspicion. "And you'll come with me? We'll hike back to the road together?"

Careful. Her brain groped for an answer that was the truth but would also appease her husband. "The road isn't our best option. We've heard search helicopters flying over. We need to stay in a place where we can be easily spotted and picked up. Like a clearing on the top of a hill or a rock outcropping."

Joseph nodded. "Fine. We'll do that."

"But I'm staying here for now." Her stomach somersaulted. Her voice trembled as she explained, "If you mean what you say about changing, doing better, then don't start another fight with Luke. You go that way—" she pointed back up the mountain "—and let the SAR find you. I'm staying with Luke until we get rescued. After that, we'll talk again. That's my offer."

"Your offer?" He chuckled wryly. "So now you're dictating terms to me?"

The rustle of branches and crunch of boots on gravel reached her. Luke was coming.

"Please, Joseph. We'll talk again when we get back to Boyd Valley. I promise. But, now…go! Don't force your hand with another fight with Luke."

He wiggled his bottom jaw back and forth, his gaze black. As willing as he was to knock her around, having a size advantage, she knew from previous experience that he was reluctant to take on other men. Last night Luke had instigated the confrontation and Joseph had had his gun to swing things in his favor. The fact that Joseph hadn't flashed it around today led her to believe he'd lost it or the gun was out of ammunition.

This morning, Joseph had thought he'd had the element of surprise on his side, that one blow from the rock he'd wielded while they slept would incapacitate Luke—or kill him.

But she'd seen him back down from altercations often enough when confronted by men he'd irritated in restaurants to know Joseph didn't like to fight if he thought he could lose. And she needed to bank on that fact now.

"Another fisticuffs is not going to solve anything. Show me you mean what you just promised, and I promise I'll find you when we get out of here."

He huffed loudly and aimed a finger at her. "All right. But this isn't over, Carrie. Far from it. I will find you in Boyd Valley or wherever you go. And we will go back to Aurora together."

It was a statement, not a question, but for the sake of

expediency, she bobbed her head in agreement. She'd worry later about how to get out of the agreement, but right now, she had to get rid of Joseph before Luke arrived on the scene.

The footsteps behind her grew louder, and with a final scowl, Joseph turned and marched off into the brush.

"There you are. I was afraid you'd gotten lost." Relief filled Luke's tone. The snap of a branch as Joseph retreated snagged Luke's attention and drew his gaze. His body stiffened.

"Nope. Not lost," she chirped, infusing her reply with as much carefree cheer as she could.

"Is that Joseph?" he hissed, angling his body for a better look.

She raised both hands and stepped in front of Luke. "It's okay. He's leaving. We just talked."

He shot her a look of dismay. "Talked? About what? What did you say to get him to leave?"

"It doesn't matter. He's gone, and we can go back to the stream to wait for the search and rescue team." She tried to guide him that direction, but Luke stood firm, staring in the direction Joseph had gone.

"I don't trust him. Maybe he's gone now, but what's to say he won't circle around and approach us from another direction?"

"Nothing. But I don't believe he wants another physical confrontation with you. He knows he'd lose. You've beaten him twice already, and I think he's lost his gun."

Luke grunted. "I was wondering about that. I tossed it away last night, down a ravine. I was praying he wouldn't find it." His gaze found hers, then scanned her body as if searching for new injuries. "You aren't hurt? Did he hit you? Grab you?"

"No." She hitched her head toward the stream bank, urging him with another nudge to follow her. When his expression remained skeptical, she launched into the explanation she knew he'd find difficult to fathom. "He wanted to apologize. He was promising me things would be better at home if I'd return with him. He wanted me to go with him and try to find a road where we could get picked up."

As she'd expected, Luke's face crinkled in disbelief. "He apologized?"

"Well, surprisingly, the word *sorry* did cross his lips for a change. Usually he makes excuses and promises he'll never hit me again. Promises things will change... but also puts half or more of the onus on me to change my behavior and stop provoking him."

Luke snorted. "What a crock. Please tell me you didn't buy that line of bull. A tiger doesn't change his stripes. He's shown you who and what he is. Do *not* go back to him!"

"I don't intend to."

With that assurance from her and no further sign of Joseph, Luke finally turned and walked back to the creek with her. What she didn't tell him was that she'd meet with Joseph, as promised, in order to keep the people she loved safe. Between now and that meeting, she had to figure out what to tell her husband, how to appease him and still get the divorce she wanted. Her heart sank, knowing the near impossibility of that scenario, but she was taking this debacle one moment at a time. Before she dealt with the terms of a divorce, she had to get out of this mountain wilderness alive.

Chapter 16

"It's a cycle," she explained to Luke hours later as they stood beside the stream, splashing themselves with water to cool off. "One I learned to recognize but didn't understand was characteristic until I read about it on websites about domestic violence. He builds up a rage, little by little. Then something, maybe something most people could ignore, would set him off. Burned toast, a spot on his shirt, being late to a concert, a smile he thought was mocking him."

"Geez, Carrie," Luke said. "You had to have been walking on eggshells all the time. That's no way to live."

She hummed her agreement as she watched the cold stream water drip from her fingers. "Then in a few hours, a few days, he'd settle down and come around with promises that it wouldn't happen again. He'd, of course, point out all the ways it was my fault, never owning the violence, per se. But he'd swear he could keep his temper in check this time, would tell me I had to do better not to goad him, and the cycle of guilt and me trying to maintain the peace and his simmering anger would start again."

Luke pushed to his feet from the crouch where he'd been dipping up water in his cupped hand. He grasped her elbow and helped her stand, as well. Drawing her close, he framed her face with his damp palms and pinned her with his sterling stare. "You never have to live that way again. You're free now, and I will make sure the rest of your days are spent knowing you are treasured, and you are respected, and you are safe."

"Luke…" she began, but he silenced her with a kiss that spiraled straight to her core. She could barely imagine an existence where she didn't measure every word, second-guess every decision and quake every time her spouse walked through the door, waiting, holding her breath. What kind of mood was he in? Had he had a good day at the office?

Never again. Oh, how she wished that could be true!

Carrie rose on her tiptoes to deepen the kiss and clutched at Luke's broad, steady shoulders, a physical manifestation of the kind of solid strength and stability he offered. If only…

The stuttering thump of her heartbeat filled her ears, growing louder as she angled her head and drew harder on his lips. More. She wanted more of him, more of his touch, more of—

He raised his head abruptly, his body tensing, his grip on her tightening.

"Luke? What—"

"Shh. Listen."

She did, and she realized the thump she'd been hearing wasn't her heartbeat. Not entirely, anyway. "The helicopter!"

Stepping back, he scanned the sky. "Take off your shirt. We need to flag them down, and it's the brightest-colored thing we have."

She snatched it off, and taking it from her, Luke walked into the stream and waved the pink top. "Hey! Down here!"

Carrie darted back under the rock overhang to grab the windbreaker Luke had balled under their heads as a pillow while they napped. Without bothering to unzip it, she slipped the jacket on like a shirt. Joining him at the edge of the stream, in full view of the rescue team, she added her own shouts and flagging motions.

The helo passed by, and disappointment gut punched Carrie. "They didn't see us? How could they not see us?"

Frustration dented Luke's forehead, as well, but as they stared after the rescue copter, it swung in a wide arc and headed back toward them. "Hold the phone…"

"Oh, thank God!" Carrie waved her arms again and repeated her shouts, even though she knew the rescuers couldn't possibly hear her over the rotor and engine noise.

She sent Luke a smile of relief as the SAR helicopter approached, slowed, then hovered over them.

A side door opened, and a man in a harness was lowered to where they stood. "Are you Carrie and Luke?"

She nodded at the man whose jumpsuit bore a pocket patch that read Jim Peterson.

Jim pulled a bit of slack in the attached line, unhooked the harness he wore and stepped out of it. "Everybody okay? Any serious injuries I should know about?"

"Nothing too bad." Luke waved the search and rescue

man off when his gaze narrowed on Luke's bruised face. "It looks worse than it feels, I'm sure."

Their rescuer faced Carrie. "Ladies first?" Jim held the harness out. "The bottom loops are like a diaper sling. They go around each leg and fasten at the waist. Step in and then we'll hook up the top straps."

Her stomach flip-flopped. She didn't much like the idea of dangling from a helicopter by a rope like a worm on a fishing line. But when she glanced at Luke, he gave her a confident grin and a nod. Even that little encouragement from him was enough to help steel her nerves and face the intimidating task. Between Luke and their rescuer, Carrie was buckled up in a matter of seconds.

"Ready?" Jim asked.

She took a deep breath and nodded, and before she could say anything else to Luke, Jim gave the long line a tug and flashed a thumbs-up. The harness tugged taut, and she was lifted off the ground.

Feet dangling, she gripped the line and tried not to look down as she was reeled up to the side door of the helicopter. When she bumped against the landing skids, another SAR member, wearing a headset and sunglasses, reached down to help her scoot inside the bay.

"Thank you!" she called to him but couldn't hear herself. The noise, loud on the ground, was deafening inside the helicopter. And after being in the bright sunlight, her eyes couldn't make out much of the interior. Didn't matter. Other than the man at her side, helping her unhook from the long line, her attention was focused on not falling out the side door as she removed the harness and gazing down at Luke below her.

The man beside her took the long line he'd just helped

her remove, attached a canvas-wrapped bundle to the main carabiner and shoved it out the door.

"What's that?" she asked, and again her voice was swallowed by the racket. Of course. Frowning her curiosity, she squeezed a hand grip affixed by the side bay door and watched him lower the bundle to Luke and Jim. First aid? But Luke had told him he didn't need immediate attention.

Maybe—

Jim unhooked the package and gave a thumbs-up. The second man began reeling in the line. When she began using hand signals to ask what was happening, the SAR man paused long enough to hand her a headset like his with a small microphone attached. She took them with a nod and a smile of thanks. The earpieces looked like the noise-canceling kind she'd seen millennials wear at her favorite coffee shop and on airplanes. Sure enough, when she put the headset on, the roar of the engine was tamped down and a male voice sounded in her ears.

"My name is Keenan Matthews. That pack was supplies for Jim and your friend until we can get back for them. Do you have injuries that require attention before we reach the hospital? I'm a medic."

She dismissed the need for first aid with a shake of her head, focusing on the oddity of his statement instead. What did he mean by "until we can get back"?

Keenan turned and signaled to the pilot. The helicopter rose and headed away. Without Luke. Carrie's chest constricted.

"Wait!" she cried, hearing her distressed voice through the headset. "What about Luke and Jim? Why are we leaving?"

"Not enough room for them on the helo. Don't worry.

After we drop you two off at the hospital, we'll head back for Jim and Mr. Wright. Shouldn't be more than two or three hours."

Disappointment that she couldn't make the trip with Luke weighted her chest. She sucked in a deep breath, searching for calm, for courage. Then his wording hit her. "You *two*? Who—"

A familiar voice came over the headset. "Hello, darling."

Shock slammed into her. She pivoted to scan the dim interior of the helicopter. On the far side of the bay from her, Joseph sat buckled in a passenger seat. His smile was smug and chilling. "So glad you're all right."

Her heart plummeted, and bile rose in her throat. Not only was she being taken away from Luke, she was trapped with Joseph—again.

Chapter 17

"Hey, whoa!" Luke pointed to the departing helicopter. "Where are they going? What about us?"

"They'll be back for us. Limited space on board."

Luke frowned at the SAR guy. "Limited space? You can only rescue one person at a time? Isn't that rather inefficient?"

"Two people. We rescued Mrs. Zimmerman's husband a few minutes ago. He was about a mile south of you."

While the name Zimmerman stumped him for a second, the word that Luke keyed in on was *husband*. His heart jolted, and he stepped closer to his rescuer, his body tense. "Joseph? You had Joseph on that helicopter?"

"Yes," Jim replied, his expression wary and oddly accusing. "I believe that's what he said his name was."

Luke cursed. "That's a mistake. A huge mistake." He pointed to his face. "Who do you think did this to me?"

"We're aware there was trouble between you two. That's another reason we took Mrs. Zimmerman in first."

"French. Her name is Carrie French. Not Zimmerman."

Jim lifted one eyebrow to express his skepticism.

Luke hesitated as he began to fill in the blanks. "What did that creep tell you happened?"

"For starters, that *you're* the creep. That you beat him up last night and kidnapped his wife. That he's been following you as best he could to rescue her ever since."

Luke wheezed a humorless laugh. "Kidnapped? Hell, no! I saved her from him! Did you see the bruises on her neck?" He waved a hand toward his own neck in a terse and frustrated motion. "He was choking the life from her last night when I came across them near our camp! He's been abusing her for years!" His volume was growing louder as his panic grew.

Joseph was with Carrie. *Damn, damn, damn!*

Jim squatted and opened the bundle that had been sent down. "I have bottled water and energy bars." He took out a bottle of water and held it up for Luke.

Luke slapped it away. "Are you listening to me? You just handed her back to the man who was trying to kill her!"

"Not according to Mr. Zimmerman. He said exactly the opposite."

"And you believed him?" Luke plowed a hand through his hair.

The SAR man took a breath, clearly trying to stay composed and professional. "I have no way of telling whose story is the truth. I don't know you or Mr. Zimmerman. Fortunately for me, it's also not my job to figure that out. It's my job to find folks reported missing and bring them safely back to civilization."

Typically, Luke respected professionalism, admired people who could remain calm in the face of the worst situations. But at that moment, he wanted to see some sign that he was getting through to the guy. A little concern or anger that might tell Luke the rescuer understood even a fraction of the screw-up that had just happened and would help rectify it before it was too late.

Instead Jim said flatly, "That is a matter for the police to sort out when you get back. Mr. Zimmerman has already asked that we notify the local police department of your alleged crimes, and they'll be on hand when we get back to decide who's telling the truth."

Luke blinked and replayed the guy's statement. "Hold up. Are you saying you plan to take me from here to the police station on suspicion of kidnapping?"

The SAR guy had the decency to look sheepish. "That's what he alleges. Among other charges. But we'll take you to the hospital first to get checked out." He shoved to his feet again, protein bars in his hand. "Look. I'm not law enforcement. It's not for me to decide. But if you didn't anything wrong, you have nothing to worry about. Right?" He held out a snack bar. "Do you want this or not?"

Luke held Jim's gaze with a hard stare as he took the offered food with a huff. "This is insane."

"I have a first-aid kit with me if you'd like to reconsider me taking a look at your injuries."

Surely Carrie would tell the police what had really happened last night. The truth. He'd have nothing to worry about. Right?

A ripple of unease spread through his gut. How much sway did Joseph have over her now? Could the bastard intimidate her into filing charges against him? Would she stand up to Joseph? He hated even putting her in that position.

He paced a few steps away then back to Jim. Blowing out a slow breath, Luke collected himself. The SAR guy wasn't to blame for the situation. And he was offering his help.

"Sure, thanks." Luke bent to pick up the bottle of water he'd knocked to the ground, gritting his teeth in frustration and remorse as he wrenched the cap off. "Sorry about chewing your ass. I do appreciate your help. This whole situation is just…nuts."

Jim squatted again and dug more supplies out of the bundle. "All right. We've got a couple hours until the helo returns. If you need to let off steam, you can tell me your side of events."

"Ma'am, I need you to sit down now and fasten the seat belt." Keenan Matthews's voice in Carrie's ears was still polite, but firmer this time, more commanding.

She snapped out of the daze that had seized her when she spotted Joseph's battered face. Her distress and despondency overshadowed even a smidgen of satisfaction seeing the evidence of Luke's defense of her swelling and discoloring her husband's face. She moved slowly toward the seat adjacent to Joseph's, the one Keenan indicated, right under her husband's watchful gaze.

After she'd sat, frozen, for several long seconds, the medic moved in front of her and started buckling her seat belt for her, his voice sounding in her headset again. "Mrs. Zimmerman, I know recent events have been traumatic, but you're safe now. I need you to cooperate for your safety."

"Please, darling. Cooperate," Joseph said.

Her stomach roiled, and her gaze shifted to his.

"And I promise that when we get back to town, I will see that Luke pays for what he did to you. We'll go home, and everything will be back to normal."

A shudder rolled through her. She'd seen the subtle message in his eyes before. The one that said, *I'm warning you. Don't make a scene or you'll pay.*

Don't make a scene. Her gut soured. How many times had she meekly caved to his will to avoid his wrath, to avoid a scene, to keep his dark side a secret? Too many. And now he was threatening Luke, a truly kind, gentle man, with punishment for helping her? It was too much. Just…too much to swallow.

Never again.

Cold rage swelled in her. Years of cowering and suppressed hatred erupted in a roar. She shoved Keegan Matthews out of her way, freeing herself from the seat belt. Ripped the headset from her ears.

And lunged at Joseph.

She swung her fists. Pummeled him. Clawed at him. Screamed and thrashed.

Until strong hands grabbed her shoulders, pulling her off him. Restraining her. She tried to fight her way free. Then amid her wrath and struggling, she felt a sting on her upper arm.

She jerked her gaze to her arm in time to see the SAR medic extract the needle of a syringe. Alarm spiked through her. "What was that?"

But the wooziness that spun through her head and buckled her legs told her all she needed to know. As she wobbled and grabbed for something to hold on to, the medic put an arm around her, steadying her.

"…get…your seat" was all she heard over the cacophony of the helicopter.

As she collapsed, her gaze drifted to Joseph.

He dabbed at his bloody nose and shook his head. His eyes were dark, accusing.

Drowsiness settled over her quickly.

Wings of panic still fluttered inside her.

Trapped…sedated…lost.

Luke…

Carrie woke slowly. Her head felt thick. Her heart was heavy. And a nebulous, underlying sense of anger or danger or anxiety buzzed along her nerves. She didn't recognize the room where she was, but the stark, pale green walls, array of looming medical equipment and antiseptic scents told her she was in a hospital. She tried to raise a hand to rub her eyes…but couldn't. Her wrists were strapped to the bed frame with wide Velcro bands.

The uneasiness morphed into panic, and she jerked against the restraints, her breath sawing from her in uneven rasps. "No! No…"

A man in scrubs was beside her instantly, pushing her back against the thin mattress. "Easy. Calm down. You're safe."

"Why are my hands tied down?"

The young man gave her an even look. "We had to be sure you weren't going to hurt yourself or someone else when you woke." He flashed a half smile. "I'm sure they'll take them off after your evaluation."

"Evaluation?" she repeated, her brain still slow to process.

Rather than elaborate, the man asked, "Are you in any pain?"

She shook her head, then when her temples throbbed, she amended, "My head hurts a little."

"Some of that is from dehydration and low blood sugar. The glucose drip will help with that." He nodded to a clear bag hanging beside her bed, and she followed the attached tubing to an IV in her arm. "But I'll ask about pain medication when I see the doctor."

"Please," she said, tugging against the restraints again, "will you free my hands? I'm not going to hurt anyone! That's ridiculous!"

"I'm sorry. I'm not authorized to do that. But I'll go let both the doctor and your husband know that you're awake. Dr. Malvese should be here soon for your evaluation."

And then she got it. Her blood went cold. "You mean a psych evaluation! What did Joseph tell you?"

The look he sent her was apologetic. "The doctor will discuss that with you. I'll be right back. Do you need anything? A blanket? Do you want to sit up more? I can adjust the bed."

She battled tears and rising panic. Joseph was going to win. He was feeding the hospital lies. "I want my hands free. I want out of here! I don't know what my husband told you, but it's lies. All lies. I'm not dangerous to anyone!"

The nurse didn't respond, and as he slipped out the door, a new thought pierced the muddle of confusion and distress clouding her brain. "Wait! Where's Luke? Have they rescued Luke Wright yet? Did they bring him here? Please, I want to see Luke!"

"I can check, but I can't discuss another patient's condition or treatment with you."

"Just…find out if he's here. And can you take him a message for me?"

Again, the nurse's face was dubious. "I'll be back in a moment."

When the exam room door closed, Carrie's heart sank. Tears spilled from her eyes, and her nose grew stuffy. She wiped her face on her shoulder, the best she could do with her hands bound. She gritted her teeth as the desperateness of her situation crashed down on her. Her hands were tied as if she were a criminal! Why would they think—

Then she flashed back to the last moments she remembered. In the helicopter. Joseph's taunting grin. The comments about Luke being at fault, having kidnapped her. Her tirade…

Damn it! No wonder the hospital staff thought she was a danger. She'd snapped and gone off on Joseph in front of the SAR team. No doubt Joseph had capitalized on her tantrum to convince the medic and the hospital staff that she was unstable. That violence was her MO instead of his.

Closing her eyes, she sank deeper into the pillows, deeper into herself.

Luke. Luke would tell them the truth.

But would they listen to him? Based on what she'd heard on the helicopter, Luke could be facing criminal charges, all because he'd helped her.

An ache split her chest. She'd avoided telling anyone her dirty secret about her marriage for this very reason. She'd not wanted anyone else to get hurt. Joseph had power and connections. He was merciless and cruel. And he had an uncanny ability to fool people with his charm and get what he wanted through his manipulative persuasion.

The bitter bite of regret gnawed her gut. Luke had risked so much for her sake. How could she do any less for him? Now she had to do everything in her power to protect Luke. Even if it meant giving in to Joseph's demands.

"I'm sure he told you I attacked him and kidnapped Carrie, but that's not how it happened!" Luke growled when the officer who appeared in his emergency exam room to question him asked for his account of the last twenty-four hours. "Joseph was strangling her when I came across them in the woods that first night. I saved her from him!"

The officer lifted an eyebrow, clearly dubious of Luke's story. "How did you save her?"

"Well, I...I grabbed his shirt to get him off her. And I may have punched him. But it was self-defense. Or justified defense of another or... I don't know what term you guys call it, but..."

The policeman was making notes.

Luke's frustration grew. "He pulled a gun on us! Did he tell you that?"

The cop looked up, that one eyebrow sketching up again. "Do you know where that gun is now?"

Luke's shoulders sagged. "No. Out on the mountain somewhere, I assume. I threw it away from where we'd been scuffling, down a ravine. He didn't seem to have it when he attacked us later. At least he didn't pull it on us."

"Later?"

"The next morning. He caught up with us. I fell asleep." He gritted his teeth in self-recrimination. "I didn't intend to, but I must have closed my eyes for too long and…"

The cop wrote again on his notepad, and an uneasiness rippled through him.

"Should I be calling a lawyer? You're not seriously buying Joseph's story, are you? Have you talked to Carrie yet? She'll tell you what happened! How Joseph has been abusing her for years. How she ran from him because she feared for her life. How he shot at us that night on the mountain, and we had to run for our lives." He plowed his hand through his hair and winced when he hit a sore spot. One of many places he'd banged his head—or had his head bashed for him—in the last twenty-four hours.

"You're not under arrest at the moment, Mr. Wright. But as I mentioned earlier, you do have the right to have an attorney present while we take your statement."

A chill slithered through Luke. He was in unknown territory here. Did calling a lawyer make him look guilty? Like he had something to hide? And if he didn't get representation, what kind of trouble was he facing? What kind of underhanded tactic could Joseph employ to hurt Carrie via charges against him?

"Can I see Carrie now? I want to see for myself that she's okay."

"Not until we're finished here and I've had a chance to question her as well."

"Can you at least tell me how she is? Where she is? She's at this hospital, too, right? I mean, the SAR team said this was the closest hospital with a helo landing pad on the roof."

Rather than answer Luke's questions, the officer flipped a page in his notepad and asked, "You say Mr.

Zimmerman attacked you the next morning? Tell me about that."

Luke took a breath, searching for his composure. The only way to help Carrie now was to give the authorities what they wanted, cooperate with the investigation and pray he could convince them of the truth.

He'd promised to keep her safe. And failed. Like he'd failed with Sharon. Luke's gut wrenched and filled with acid. No matter what it took, he would not lose another woman he loved due to his own failure. As soon as he could, he'd search the hospital—hell, the whole damn city, if needed—until he found Carrie. No matter what, he would get her away from Joseph.

When she heard the exam room door open, Carrie looked up, expecting the nurse's promised return or perhaps the ER staff doctor. Instead, Joseph entered and closed the door firmly behind him.

Her stomach twisted, and she held her breath, not knowing what to expect from him. Surely he wouldn't hurt her here, in the hospital, where so many witnesses could learn of his ill deeds if he lashed out at her.

Carrie's mouth dried as he studied the restraints on her hands for a moment before sitting on the edge of the bed. Trussed as she was, she was at his mercy if he flouted the risk of discovery and inflicted his version of punishment.

He shook his head. "Your little tantrum on the helicopter was a tactical mistake, my dear. Not being one to miss an opportunity, I've told them that rages of this sort are common for you. I said that I feared you might harm yourself. And that you'd threatened to hurt our baby."

Carrie swallowed the urge to throw the fact that she was no longer pregnant in his face. But being restrained, vulnerable, that course of action was unwise. Soon enough, the doctors would reveal her secret. Surely in all the tests they'd run since she'd landed at the hospital, they'd have discovered her miscarriage. She lowered her gaze, afraid he'd see the truth in her eyes, and fought down the bitter swell of panic from her gut.

"This can go a number of ways, darling."

"Don't call me that," she grumbled.

"What's that?"

She fisted her hands and swallowed hard to keep down the bile that rose in her throat from choking her. Taking a slow breath, she raised her gaze once more to Joseph's. "Don't call me darling. *Darling* implies you care. That you cherish me. That I matter to you. Clearly I don't. I probably never have."

He gave a small shrug and nod as if conceding her point. "Cherish? No. But you do matter. You and, especially now, the baby are my ties to the French name and, therefore, my right to be on the company board as part of the family. That's always been your role in my life. I thought you understood that."

"Oh, I do. I have for a long time."

His snort of disdain said he now considered her the stupidest of fools. He folded his arms over his chest and canted his head to the side as he stared coolly at her. "So if not darling, what then? Deceitful slut? Lying whore?" He raised a finger as if struck by inspiration. "Ungrateful bitch. I like that one."

Instead of being stung by the vile names, Carrie ached because of the contrast that sprang to her mind. Luke's gentleness. His warm smiles. The tenderness in his touch. The heat of his kisses. Real affection. True feeling and kindness. Would she ever find that again?

"So here's how things will be now." Joseph shoved away from the bed and began pacing the tight confines as he lectured her. "When you are discharged from the hospital, you will return home with me until the baby is born. At that time, I'll allow you to leave, if that's still what you want."

Carrie's pulse thumped so hard, she could feel the throb in her throat. She frowned. Surely she'd heard him wrong. Joseph didn't relinquish control. Control was his motivation for everything and with everyone.

"However," he continued, pivoting on his heel and shooting a steely glare at her, "the baby will stay with me. You will sign over full custody to me and give up any and all parental rights."

Even knowing there was no child coming, making his proposal moot, his demand to keep their offspring was stunning and untenable to her. "What?"

He shrugged. "Once the baby comes and I'm given full control over the kid's legacy inheritance shares of French Industries, I won't need you anymore."

"I would never abandon my child!" She shuddered at the mere suggestion, nausea roiling in her gut. "Especially not to you!"

"Then stay. It will save me the cost of a nanny or boarding school." He took a few steps closer and aimed a finger at her. "The point being, I *will* have complete authority over everything regarding this baby. Is that understood?"

Hatred surged in her with such vengeance, she could no longer keep her secret, and she wielded it like a weapon against him. "There is no more baby, you bastard! I miscarried a month ago."

Chapter 18

Joseph blinked as if stunned as much by her courage to speak to him with that much fire in her tone as he was startled by her news. "You're lying."

She huffed a humorless laugh. "No, I'm not. We're in a hospital. Ask any of the doctors to run a pregnancy test. That will prove it."

Joseph's jaw tightened, and spleen filled his eyes. "You killed it to spite me."

If she thought she'd finished being shocked by her husband's vileness, she'd been wrong. "Are you insane? I risked everything to escape our marriage so I could save my baby from a life with you! I grieved for it when I lost it. I still do. I'd never hurt my own child, even if it did share blood with the devil himself!"

Carrie saw the ire that was building in Joseph. The muscle jumping in his jaw, the flare of his nostrils, the tension that vibrated through him like a pressure valve ready to blow. He stalked away, his hands jittery at his sides before he swung around and strode back to her, his eyes feverish. "In that case, you will go home with me, and we'll make another baby."

Her heart jolted. "What? No!"

"Oh yes." He wrapped his fingers around her re-strained wrist and squeezed until she thought her bones might crack. "We *will* keep trying until you are pregnant again. You *will* give me a kid, or you will never be rid of me. If you want to run away and play cowboy's whore or whatever the hell you thought you were doing on that ranch, then you'll give me what I need to secure my investments and my place at the table with French Industries."

"You're despicable," she hissed, unable—or maybe unwilling—to shove her feelings down.

Predictably, he raised a hand, as if to slap her, and she braced for the impact. But outside the closed door, a page for a doctor sounded over the intercom, and Joseph froze, obviously reminded he'd not easily hide his transgressions in the hospital.

Instead, making a fist, he aimed one finger in her face and said slowly, darkly, "Do. You. Understand?"

Returning to the house in Aurora with him—she couldn't even think of it as her home anymore—was re-pellent, abhorrent. Never in a hundred years would she have expected to be even considering going back to Joseph and the dysfunctional life they'd had. But that was before she knew Luke, before someone else mattered to her, before someone else had become ensnared in her twisted scenario. She wanted to reject everything about Joseph's sick proposal, but she heard herself say, "All charges you've made against Luke will be dropped. He will walk away from this situation free and clear, unscathed, and you will never do anything to hurt him or accuse him ever again."

Joseph's brow furrowed. "I'm sorry. Did I lead you to believe this was a negotiation?"

"I mean it, Joseph. Luke has done nothing wrong. If you continue to levy false charges against him, you will never have the child you want." She paused, uncertain where she'd found the courage to challenge him. Except for the deep feelings and gratitude she felt for Luke. "Correction—because I know it's not the baby you want—you'll never have the permanent stake in French Industries that you want. Ever."

Carrie could see the rage that filled Joseph's eyes. He shook with it. "You little bitch."

"Am I clear?"

Her husband studied her, his expression icy and calculating. Finally he said, "Yes. Fine. Your cowboy is nothing. But if I clear him, you never see him again."

Even though she hadn't thought she would have a future with Luke, the prospect of never holding him, never being able to tell him how she felt or explain her choices to him, flayed her heart. She gave a tiny nod.

Joseph leaned close, sticking his nose right in her face. "Maybe I should have the hospital run that pregnancy test after all. To make sure your cowboy didn't knock you up."

Shock rolled through Carrie. Her face must have revealed something to Joseph, because he curled his lip in disgust. "You spread your legs for that cowboy, didn't you, slut?"

"No!" she rasped.

"Liar. I can see the guilt on your face." He grabbed a fistful of her hair. "You screwed him! Didn't you?"

Her own fury boiling from her core, Carrie spit in his face.

He released her hair long enough to wipe his cheek, his countenance twisted and bitter.

Then the room door opened, and in an instant, Joseph schooled his expression, calmed his tense facial muscles and pasted a fake smile on his lips. The transformation was radical. Chilling.

"How are we doing in here? I'm Dr. Holt." The doctor with a neatly trimmed beard and wire-rimmed glasses sent Carrie a brief glance and smile before shifting his attention to the machine at her bedside that displayed all her vital signs. His smile quickly faded, and he gave a low grunt. "Your pulse is awfully high. How do you feel?"

"A panic attack," Joseph said, answering before Carrie could say anything. "I was just about to call the nurse. She gets them now and then when she goes off her meds."

The doctor consulted the clipboard in his hands. "What med would that be?"

"I don't recall the name. Something for anxiety and depression."

"I'm fine," Carrie said, taking care to even her breathing. "I just got upset for a moment. It's these restraints. Can't we, please, take them off? I'm not a danger to anyone." She gritted her teeth but avoided Joseph's gaze. "And I'm not off any meds." Then to Dr. Holt, "Not long-term, anyway. I take an antianxiety med, but I only missed one dose while lost on the mountain." An antianxiety med she'd started taking to cope with the fear and stress Joseph had instilled in her.

The lean man stroked his short beard and nodded.

"I see it here on your chart." The doctor wrapped the blood-pressure cuff attached to the monitor around her arm and hit a button to start it inflating. "We'll get you a dose right away. I can also order a dose of something to relax you if you think it will help."

"Yes. Thank you," Joseph said at the same time Carrie replied firmly, "No."

The doctor gave Carrie a long, steady look before glancing again to the monitor. "Your numbers are already coming down. Still a tad high. What do you say we monitor your blood pressure for the next half hour or so, and if it continues to come down, we'll skip the sedative."

"Yes. That sounds good." Carrie dug deep for a smile to reassure the doctor and continued to focus on taking slow, steady breaths to calm her pulse.

Joseph folded his arms across his chest, clearly not happy about being outvoted.

"So can you remove the restraints? Please?"

"Have you spoken to Dr. Malvese yet?" Dr. Holt asked. "She'd be the one to make that call."

Carrie shook her head. "No. Since I woke up, I've only seen you and a nurse."

Another knock sounded on her door, and a petite woman in a casual pantsuit poked her head in the door. "Knock, knock. I'm looking for Carrie Zimmerman."

"Ah, speak of the devil," the doctor said.

"Well, not quite the devil, although my kids think I'm evil when I insist they clean their rooms before bedtime." The woman with short-cropped, prematurely gray hair flashed a bright smile and shook the first doctor's hand. Turning to Joseph, she offered her hand, saying, "Betina Malvese."

Joseph gave the newly arrived doctor his most engaging grin and introduced himself. When Dr. Malvese faced Carrie, she placed a warm hand on Carrie's forearm. "You must be Carrie. If we could get these gentlemen to give us the room—" she gave Dr. Holt a meaningful glance "—we'll chat a bit. Okay?"

Dr. Holt was busy scribbling on the clipboard, but he nodded his agreement. "Certainly. Mr. Zimmerman?" He opened the door and motioned for Joseph to precede him to the hall.

Joseph waved him off with an affable grin. "Thanks, but I'll stay with my wife."

Dr. Holt passed the clipboard to Dr. Malvese as she was saying, "I'm sorry, but I need to speak to Carrie alone. You can wait in the family seating in the lobby."

"I'm sure Carrie won't mind me staying," he countered.

"I'm afraid I can't allow that. This conversation is just between your wife and me."

Carrie wondered if either doctor saw the cold flicker of irritation that passed over Joseph's eyes, the tightening in his jaw as he faced Dr. Malvese. The woman didn't flinch, didn't bat an eyelash under Joseph's hard stare. Carrie tried to appear equally calm when his gaze shifted to her. "All right then. Carrie darling, regarding our discussion moments ago… We have an agreement." His smile was stiff. "I'll take care of everything you asked about as soon as we get home." He winked and blew her a kiss, playing the charming, loving husband, before stepping out of the room with Dr. Holt.

Carrie stared numbly at the closed door, digesting Joseph's parting words. They had an agreement? Her chest squeezed as she replayed the argument they'd been having before the doctors arrived. Joseph had been making crude assumptions about her relationship with Luke.

And she'd been negotiating for Joseph to drop all allegations and criminal charges against Luke. *An agreement...*

She'd never known Joseph to agree to anything she'd requested. Could she believe him? Could she trust that he would clear Luke of any wrongdoing? If there was any chance that Joseph would keep his word and let Luke return to his life, free and clear, Carrie's part of the bargain started now—convincing Dr. Malvese that all was well in Carrie's mind, life and marriage. She shuddered as she turned her attention to Dr. Malvese, whom Carrie had no doubt was from the clinical psychology department, even though the print on the ID card clipped at her waist was too small to read from where Carrie was.

Dr. Malvese studied whatever Dr. Holt had written on the clipboard. When the doctor looked up, she gave Carrie a calm, encouraging smile. "So. Let's talk. Just you and me. And be assured that anything and everything you discuss with me is confidential. I cannot legally and will not ethically share anything you tell me with anyone else." Her gaze was direct but nonconfrontational as she added, "Including your husband."

Carrie's pulse stutter-stepped. Was this the opening she'd been waiting for, the chance to tell her story and really be heard? A bubble of hope swelled in her chest, but immediately doubt demons dug their claws in and popped the ballooning promise. If she told the doctor everything, what good would it do? She still had to appease Joseph in order to protect Luke. What if by telling her dark secret, she set in motion events she couldn't control?

"Carrie, you're safe. It's okay to talk to me."

She furrowed her brow. "Am I safe?" she asked, her

tone dripping sarcasm. "I'm tethered to this bed like a rabid dog. I feel like a prisoner."

"I can understand that. Answer a few questions for me, and let's see about removing those restraints. Why did you attack your husband on the helicopter?"

Carrie weighed her answer, considering how her words might be misconstrued. *I snapped* wouldn't help her cause. *He deserved it* seemed equally unhelpful, even if both statements were true.

"It was a mistake," Carrie said in a measured tone. "I'm sorry I did it. I'm more sorry for any danger I put the SAR team in for having lost my temper. I shouldn't have let Joseph push my buttons, but I did. It won't happen again."

The doctor nodded and asked, "What buttons did he push, Carrie?" When she didn't answer, Dr. Malvese said, "Tell me about the bruises on your neck. They look like finger marks. Am I right?"

Carrie didn't answer, but gave the doctor a *do I have to spell it out?* look.

"Did your husband do it?"

Silence. She turned her head to avoid the doctor's eyes.

"Did Luke Wright?"

Carrie jerked her gaze back to the doctor, her eyes widening in dismay. "No! Luke did nothing wrong! He protected me!"

"Protected you from…what?"

To her horror, tears bloomed in her eyes and trickled onto her cheek. "Don't be cagey, Doctor. You know what's going on here. Don't make me spell it out."

"I'm afraid you have to. I can't assume. I need verbal verification from you."

"And I can't verify without putting Luke at risk. He protected me, and now I have to protect him."

Dr. Malvese placed a warm hand on Carrie's. "And I want to protect you, but I can't without some confirmation from you. Carrie, does your husband hurt you physically or verbally? Do you fear for your safety with him?"

One word. All she had to do was speak up, give a nod, anything to confirm the doctor's assertion. But she'd made a pact with Joseph. Made a deal with the devil. And if she didn't give Joseph what he wanted, Luke would pay the price. She couldn't live with that.

And so she said, "No."

Chapter 19

Dr. Malvese stayed for thirty more minutes, talking to Carrie about her marriage and the incidents in the mountains and on the helicopter and asking about her feelings, her state of mind. Through it all, Carrie maintained her story that her marriage was fine, Luke was innocent of wrongdoing, and she'd simply been tired, hungry and short-tempered when she attacked Joseph. The doctor was clearly dubious of the claims regarding her marriage, but she called the nurse to unfasten the wrist restraints, deeming Carrie no threat to anyone.

After the nurse left, Dr. Malvese turned back to Carrie with a sad, defeated look on her face as she pulled out her business card. "I've written the phone number for a domestic violence hotline on the back. If you ever need help, please call me or this crisis line. I know it is frightening to think about leaving, but nothing will change until you find the strength and courage to face your fear. When you *are* ready, Carrie, if you call—" she tapped the card with her fingernail before handing it over "—you won't be alone."

Carrie accepted the card with a skeptical half grin. She didn't bother telling the doctor she *had* found the courage to leave once. And for weeks she had been alone. Until Nina had pulled the truth from her. Until Luke risked his life to help her. Now she had to do everything in her power to return Luke's life to him.

After Dr. Malvese left, the nurse returned to check Carrie's blood pressure again. "Not bad. High end of normal range." He paused, then added, "I know you're tired, but the police want to ask you a few questions. Do you need anything before I let them in? Something to eat?"

The police. The thought of giving her statement squelched any appetite she had. And so much for lowering her blood pressure!

"No. Thank you."

Even knowing she'd done nothing wrong, she trembled at the notion of repeating her story to the cops. What had Joseph told them? Had they questioned Luke yet? She had to find a way to tell the truth in a way that walked the fine line between clearing Luke and not casting Joseph in a light that would earn his wrath. If her story differed dramatically from what Joseph had told the police, what sort of repercussions could she face? She had to stick as close to the truth as possible. She couldn't risk—

A knock cut into her mind-scrambling deliberations. Her head buzzed with adrenaline as the officers entered the exam room. She knew her pulse, an indicator of her stress level, was displayed on the machine at her bedside. She fought internally to stay calm, to regulate her breathing.

After a few introductions and pleasantries, the older of the two officers, a man with silver hair and a bit of a gut hanging over his utility belt, asked for her account of events.

She squeezed handfuls of the sheet covering the gurney she lay on and inhaled a slow, deep breath through her nose. "It was just a big misunderstanding, really." She forced a dismissive grin. "Luke heard me arguing with my husband in the woods near our campsite and thought I was in danger. He came to my aid. Tried to calm tempers. Joseph and Luke tussled, but once the misunderstanding was cleared up, everything was fine."

"Then what happened?" the older officer asked.

Careful. She forced herself to maintain eye contact, not give any physical cues she was stretching the truth.

"Well, Joseph needed time alone to calm down before returning to camp, so Luke and I left without him. But we got turned around in the dark and got lost." She flashed a chagrined smile. "I guess Joseph did, too. We were found by the SAR team a few hours ago after Luke and I had wandered who knows how far. We were trying to find the spot on the river where the tour group would launch for rafting. Obviously we didn't." Again she gave the policemen an embarrassed grin.

"What about your husband? Where was he while you were wandering on the mountain?"

"I can't say everywhere he went, but he was already on the helicopter when I was rescued by the SAR team."

When the officer asked about her attacking Joseph on the helicopter, she frowned and bobbed a nod. No point denying what the SAR men had witnessed. As with Dr. Malvese, she claimed fatigue and hunger had reignited her hurt feelings about the argument the night before.

"But everything's been worked out now. You can ask my husband yourself. He's out in the waiting room." She silently prayed Joseph had kept his end of the bargain and that his story matched hers closely enough to satisfy the policemen. To clear Luke of criminal charges.

The policemen looked at each other. "We will ask him as soon as we can. Your husband has been hard to pin down for an interview."

Again she forced a smile to her face, wondering how Joseph had dodged the police and how he would characterize the last twenty-four hours' events.

"What can you tell me about the bruises on your neck?" the younger officer asked.

She jerked her gaze to him, fighting to keep her expression as neutral as possible. Her heart was thumping hard, and she could hear the increased pace of the beeping on the bedside monitor. *Deep breaths. Calm down. For Luke's sake, don't blow this. If Joseph thinks you didn't keep the bargain...*

"Well...the argument Joseph and I were having outside the camp..." She paused. Swallowed when her mouth grew arid. "...got physical. That's one of the reasons Luke stepped in. But—" she waved a hand, minimizing the event. She knew Luke's story would differ. So would Joseph's. How did she walk the fine line between convicting her husband and doing what she'd promised Joseph in order to protect Luke from false charges? "—it wasn't as bad as I'm sure it appeared. He didn't really hurt me. I just bruise easily and, well...it was nothing. I'm fine."

Her gut roiled. Oh God...would they believe her? Did she want them to? Their stoic faces revealed nothing. She wished she was half as good at hiding her emotions.

The older policeman looked up from his notepad and

angled his head as he looked at her. "Has your husband ever choked you like that before?"

"No." She shook her head, grateful the officer phrased the question as he had. Joseph had not, in fact, choked her previously. Small wonder, among the other injures he'd inflicted, but a fine point she wasn't going to raise.

The two men exchanged a look, the younger cop heaving an audible sigh.

"Anything else you'd like to add to your statement before we talk to your husband?" the senior officer asked.

She hesitated. The less said the better, right? Stop while you're ahead. Or was she behind? She shrugged a shoulder. "Not that I can think of."

The policemen finished jotting their notes and thanked her for her time, leaving her to fret over what would happen next. With the police and the psychologist both finished talking with her, she had no doubt Joseph would be back soon. He was bound to be hovering near her exam room so he could make sure she returned home with him.

The room door burst open again, and her heart stilled.

Until she saw Luke standing at the threshold, his battered face full of worry.

Relief and affection flowed through her with the force of the tumbling rapids in the mountain stream they'd hiked. "Luke!"

He rushed to the bed, and she opened her arms to him, embracing him with a fierce hug. Clinging. Never wanting to let go.

He held her just as tightly. "Thank God. Are you all right? What happened with Joseph?"

He pulled back and framed her face with his hands. "Let me look at you. Oh, Carrie, I was so worried I'd lost you."

His words pierced her heart. Because she was lost to him.

Her promise to Joseph, her deal to earn her husband's cooperation regarding Luke's innocence, had sealed her fate.

"I'm okay." She stroked his cheek, savoring the scratchy-soft stubble beneath her fingers. "What about you? What did the doctor say?"

"Nothing broken. I got IV fluids like you." He nodded to the hanging bag beside her that was nearly empty. "Recommended I take some time off to rest."

The door opened again, and, once more, Carrie tensed, then sighed her relief when the visitor proved not to be Joseph returning. Yet. She had to get Luke safely away from her room before that happened.

"Okay. Let's see how that BP's doing," Dr. Holt said. The doctor's gaze landed on Luke, and his eyebrow sketched up for a moment.

The male nurse had followed Dr. Holt into the room and started the blood pressure cuff inflating again. The room remained silent until the cuff hissed, releasing the pressure around her arm, and the nurse read out the reading. "One twenty over seventy-eighty."

Dr. Holt nodded. "Much better than before, but I still recommend you have your regular doctor keep tabs on it. And do your best to avoid stress, watch your sodium intake, get plenty of exercise." He scribbled on the clipboard he carried. When he finished, he handed her the top sheet. "Dr. Malvese has signed off, says she gave you her contact information, so you are discharged and free to go."

Carrie exhaled, easing the constriction in her chest.

The nurse removed the blood pressure cuff from her arm and gently pulled at the tape covering the IV needle.

Crossing his arms over his chest, Dr. Holt sent her a dark look. "For the record, the fact that I'm discharging you doesn't mean you don't need to rest and take better care of yourself. Drink plenty of fluids and follow up with your regular physician this week, especially if any new symptoms crop up."

"I'll make sure she does," Luke said, folding her hand between his.

With a final concerned look and valediction, Dr. Holt pivoted and left the room. The nurse finished disconnecting tubes and wires, stuck a small bandage over the IV puncture and bade them goodbye, as well.

"Let's blow this joint, huh?" Luke said. "Before Joseph learns you've been discharged."

She squeezed his fingers. "Luke, I…I have to talk to you about Joseph. I—" Her throat closed. How in the world did she explain her choice to Luke? He'd never understand, never agree.

He frowned. "If we have to talk about him, can we at least wait until we get back to the ranch or, better yet, to my place?"

"That's the thing. I can't go with you. I told Joseph I would—" She choked on the words, and Luke cut her off, mumbling an earthy curse.

"Don't let him get in your head again! You cannot trust anything he says." He exhaled sharply then tugged her arm. "We'll talk about this later. Right now we have to get out of here. Go somewhere safe before he learns you've been discharged and comes looking for you."

"Nowhere is safe," she said on a sigh.

He shook his head. "That is defeatist talk. I promised you that I would protect you, and I will. Trust me, honey. Please."

"Luke—"

He towed her out of the exam room with a firm but careful grip on her arm. She trudged behind him, past other patients, orderlies and hospital staff until they reached the ER waiting room. Nina and Zane were there, their anxious looks stabbing Carrie anew. She'd caused the strain and worry for these people she cared about.

Nina embraced her. "I saw Joseph earlier," she whispered as she hugged Carrie. "Don't think he recognized me, but… Geez, it took everything in me not to walk up to him and slap his smug face."

Carrie shuddered. "Nina, no. Don't put yourself in his line of fire."

"He doesn't scare me."

"He should. He's dangerous." Carrie cast a furtive glance around the waiting room. "Where is he now? Do you know?"

"The policemen escorted him through those doors, presumably to interview him in private." Nina levered back from their embrace. "So we have a chance to sneak you out of here. Let's get you home."

Carrie furrowed her brow. Her friends' best intentions were going to ruin the agreement she'd made with Joseph. As much as she hated the notion of living under her husband's thumb, conceiving another baby with him, she had no choice. Joseph could hurt Luke in any number of ways. Physically or with lawsuits. False criminal charges. Sabotaging his livelihood. Going after his family. Joseph knew too many ways to inflict pain beyond just the physical. "Nina, I can't—"

"Zzzbbbt!" Nina said, cutting her off. "You can."

Her friend looped her arm through Carrie's, and Luke moved to her other side. The two escorted her out while Zane jogged ahead to unlock his SUV for them.

"Wait, guys," she pleaded half-heartedly. "I know you mean well, but I made a deal with Joseph."

Luke sent her a shocked frown. "Well, you're breaking the bargain. I won't let him get near you."

She tried to slow their pace, her pulse beating a frantic rhythm when she considered how Joseph would react to her slipping away from the hospital. "You don't understand. He's threatened to come after you, Luke. And I can't let him hurt—"

Luke tightened his grip and shook his head. "Forget it, Carrie. This is an intervention, and you won't change our minds. I won't turn my back on you like I did Sharon. I *won't*."

An ambulance pulled into the ER driveway, sirens screeching, jangling Carrie's already frayed nerves. When the blaring whine was silenced, she argued, "I'm not Sharon. I'm not planning suicide. You don't have to—"

"Aren't you?" he asked bluntly, stopping to face her. "Because it seems to me going back to that bastard for even a minute is suicide. Even if he doesn't murder you, which he very well could, it would certainly kill your soul. I won't allow it. I love you too much to—"

He cut himself off abruptly as if realizing what he'd said.

Love. Her heart jolted, and tears filled her eyes. "Luke…"

"Um, can we do this in the car? Or back at the ranch?" Nina jostled her arm and cast a worried glance back to the ER entrance.

"I, uh—" Carrie stumbled along as Nina towed her the rest of the way to Zane's waiting SUV. She climbed in the back seat between Nina and Luke, feeling like she was in witness protection. Her nerves jangled, knowing how desperately bad things could get for these people she cared about. The car was largely silent as Zane negotiated the streets near the hospital. When they were finally on the highway, headed back to the Double M Ranch, Carrie said, "Zane, I'm sorry. I know how much I messed things up for you and the company. For the tour group."

Zane met her gaze via the rearview mirror. "Are you kidding? I should be apologizing to you. I had no idea who he was—or what he was—when I sent your husband out to the camp late like that."

"You couldn't have known. I don't blame you."

"We usually don't allow late sign-ups like that, but it's the end of the season, and he convinced me to bend the rules. Said how much it meant to him to go, and…" Zane banged the steering wheel with his palm and shook his head.

"That's how he is," she said quietly. "He's a master schmoozer and manipulator. He's charming and ingratiating in public."

"And a monster in private," Luke finished for her.

The group fell silent again, as if nothing more needed to be said on the matter. When they reached the outskirts of Boyd Valley, Zane asked, "Where am I taking you, Carrie?"

"I, uh…" Where was she going? She was away from Joseph, could run again. But doing so would almost certainly mean Joseph would seek revenge against Luke and Nina for helping her.

Nina turned to her. "You're welcome to stay with me for as long as you need. We'll figure this out together."

"I don't know. Thank you, but—"

"Same offer," Luke said, putting a hand on her knee. "In the mountains, I promised to keep you safe. That hasn't changed. Stay with me, Carrie. I want you near me where I can protect you."

"And the guesthouse at the ranch is open to you as long as you need it," Zane added. "Anything you need, my family and I will help you."

A core-deep warmth puddled inside her at having so many people offering assistance, shelter and support. She treasured the offers, the friendships like rare jewels. Joseph had seen to it during their marriage that Carrie was isolated and estranged from most of her friends.

"Thank you all. I'm moved by your generosity and kindness." She took a deep breath, trying to calm the ragged thumping of her heart, searching for the courage to do what she had to in order to protect these people she cared about. "But…"

Luke's hand tensed on her knee. "Carrie."

His tone, his expression held disappointment. Warning. Pleading.

"Like I tried to explain earlier—" she gulped a breath "—I made an agreement with Joseph that I'd go back to—"

"No!" Nina said, grabbing Carrie's arm.

Luke's response was a bitter curse word, then, "You can't let him get in your head! Carrie, don't be stupid!"

She shot him an irritated look. "I'm doing it for you!"

Luke's eyes widened, and his expression blanked with incredulity. "What?"

She blinked back tears of frustration. Anger. Grief. "He promised not to follow through with the trumped-up charges against you, not to harm you or take any measures against you for helping me if I came back to him. Temporarily."

Luke shook his head. "Carrie, he can't hurt me. I've done nothing wrong."

She scoffed. "You think he cares? *He thinks we're lovers.* I told him we weren't, but he's jealous and wants revenge. He wants to lash out at me by hurting you. I can't let him do that!"

Luke faced her fully, taking both of her hands in his. "Carrie, I'll be fine. Don't let him win!"

She tightened her grip on his hands. "It's not forever. He's given me an out. He wants a baby. An heir with inheritance rights to my family's business. He wants a permanent claim to his position and power on the board. If I have a baby with him, he said he'd let me go."

Beside her, Nina grunted. "Oh, Carrie…"

Luke's face crumpled with dismay. "Do you hear yourself? You would barter your own child to him as some kind of ransom for—"

"No!" She shook her head and shot him a fierce look. "I could never do that! But by agreeing to his demands, I've bought you time. I've bought *myself* time to find another way out."

Luke growled his frustration. "You don't need another way out! You *are* out! Stay with me and let me protect you!"

The vehicle stopped, and Zane cut the engine. Carrie tore her gaze from Luke's to glance out the window. Somehow, while she was debating her future with Luke, they'd arrived back at the McCalls' ranch.

Zane folded the ignition key up behind the sunshade and twisted to face the back seat. "I'll let you two finish discussing things. My offer of lodging and protection here at the ranch stands. You've got a bunch of men here who'll stand between you and your abuser if he comes after you."

"And women!" Nina added, tugging on Carrie's arm. "He'll have to get through me, too!" She gave a dry laugh. "And the McCall ladies are not to be trifled with, either. Never met a better, braver bunch of women."

"Amen," Zane said.

Carrie thanked them again for their offers, and after Nina and Zane had departed, Luke sat motionless beside her, his expression brooding.

Finally she exhaled a frustrated sigh. "I need to pack my things."

Without any further discussion, he escorted her back to the guesthouse. The front room was quiet, empty, since the rest of the guests were still out on the delayed adventure trip with Josh.

After clicking on a small lamp that cast a golden glow around the living room, she dropped wearily onto the couch. "I need to get out of here, but I can't muster the energy."

Luke sat beside her, his body angled so they could talk. "So don't go. Maybe Zane and Nina have it right about you staying here, surrounded by lots of people who will all protect you. Including me. I intend to stay right here with you for as long as needed."

She shook her head sadly. "No, Luke. That's exactly what I don't want."

His expression reflected hurt. "You don't want me around?"

"What I want and what I know is best for you are two different things."

"Bull."

She blinked, startled by the succinct heat in his response. "I can't be with you, Luke. You know I can't put you in harm's way, but beyond that, I can't ask you to make that kind of sacrifice for me. You may think everything will be fine as soon as I divorce Joseph, but you're wrong. Even if I run from him again, I will spend my whole life looking over my shoulder, waiting for him to pop out of the shadows. Always on guard, always on edge, always wondering when and what will happen when he comes back around. When, not if. He will always be a threat and a lurking menace in my life. And I can't… I *won't* ask you to live like that."

"What if I'm willing to take that risk? What if you are worth the sacrifice to me? Shouldn't it be my choice whether I'm willing to deal with the inconvenience of your ex in exchange for a future with the woman I'm falling in love with?"

Carrie's breath caught. "Love? You said that before. I—"

"Why do you sound surprised?"

"I guess I am." She bent her head and studied her torn fingernails and scraped hands, evidence of the last two days' rough treatment. "How can you love me when all I've been is trouble for you?"

Luke shifted closer to her, wrapping his larger hands around hers. "Because what I feel for you isn't about what's happened to us. It's about who you are. The caring, courageous woman who—" She snorted her disagreement, and he stopped. "What?"

She shook her head, her gaze still cast down. "I'm not courageous. I'm scared to death."

"That just makes everything you've done all the more brave! You left Joseph when—" Again he stopped and raised a hand to grasp her chin, lifting her head so he could meet her eyes. "Listen to me, Carrie, and listen good. You had great courage to leave him when you learned you were pregnant. You wanted to protect your baby, just like you want to protect me now, no matter the cost to yourself. That's true love and real bravery, and while I don't agree with your methods now, I admire your willingness to protect me. You're a good person. You're beautiful inside and out, and I don't need months of dating to tell me you're the kind of woman I want to spend my life with."

A sob hiccupped from her chest. "Oh, Luke, I'd love nothing more. But—"

He pressed his mouth to hers, stalling her protest. Her head swam as pure, sweet pleasure and heartbreak swirled through her, a whirlwind of longing and regret. Too tired to fight the storm within her, she sagged against him, draping her arms around his neck. His kiss was at the same time demanding and gentle, fervent and tender. With the tip of his tongue, he sought a deeper exploration of her mouth, and she opened to him.

His hands swept down her body, caressing, enticing, inviting her to yield to the emotions that clamored inside her. For precious minutes, she simply savored the taste of him, the feel of his lips on hers, the heat that filled her and pooled at her core.

When he eased her back against the cushions of the couch, she opened her mouth to object, but the words snagged in her throat. Joseph already believed she and Luke were lovers. So why not allow herself the chance to know what it was like to be with someone she fully trusted, without fear or shame or regrets? She wanted

Luke with a desperate urgency, and a rebellious part of her refused to consider anything but the moment at hand.

As always, Luke was attuned to her mood and sensed her hesitation. Levering back, he narrowed a concerned look on her. "Carrie?"

She stroked his unshaven cheek, the quiet scratching sound sending shivers of delight over her skin. "As I recall, you promised that the first time we made love would be in a bed."

He blinked, and she lifted a corner of her mouth along with one eyebrow.

The smile that blossomed on his face melted any reservations she might have had. "That I did, my dear. And so we shall."

Chapter 20

In a fluid motion that belied the aches he had to be suffering after his combat with Joseph, Luke rose to his feet and scooped Carrie into his arms. He carried her down the hall to her guest room and kicked the door closed with his foot. As he placed her carefully on the bed, Carrie chuckled, enchanted by the romantic gesture. "How gallant!"

He waggled his eyebrows. "You ain't seen nothing yet."

Catching her by the ankle, he removed first one shoe then the other before sitting to unlace his own boots. Next he shucked his jeans, his shirt and his socks, until he stood before her wearing only his briefs and an expression of love and desire in his eyes that made her toes curl. She followed suit, sitting up on the bed to shimmy out of her clothes. When she unhooked her bra and let it drop to the floor, Luke's gaze drifted over her, and he pressed a hand to his chest. "My God, Carrie. You are so lovely."

She smiled shyly. "And so stinky. Join me in the shower?"

"Excellent idea."

Any quip she might have returned died on her tongue when he whipped off his briefs and stood before her in all his naked, manly beauty. A lean torso, marred with bruises, muscular shoulders and powerful thighs. Her own Greek god. No, her own heartthrob cowboy.

They lingered in the shower, long after the hot water was used up, kissing, touching, learning each other's bodies. Finally, when goose bumps rose on her arms from the cooled water, he once again carried her to the bed and made sweet, slow love to her. Worshipping her body with his, not using. Cherishing her, not possessing. Arousing her, not selfishly taking.

When he joined their bodies, it was a marriage of spirits and a celebration of the love she'd found. The kind of love she might only know this once. She held his gaze, memorizing everything about the moment, storing up the memory to revisit in days to come.

Because as precious as their lovemaking was, as much as she wanted to stay in Luke's arms forever, their union only made her more resolved to protect him. She knew now without a doubt how much she cared for him. And she had to do whatever it took to keep him safe from Joseph's inevitable wrath.

When she woke the next morning, she lounged in the peaceful stillness of the room while Luke dozed and she lay cuddled against his warmth. But all too soon, her mind betrayed her tranquility, and Carrie replayed the threats Joseph had made in the hospital. The deal she'd made with the devil.

Joseph would never be appeased until he had their child as his linchpin to secure his stake in her family's business. The irony was, no matter how terrible he was as a husband, he was actually a good businessman.

Before he'd died, her father had told her what a good job Joseph was doing at French Industries, how he'd felt confident the family's company would thrive under Joseph's leadership. Could she take any small measure of comfort knowing her sacrifice would be good for the company her father and grandfather had built?

She scoffed at her thin justification. *You really are digging for some scrap of rationalization, aren't you?*

If only there were a way to give Joseph what he wanted without having to lock herself in that hellish marriage with him or create a child that—

The idea came to her like a lightning bolt. She felt the shock to her marrow, the seeds of a plan stunning her with its potential.

Give him what he wants... Of course!

Her mind spinning, she slipped out of Luke's arms and tiptoed to the bathroom. She braced her arms on the edge of the sink, her limbs quivering with adrenaline.

She gaped at her tousled reflection, feeling stupid for not thinking of the answer sooner, but refused to chastise herself. That alone was progress. No more self-reproach. She could blame fear and self-preservation, fatigue and distractions for muddling her brain until now. And while it may have taken far too long to come around to her decision, she had finally reached it. That was the important thing.

Assuming it would work.

She knew Joseph craved control. He needed to feel he'd won. She needed to execute her plan in a way that gave him that sense of dominance, authority and victory, so that he'd agree to her terms.

Carrie hurried through her ablutions and threw on her clothes. She had her work cut out for her, and the sooner she started getting the details arranged, the better.

Chapter 21

Luke hadn't set an alarm to wake him. Thanks to the blackout curtains in the guest room and his sheer exhaustion from the tumult—and lovemaking—of the day before, he slept until almost noon. He groaned, feeling somewhat guilty for the laziness, but, damn, it had felt good.

Carrie was not next to him in the bed. As he stretched his stiff muscles, a niggling doubt tickled his nape. He sat up, frowning, his stomach pitching. Surely she hadn't gone back to Joseph. Their lovemaking last night had convinced her to stay with him. Hadn't it? She'd whispered words of love to him as they'd held each other, and he'd repeatedly promised her his own love and loyalty.

Rubbing his eyes, he tried to shove his concerns aside. *Be sensible.* The more likely scenario was that she'd risen hours ago and left him to enjoy the chance to sleep in.

She was probably reading or checking her email on her phone in the living room.

Just in case, he called, "Carrie?"

Throwing back the sheet, he crawled stiffly out of bed and ambled in his underwear to the front room of the guesthouse. "Yo, Carrie? You here?"

Empty. No answer.

The main house then. Or maybe in the stables with Nina?

He scrubbed his hands over his face and stumbled to the shower, needing a blast of cool water to clear the cobwebs. When he was finished cleaning up and dressing, he whistled a bouncy pop song that was stuck in his head. Sappy and trite as it sounded, making love to Carrie had given him a new lease on life. He was happy, truly happy for the first time in months. He headed out of the guest quarters, intending to stop by the stable in search of Carrie before checking the family's home, but he only made it as far as the front guesthouse door when he spotted the note with his name written on the front in a flowing print. His breath stuck in his throat, his tune abruptly silenced. The prickly premonition scraped the back of his neck again.

He snatched the note down, acid pooling in his gut even before he read Carrie's words to him. He knew, just knew, what she'd done. Knew that he'd failed her, like he'd failed Sharon.

He read the first few lines, and his knees buckled.

Dear Luke, I'm sorry for leaving like this without a goodbye. I know now what I must do. Please do not come after me. I need to do this alone.

He staggered back a couple steps, collapsing in a stuffed chair by the front window, his heart aching, before he found the courage, the strength to read the next lines.

I must give Joseph what he wants in order to protect you and to have any chance of happiness in the future. I've gone to confront him, to make peace with him, as I should have before I drew you into this terrible mess. I will be all right. Please, please, do not try to follow me. Your presence will only inflame Joseph. I can—no, I *must* do this for myself if I am ever to look myself in the mirror with my head high. I love you, Luke. Carrie

He lowered the note, his hand trembling, and muttered one dark curse word before charging out the door. He had to stop Carrie before she put herself in Joseph's reach, in Joseph's sadistic control again. He only prayed he wasn't too late.

Trepidation filled Carrie as she approached the front door of the Aurora house she'd shared with Joseph for five years. The mansion, equipped with every modern luxury and decorated by the best interior designers in the city, didn't feel like home to her. Familiar, yes. But not home. *Home* implied a love, peace and security that she'd never really known since the first time Joseph raised a hand to her.

She stood on the stoop, hesitating, taking so long to prepare herself that one of the men she'd brought with her asked, "Carrie, are you all right? Don't you have your key?"

She turned to George Collum, the chief legal counsel for French Industries, whom her father had hired and been friends with for decades, and gave him a strained smile. "I'm fine. Just…thinking."

George shifted his briefcase from one hand to the other and tipped his head in concession.

"I know we promised not to question your reasons for this move," Nick Burrows, the chief financial officer for the company, who'd also accompanied her, said, "but I've been a part of this company too many years and I knew your parents too long to dismiss these changes out of hand. I know your family would be concerned first and foremost with your welfare." He put a fatherly hand on her shoulder, his bushy gray eyebrows knitted. "Are you certain this is what you want? Are you under some kind of duress?"

She smiled. "No. I made this choice on my own. It's what I want."

The front door opened, and Carrie whirled to face her husband.

"Finally found your way home, did you, dear? I was beginning to think you'd broken our bargain." Joseph's tight mouth softened and the diamond-hard glitter in his eyes eased when his gaze shifted to her three companions. He blinked and drew his shoulders back, clearly startled by the presence of the executives who stood with her at the door. "Gentlemen, I— This is a pleasant surprise. What brings you by today?"

"Your wife does. What bargain is she breaking?" Nick asked.

The third man with her, Bill Fredericks, the head of the company's accounting department, motioned to Joseph's black eye, swollen nose and split lip. "What in God's name happened to your face?"

"Well, not so much a bargain as...well, we have reservations for dinner, and I was afraid we'd be late. As far as this—" Joseph waved vaguely to his face "—long story. Not important." He stood back and swept an arm to invite them all inside. "Please, let me get you a drink." Then to Carrie, the steel returning to his stare, "Darling, why don't you get changed for dinner? I'll entertain the men. Then we must make dinner a party of five. Yes?"

Everything in her wanted to concede to Joseph, to scurry to her bedroom and avoid the confrontation to come. But she fought her learned habits, the voice of self-preservation that shouted for her to submit, to avoid trouble. Instead, she pulled her shoulders square and raised her chin, actions that Joseph's raised eyebrow said he hadn't missed.

"I'm not going to dinner with you tonight, Joseph. In fact, I'm leaving after I make my offer to you."

Suspicion colored his face, along with the kind of irritation that she'd learned long ago spelled danger. He flexed and balled his hands at his sides, and with a quick glance to the men behind her, he flashed a tight smile. "What offer are you talking about? I thought when we spoke earlier we'd settled our differences." His nostrils flared slightly. "Remember that?"

Carrie gave a curt nod. "Of course I do. I think you'll appreciate this offer more."

His brow furrowed, and he stepped back, allowing her and the French Industries executives to enter. After he'd closed the door, Joseph said, "Gentlemen, I need a moment alone with my wife. Would you excuse us?"

When he wrapped his fingers around her arm, the

contents of her stomach curdled. Digging deep in her heart for the strength she'd rediscovered thanks to Luke's love and support, Nina's faith and encouragement, she wrenched her arm free. Had the men from the company's board of directors not been there, she doubted he'd have released her so easily. She straightened her spine, despite the quivering in her belly. "No. Anything you have to say to me can be said in front of them."

A muscle in his jaw ticked, and his steely glare narrowed on her. Behind her, she could hear the men shifting their weight and clearing their throats with ill ease. Finally, Joseph huffed a sigh and jerked his chin higher. "Fine." Turning on his heel, he marched into the living room and walked straight to the wet bar, where he unstoppered the scotch in its crystal decanter and poured himself a drink.

Carrie cast an apologetic smile to the executives as they followed Joseph into the house. The men's frowns and worried glances clearly said they were uncomfortable with the private tension she'd exposed them to.

Joseph downed the drink and poured another for himself before facing her and the men, his amiable smile in place again. "Carrie, get these fellas a drink, huh?"

All three men declined quietly, and Carrie sat on the edge of the couch when Joseph waved a hand inviting the men to sit. George laid his briefcase on the coffee table and sat next to Carrie. For his part, her husband prowled the living room restlessly.

Carrie took a deep breath. "I have thought a great deal about the proposal you made me earlier regarding our future, and I'm prepared to make a counteroffer that I think you'll like better."

Joseph shook his head and sent her a disappointed

scowl. "Reneging on our agreement already, Carrie?" He laughed without humor. "I'm disappointed in you. What would your father say about this disloyalty and faithlessness in bargaining? Integrity was the backbone of his business model."

Bile filled her blood hearing him using her father's scruples as a weapon against her when he was the one who lacked true moral fiber. "If my father knew the truth of our agreement, he'd roll over in his grave," she said softly, a chill in her tone. "And he'd want me to do anything and everything in my power to get far away from you."

George Collum turned to her, a dark concern in his rheumy eyes. "Carrie, dear, what does that mean? What haven't you told us?"

"Yes," Nick Burrows agreed. "I'm not at all comfortable with the direction this conversation has taken or the mood I'm detecting."

She gave them the best reassuring grin she could muster. "It's fine, gentlemen. I've just caught Joseph unaware is all."

Joseph grunted, and his nose flared again. He took a long swallow of scotch before striding to the double French doors to the balcony. Through the plate glass in the doors, he stared out at their swimming pool and lavishly landscaped patio. A window in the dining room was open, and the scent of gardenias and roses in her garden drifted in on the evening breeze. The aromas that had once been a joy to her now harkened back to summer nights when pain racked her body and bitter shouts filled her ears. Carrie shoved those memories away, needing to keep her composure.

Even with his back to her, she could sense the fury

Joseph battled. In deference to the leadership of French Industries in their presence, he was obviously struggling to rein in his temper and present a demeanor of calm and reason. But she'd taken a huge risk. She'd openly challenged him in front of people he lived to impress. She'd tipped off his colleagues to his darkest secret. He'd make sure she paid for her impertinence. She shivered imagining what form that retribution would take.

She tried to close her nose to the cloying floral scents and took a fortifying breath through her mouth. She pictured Luke, his steadying faith in her, his love, his gentleness. He was the reason she was here, and it gave her courage, strength. Slowly, she released the breath she'd held and said, "I'm offering different terms, Joseph. I'm prepared to give you what you *truly* want, without any end around. I'm giving you my shares of French Industries in return for a divorce and your promise never to contact or come near me again."

Chapter 22

Joseph spun. Glowered at her. "Come again?"

Before she could answer, a loud pounding rattled the front door. "Carrie, open up! Don't do this!"

She gasped. *Oh no! Luke.*

The black look that filled Joseph's face told her what she'd expected. Luke's presence would agitate Joseph and throw her negotiation into a tailspin. Her husband might sign away his claim on her to win more control at her family's business, but his pride wouldn't let him concede her to another man.

The company executives exchanged puzzled, disquieted looks.

"Carrie!" Luke shouted again, pounding the door harder.

She shot up from the couch and scurried toward the door, needing to get there and send Luke away before Joseph—

"Sit!" Joseph barked, marching toward the front door. "I'll handle him."

Again she defied Joseph, ignoring his command as she yanked open the door and shook her head desperately. "You have to go! Now! Please, Luke, trust me. Just go before—"

Joseph jerked the door from her hand and stepped out on the stoop, his chest puffed out and his glare glacial. "You son of a bitch! You have a lot of nerve showing up here." He cut her a sour look. "I should have known this was all a ruse to allow you to shack up with your lover."

As Joseph jostled into Luke's personal space, bumping him aggressively, Luke rose to the challenge and stood taller. He used his height advantage to stare down at Joseph with granite eyes.

Panicked, Carrie threw herself into the fray, something she'd never have dared to do even a few months ago, but she had to stop the escalating confrontation. Luke meant too much to her to stand aside and see him get into another altercation with Joseph, to risk real charges of assault being levied against him.

"No! Please stop!" She wedged herself between the men, placing a calming hand on Luke's chest, knowing him to be the more reasonable of the two. "Please, Luke, just go. I know what I'm doing."

"Well, I don't know what you're doing, but I know it's wrong. You can't go back to him! You can't let him win!"

"Wrong, cowboy," Joseph said, shoving her aside. "I always win. So either you leave now, and stay far away from my wife, or I call the cops."

"Joseph, no!" She reasserted herself, turning to face her husband's dark countenance. "Please, let me—"

Joseph poked his finger in Luke's face. "I can still

file those charges against you for kidnapping and assault, you know."

A shrill whistle sounded from the foyer.

She, Joseph and Luke all quieted, shifting their attention to the older gentleman watching the confrontation with dismay and disapproval. Nick adjusted his necktie and in a stern, fatherly tone said, "I don't know all the dynamics of what is going on here, but I know this—this bickering and chest beating is unseemly and beneath you. All of you." His eyes were fixed on Joseph, but once Joseph's combative stance eased and he took a step back, Nick spared Carrie a disconcerted glance, as well.

"Carrie?" Luke said, his quiet tone and querying look asking who this well-dressed, paternal figure was and if she trusted him.

She jerked a head bob.

"Let's all step into the next room and hash this out peacefully." Nick waved a hand, directing them back to the living room. "Like civil adults. Like respected members of French Industries' board of directors."

Joseph's spine stiffened and, raising his chin, he gave Luke and Carrie access to precede him into the house.

As they moved inside, she whispered to Luke, "Please, just stay calm and let me and the men talk to Joseph."

"If he puts a finger on you—" Luke whispered back.

"He won't. Not with so many witnesses, men he respects and wants to impress." She knitted her brow. "How did you even find the house?"

Luke scoffed mildly. "Everything's on the internet, Carrie."

Joseph had returned to the bar and poured another two fingers of liquor in his glass. "All right, Carrie. You called this meeting. Get on with it." He gestured with the hand holding the highball glass, and the contents sloshed. "You were saying something about giving me your shares of French Industries?"

Luke jerked his head toward her. "You *what*?"

With a raised palm, she silenced Luke, then sat on the couch next to George again, giving the attorney a nod.

George leaned forward to unlatch the brass fasteners on his briefcase, and he lifted the top. After removing a thick file, he closed the briefcase, set it on the floor and opened the file on the coffee table. "I've drawn up a simple contract here that transfers ownership of all of Carrie's shares of French Industries to Joseph."

"Carrie..." Luke's tone was stunned.

"With conditions," she added, to be sure not only Joseph understood, but Luke, as well.

Joseph grunted. "Conditions. Now we're getting to the real truth. You want to be free to play the whore to this nobody." He jerked his head toward Luke.

When she heard a growl-like rumble from Luke's direction, she shot him another pleading, silencing glance. Then to Joseph, she said, "This is not about Luke. Leave him out of it. It's about ending a marriage I haven't been happy in for years."

Her husband sneered at her. "If you think you're getting half of our bank account or this house or alimony, then think again."

Carrie bit the inside of her cheek and swallowed the bitter reply that sprang to her tongue. Stooping to nastiness would serve no purpose but dragging her down to Joseph's level. Squeezing her hands into fists, she replied, "No. All I want to take with me are my clothes, my mother's pearl necklace and my grandmother's candy dish."

Joseph wrinkled his nose and glanced across the room

to the sideboard where the depression-glass candy dish was on display. "That ugly thing?"

"It has great sentimental value to me." Memories of visits to her grandmother's home and sharing sweet treats with her grandfather after dinner filled her head and heart. "You can have everything else, in exchange for a complete severance of our relationship. No contact, no threats or punitive actions against me or my friends ever. Not a sniff."

Joseph's glare was all the more menacing with his left eye squinting through the blue-black bruise. Without breaking eye contact, he raised his glass to drink again. She could almost smell the rage simmering in him like short-circuited wires smoking.

Nick cleared his throat. "Are you sure about this, Carrie? You brought ninety percent of your current assets into the marriage. You have a legal right to—"

"I'm sure. I want to make the offer as lucrative as possible for Joseph. To give him every reason to accept." She turned the contract to face him on the coffee table. "All you have to do is sign and stick to the terms, and you'll have everything you ever wanted from me."

Joseph downed the rest of his drink, then stood glowering at the room full of men, his jaw tight, his fingers squeezing the crystal highball glass so hard Carrie was surprised it didn't crack. "I don't appreciate being ganged up on in my own home, Carrie."

She shook her head. "We're not trying to gang up on—"

With a roar, Joseph pivoted and threw the heavy glass across the room. The crash sent a shudder of surprise through everyone gathered in the room. The plate-glass panel in the French door to the porch splintered, leaving jagged peaks that reminded Carrie of shark's teeth.

"Joseph!" she gasped. "Please don't—"

He whirled toward her. "Don't? Don't what?" he snarled. "Break things? It's my house. You said you don't want it. So I'll break any—" he snatched up a lamp and threw it in the same direction he'd sent the highball glass "—damned—" next he grabbed a decorative ceramic bowl from the side table and flung it to join the other carnage "—thing I—" he stepped toward a desk at the side of the room and swiped his arm across it, clearing all the items and sending the blotter, faux inkwell and quill and letter opener to the floor "—want!"

"For God's sake, Joseph. Get ahold of yourself!" Nick barked.

When he shifted his attention to her grandmother's candy dish, Carrie leaped up and darted across the room. "Joseph, no! Please!"

With a smirk of sheer malice, he grabbed the depression-glass dish and hurled it onto the floor, shattering the heirloom. Rage swelled inside her.

She squared off with him, snarling, "You're hateful."

"In fact," Joseph said, advancing on Carrie now, "you're still my wife, and if I want to break *you*…"

With a gasp, she scuttled away even as Luke hurried across the room to put himself in front of her.

"… I have every right to!" Joseph reached for her, and Luke blocked the move with a thrust of his arm to knock Joseph's away.

One swipe led to another, a push, a grab—

Carrie tried to step between the men to break up what was sure to lead to full-out blows soon—or worse. But instead of helping, she caught a slap from Joseph and yelped her pain.

"You son of a bitch! I told you not to touch her!" Luke yelled, shoving Joseph hard.

Joseph stumbled back a step, his expression hardening, and he lowered his head and shoulder as if preparing to charge. An enraged bull about to stampede the matador.

But a figure surged at Joseph from the periphery of her vision. Bill Fredericks swung the crystal decanter of scotch at the side of Joseph's head, smashing it and sending Joseph reeling, clutching his temple.

Carrie watched in numb disbelief as her husband tripped over the lamp, lying on the floor where Joseph had thrown it, and tumbled backward. Joseph grabbed for something to break his fall, finding nothing, as he spilled toward the French door. The shark's teeth.

Carrie gasped in horror as the largest shard of glass punctured Joseph's throat and blood sprayed from the wound. "Joseph!"

She shoved past Luke and darted to her husband's side. She wanted to stop the bleeding, but the sharp glass still protruded from his neck. "Help me! We have to move him! Get him off the glass…"

Jolted into action by her cry, the men, who'd been gaping in stunned silence, hustled forward. With assistance from Nick, Luke lifted Joseph's head and shoulders as Carrie removed the shard. Joseph's eyes were wild with pain, and he gurgled on blood as he tried to speak.

"No. Don't talk," Carrie told him, following as the men laid Joseph on the floor amid the detritus of his temper tantrum. She pressed her hands over the wound that gushed blood and whimpered her fear. As much as she hated everything Joseph had done to her, she'd never wished for his death. And certainly not now. Not like this. "Joseph. Don't die. Stay with me."

"Use this." Luke whipped his shirt off over his head and handed it to her as he knelt beside her. He covered her trembling hands with his own. Pressed. Yelled over his shoulder, "One of you better be calling an ambulance! He's bleeding fast. I don't know how long he can make it."

"I am!" one of the men called back. Carrie wasn't sure whom. Her focus was on the agonized look in Joseph's eyes.

The urge to curse at him, the temptation to gloat and ask him how it felt to be the one in pain instead of her sifted through her brain. To spew her bitterness and fury. To rub his nose in his defeat in his final moments.

But she choked back the urge. She refused to be that cruel. Refused to demean herself or allow her own character to be further destroyed by the pain he'd caused her. Instead tears blurred her vision and dripped on Joseph's cheek. Tears for what could have been, for the talented man who'd let his demons shape him, for the years of heartache that should have been full of joy and love. She could feel the weakening throb as Joseph's adrenaline-spiked pulse faded beneath her hands, and her double-edged grief wrenched in her chest. "Joseph! Hold on. Help is coming."

But her husband's eyes fixed, and the flicker of life in his gaze dimmed. His pain-contorted face settled into a blank, relaxed stare.

Carrie's breath hitched. "Oh no. Oh my God." She raised a stunned gaze to Luke, whose expression reflected her shock.

"Is he…?" Bill asked, his voice strained. "I didn't

mean to—I only—" The older man began hyperventilating and shaking. "Oh dear Lord…"

Luke stood slowly and pivoted to face Bill. "You've done nothing wrong."

"M-my father used to b-beat my mother, and I—I only wanted to stop him from hurting Carrie. I—"

"We understand you were defending Carrie," George said. "That is the truth, and it is what I will tell the police."

"You have three other witnesses here who will vouch for you, too," Luke said.

Bill's bleak eyes met Luke's, and he gave a small nod.

Carrie tried to rise to her feet, but her legs were useless. She wobbled and sank back to her knees. Harsh sobs ripped from her chest.

Instantly, Luke moved to her side and wrapped her in his embrace. Neither of them gave any mind to the blood coating their hands, evidence of their attempts to save the man that had stood between them and a future together. The man who had scarred her past.

Right now, she needed Luke's comfort and strength. A part of her brain recognized that with Joseph's death, she was free. To start her life over without fear. To choose whatever path forward she wanted. To be with Luke and love him for the rest of her days.

But she silenced that voice. She couldn't think about any of that now. Her head, her heart, her soul were too numb, too grieved, too confused to consider anything but this moment. This horror. This need to hold Luke and know she was finally safe.

"He's right," she heard Nick say and glanced up to see the older man holding Bill's shoulders. "You were defending Carrie. We all were. You saw what was happening, his rage, his violence. We all did. What you did was justified. Tragic and unfortunate, but *justified.*"

"He…he tripped on the things he threw…the glass he broke… I didn't mean for—" Bill said in a strange monotone.

Carrie peeked over at Joseph's still form and considered what the accountant had said. Joseph had died largely from the damage he'd caused with his tantrum. The lamp he stumbled over, the jagged glass that had stabbed him. An odd dizziness washed through her. A deep sadness filled her core even as she realized that, in a sense, Joseph's death was his own fault.

Chapter 23

Carrie and Luke didn't get back to the ranch until well after dark that night. Their interviews with the police were tedious and time-consuming, but in the end, no charges were filed against Bill Fredericks, pending completion of the forensic investigation of the scene. Because the other guests with the adventure tour had returned that afternoon and were occupying the guesthouse at the ranch, Carrie accepted Nina's invitation to stay with her until the police released the Aurora house from its crime-scene status.

Carrie wasn't sure she ever wanted to return to the house, haunted as it was by bad memories. For now, she simply wanted to blot the horrid images and sounds of the day from her mind and sleep for the first night in years without a cloud of fear hanging over her.

"My goodness, darling," Lylah Grace said from the

bedroom door as Carrie gathered her belongings from the guesthouse. "I'm so sorry for your loss. Can I do anything for you?"

Carrie smiled her gratitude weakly to the other woman. "Thank you. But no."

Lylah Grace opened her arms and crossed to Carrie. "I'll pray for you," she said, enfolding Carrie in a hug.

Carrie closed her eyes, savoring the maternal comfort Lylah Grace offered and fighting back tears.

Luke appeared at the door and cleared his throat quietly. "My truck's out front, when you're ready to go."

Nodding, Carrie backed out of Lylah Grace's hug and closed her suitcase. "I'm ready."

Luke took the suitcase from her, and calling her farewells to the rest of the tour group gathered in the living room, she climbed in Luke's truck.

They said nothing to each other until they were on the road to Nina's house. Finally Luke broke the silence. "So what will you do now?"

She didn't answer right away. Still feeling stunned by the surreal events of the afternoon, she hadn't thought beyond surviving the next minute, then the next. She felt Luke's gaze on her and finally muttered, "Bury him. And with him, I'll find a way to put to rest all the history we had between us." She picked at a hangnail, and he turned in at the gravel driveway to Nina and Steve's duplex.

Nina rushed out to meet her on the driveway while Luke toted her suitcase inside.

"We've finished dinner, but I can heat up a plate for you if you're hungry," Steve said, ushering her inside to the kitchen table.

Carrie shook her head.

Nina, Steve and Luke joined her around the small table, and Luke hung his Stetson on a spindle of his chair back.

Fidgeting with the fringe on the place mat in front of her, Carrie sighed. "You all don't have to babysit me. I'll be okay. I'm just...still processing."

"Understandable." Nina reached for her hand and squeezed it.

"I've already been in touch with a counselor, a woman who visited me in the hospital the other day. Made an appointment to start therapy."

Luke inhaled deeply. Exhaled slowly. "Wise move. But you know I'm here for you, too."

She glanced up at him, and the care and concern in his silver eyes arrowed to her heart. "I do. But..."

"But?"

When Carrie fumbled, Nina divided a look between them. "But...she's suffered a trauma, and she really needs a professional to help her sort out the kind of emotions that go along with abuse and death and guilt."

"I know." Luke still stared at Carrie as if expecting... something. "I only meant that—"

"Luke," Carrie wheezed, her lungs suddenly tight. "I can't..." She struggled for the breath, the courage, the love to say what she had to. "I need time."

He blinked. "Well...of course. We can take all the time you need to—"

"Alone."

Luke's eyebrows dipped. His jaw muscles twitched. He swallowed. "Oh."

The softly spoken word was full of pain and heart-break.

Carrie's throat cramped with emotion, and she needed

a moment to loosen the knot before she could speak again. "I care about you. I do. But I have a lot to figure out. About who I am. What I want. How to put everything that's happened in perspective."

At the edge of her vision, Steve touched Nina's shoulder as he rose from the table and eased away, saying softly, "Let's give them some privacy."

Nina scooted her chair back, but before she could rise, Luke was on his feet. "No. I should go. I know you're all tired."

The despondency and defeat in his expression ripped at Carrie's already tattered soul. "Luke, wait..."

He jammed his hat back on his head and avoided her gaze as he strode toward the door.

She rushed out the door on his heels. "Luke, stop. Please!"

He pivoted to face her with a strained smile. "It's okay. I get it. You warned me. I knew you weren't in the same place I was. I shouldn't have pushed."

She clutched at his arms, desperate to make him understand her choice. "That doesn't mean I don't have feelings for you. But it's all happened so fast, and my world is in tumult. I need a chance to think, to sort everything out. To *heal* before I jump into another relationship."

His thin smile still reflected his hurt. "It's okay. I get it. I'm happy I could be your champion when you needed one."

She dug her fingers into his arms. "I didn't—"

He silenced her with a deep, poignant kiss. When he pulled away, he said, "Goodbye, Carrie. Take care of yourself."

Before she could even gather her breath after his devastating kiss, he'd spun sharply on his heel and marched to his truck. As his taillights faded down the street, she couldn't help feeling she had found what she was looking for. And just lost it.

Chapter 24

Early May, the following year

"Luke!" Nina called as she ran across the ranch yard. "Thank God I found you!"

"What's wrong?" He shucked the gloves he'd been wearing while repairing a fence in the north pasture and tucked them under his arm.

Nina paused to catch her breath. "I just got off the phone with Carrie. She's in the hospital in Denver and asked you to come. It's important."

Pain rocketed through his chest as if he'd been sucker punched. *Carrie.* He hadn't spoken with her in months. At first, he'd avoided her calls because it hurt too much to talk to her. He might understand her justifications for distancing herself from him, but that didn't mean it didn't sting.

Sting? Hell, the pain of knowing she didn't return his

love, didn't want him in her life was bleach poured on a gaping wound. A gut shot. Agony.

He needed a moment to compose himself. "The hospital? What— How bad is it?"

Nina winced. "I promised not to say. But…go. Now. She needs you."

Images of finding Sharon's lifeless body, knowing he'd been too late to save her, were enough to prod him to hurry, even if he felt like ten kinds of fool, jumping to be at Carrie's side after she'd cast him off. *Glutton for punishment, I guess.*

He reached the Denver hospital Nina directed him to in record time, thankful rush hour hadn't yet started on the highways approaching the city center. After parking in the visitors' lot, he jogged to the information desk and asked for Carrie's room number.

The older gentleman manning the information desk looked her up on the computer and gave him her room number.

"Thanks," Luke said and turned to trot to the elevator. When he got off the elevator and glanced around for a sign that would direct him to Carrie's room, he hesitated when he spotted the sign that read Labor and Delivery. *What the hell?*

Certain he'd misunderstood the room number the man downstairs had given him, he approached the nurses' station and caught the attention of one of the women behind the desk. "I think I'm on the wrong floor. I'm looking for Carrie French. Do you have a way to check the database—"

"Are you Luke?" the nurse asked, her face brightening before he could finish his question.

"I—" A strange lump settled in his gut. He nodded. "Yeah."

The nurse pointed down the hall to the left, repeating the room number the man at the information desk had given him. "She's been waiting for you, hoping you'd come."

He nodded and started down the hall. Numb. Confused. And apprehensive. Through the muddle of his shell-shocked thoughts, he tried to remember. Had they used contraception the night they made love? The sex had been spontaneous. They'd been worn out from the events of the day, not being especially careful. His stomach tightened. If he couldn't remember, chances were good they hadn't. *Hell!*

He reached the door of her room and knocked quietly. "Come…urrgh…in!"

He took a deep breath and pushed through the door.

Carrie was holding her stomach, rounded with pregnancy, and panting through a contraction. When she spotted him, her eyes widened. "Luke…" she gasped between ragged breaths.

He removed his hat and walked closer. He had to try twice to get sound to come from his throat. "Hi."

Her body relaxed, and she sank back into the pillow, taking deeper, cleansing breaths. "First, we have about eight minutes before the next one hits, so if you'll just let me explain…"

"I'd say this is self-explanatory." He waved a hand toward her belly.

She nodded and flashed a sheepish smile. "But…I didn't ask you here because I expect anything from you. You are free to walk out that door and never look back if you want. I'll be all right. I'm not afraid to raise her alone."

Luke's legs trembled, and he sat down on the edge of the bed before his knees gave out. "Her? It's a girl? You're sure?"

Carrie sent him a wary grin. "Yeah. You have a daughter. *We* have a daughter." Her brow crinkled, and she added hastily, "But like I said, I only asked you to come because I thought it was only fair to give you the chance to be here when she was born, in case…you wanted to be."

"Um…of course I do," he said. "Especially seeing as how I missed the whole pregnancy. You didn't think I'd want to know sooner that I was a father?"

She closed her eyes. "I know. I'm sorry. I always planned to tell you before…well, before now. But, at first, I was worried I might miscarry. Like I did before. And then when I was more certain the pregnancy was safe, it only gave me more to consider, more to sort out, more plans to make."

"Plans." He nodded. "And you didn't think I might want to be part of making those plans?"

Her expression firmed with determination. "Yes. But I also needed to be in a healthy place, a stable, strong place, an independent place before I told you. I didn't want to come to you while I was still searching and unsure and have you feel any obligation to me or the baby."

"Oblig—" He dragged a hand over his mouth.

"I wanted," she continued doggedly, "to be sure I could take care of myself and the baby if you decided you weren't ready to be a father. And I didn't want my decisions about my future to be muddled up with the trash I was still dealing with from my past."

Fidgeting, Luke curled the brim of his hat and sighed. "And now? What have you decided? What does your future with our daughter look like to you?" He fought to keep the bitterness out of his tone.

"Depends. I want you to be as little or as much of a part of Charlotte's life as you want. No strings. No guilt. No—"

"Charlotte?" Something sweet unfurled at his core. "Is that her name?"

For the first time since he'd arrived, Carrie looked uncertain. "Do you like it? It was my grandmother's name and—"

"Charlotte Wright," he said, testing the sound of it, then nodding.

"Wright?"

He straightened his back. "You got to pick her first name. Only fair I get to give her the last name I want."

She took a couple beats before she whispered, "May I have your last name, too?"

Luke's pulse quickened. "You want my last name?"

Her hand slid across the sheets to curl around his wrist. "I want *you*, Luke. Your heart, your soul, your love. And, eventually, your name. If it's not too late."

Now he was the one who needed a moment to respond. His chest squeezed, and he replayed her words to be sure he'd heard her right. He'd dreamed of this moment so many times, imagined her back in his life in so many ways—well, except this way—that he could almost imagine this was another fantasy.

In the silence left by his muteness, she rushed on to say, "I know I don't deserve a second chance. I've handled this all badly. But I rushed into marriage with Joseph, and I had to be sure what I was feeling for you was really love and not gratitude or hero worship or…whatever. But every day I was without you, it became clearer to me that what I found with you out on that mountain, or maybe earlier in the dusty corrals of the Double M, were the seeds of a love that has never faded. You're a once-in-a-lifetime guy, Luke. You are everything I want in a husband, companion and lover. And everything I want for my child's father."

He furrowed his brow, and he angled his body to face her more fully. "And if there were no baby? What then? I'm only here with you now because you're in labor."

She nodded. "Fair question. One I have asked myself dozens of times, trust me, because I wanted to be sure I was doing the right thing for the right reasons. And if not for Charlotte, I—" She stopped midsentence, and she sat up as her face scrunched in pain. "Yowza…that was only five…minutes. They're…coming faster."

Luke stood, worry pinging through him. "Should I get someone? A nurse?"

"Not…yet."

She panted through the rest of the contraction while he stood beside her, stroking her hand and feeling worse than useless. When she relaxed against the pillow, her breathing deep and her eyes closed, he settled on the edge of the bed again.

Luke glanced around the labor room, which was decorated to resemble a posh bedroom, a homey atmosphere clearly designed to put the mothers at ease.

A labor room. He scratched his cheek and let that truth sink in. He was with Carrie. In a hospital room. Awaiting the birth of his daughter.

Damn.

He blinked.

Ho. Ly. Cow.

A smile split his face.

"Where was I?" Carrie asked, sounding winded.

He turned to her again, leaning in to brush damp tendrils of hair from her forehead. "Maybe you should rest.

Concentrate on getting Charlotte here safely, and we'll finish this discussion later?"

She shook her head stubbornly. "I've put you off too long already. I need you to know."

"Know what?"

"I love you. I know we need to spend more time together, learn more about each other before we take any more steps. But even if we didn't have Charlotte, I'd want you. I need you, Luke. Not because I want you to fix anything in my life—that's what these past few months have been about. Getting my life straight. But because you're the best man I know." Her mouth curled in a lopsided grin. "And the sexiest."

He barked a startled laugh. "Is that any way for a woman in labor to talk?"

She caught the front of his shirt and dragged him closer. "It is when she's crazy about her man."

She kissed him gently, and skyrockets fired in his blood, in his soul.

"I love you, Luke. Staying away from you these last months was miserable for me. But I had to be sure. Please forgive me for taking so long, for keeping Charlotte a secret until I was certain that what I felt was love and I knew I'd reached a good place in my life. A place where I could give you my whole heart. Not tattered and confused, but healthy and certain."

"There's nothing to forgive. It hurt being away from you, but I understand it was what you needed. And forever and always, I want what is best for you."

She seemed relieved by his words, a smile twitching at the edges of her mouth. "Then say you still love me. Say we can try again."

He cupped her cheek, and the warmth in his heart

swelled. "I never stopped loving you, sweetheart. And just knowing Charlotte's ours… I love her already."

Carrie's forehead wrinkled, and a look of dismay dimmed her face. "Oh boy…" she muttered.

He tipped his head. "That's not the reaction I was expecting to my profession of love."

"I know. It's only… My water just broke."

Luke sat straighter, panic flashing through him. "What? What should I do?"

"Well… I'm ready for you to get the nurse."

"I'm on it!" he called as he rushed out the door.

"Welcome to the world, Charlotte Elizabeth," Carrie cooed when the nurses placed her swaddled daughter in her arms.

Charlotte gurgled and gazed up at her with pale blue, unfocused eyes.

"Oh my God," Luke said, leaning in for a better look. "She's so small. And so perfect."

Carrie heard the emotion that cracked in his voice and saw the shimmer in his eyes. She sighed happily, blinking back her own tears.

"Hi, Charlotte. I'm your daddy," he said gently. "There's a big beautiful world out there, and I promise to show you all of it. We'll climb mountains and go fishing and swim in the ocean. And I'm going to teach you how to ride a horse and how to change a flat tire. And I'm going to protect you. Always. I won't ever let anyone hurt you, my sweet girl." He shifted his gaze to Carrie. "Or hurt you."

To save the moment from getting too dark or maudlin, Carrie quipped, "And I am going to teach your daddy how to push the nurse-call button on the bed rail instead of running down the hall to the nurses' station."

Luke rolled his eyes. "Funny. But I did bring a nurse back with me, didn't I?"

She chuckled. "That you did."

"See." He kissed her gently and smiled. "I told you I'd take care of you."

Carrie drew a confident breath. "But that's the thing, Luke. I don't need you to take care of me. I've found my center. I'm on my feet again. All I need from you is your love."

His answering smile and nod radiated pride and affection. For Carrie, it was like seeing the sunshine after years of rain.

"You've got it, sweetheart." Luke swiped his thumb along her cheek. "You have my love and everything else I am."

She angled her head to kiss his palm. "Then I am the luckiest girl in the world."

* * * * *

Don't miss other books in Beth Cornelison's McCall Adventure Ranch miniseries:

Rancher's Hostage Rescue
Rancher's Covert Christmas
Rancher's Deadly Reunion
Rancher's High-Stakes Rescue

Available now wherever Harlequin Romantic Suspense books and ebooks are sold!